I0637142

Black Moon Dragon

Shelley Munro

Munro Press

DEDICATION

For Paul, my husband, partner in crime, and fellow adventurer.
Every day is a good day.

Introduction

A sacrifice for love has repercussions across the centuries.

After her father dies, Jessalyn Brown's life is one drama after another, and now she has developed a mysterious and surely fatal disease. Either that or she's turning crazy. Desperate for answers, she travels to the city, and that's where her dilemmas become bigger and life-threatening.

In a deep depression after he executed his mother to keep dragons a secret from humans, Manu Taniwha's life is full of petty squabbles and a noisy faction who demand he step down as the leader. Now a young woman is setting fires and threatening his leadership. He must execute her too, for the good of his people. Except when he meets her, he discovers she is his mate. She is the one person in this world who might make his life bearable.

Taniwha politics and secret-squirrel dragon stuff create roadblocks to a romance while the mystery of Jessalyn's heritage is plain puzzling. The clock is ticking, and if Manu doesn't get his act together, he'll lose the perfect-for-him woman.

Contains a grumpy billionaire taniwha, mesmerizing tattoos, politics, and a strong, sassy woman who is about to burst out of her cocoon and kick dragon butt. Stand well back because her flames are hot!

CHAPTER 1

Fire!

D eath. It hung over the house, somber and heavy, dampening even the summer sunshine. Final and life-changing for those left behind.

Devastating for her.

Jessalyn Brown sat on her father's bedroom floor and leaned against his bed. Her hand trembled, rattling the sheet of paper she clutched.

Despair iced her veins and pressed against her chest. Despair sapped her confidence. For the first time since the funeral, tears slipped down her cheeks.

The citrus of her father's favorite aftershave lingered while the loose change he'd tossed from his pockets littered the top of a dresser. The bureau was a piece he'd carved with his own hands as a teen, and the native kauri wood gleamed with the patina of age and layers of polish.

Jessalyn swallowed hard, inhaled to center her mind. At age two, she'd barely registered her mother's death. In the passing years, her father told her bits and pieces about Humarie. He'd told her stories of how they'd met and fallen in love. He'd described her mother's favorite colors, songs, hobbies, clothes, food, and everything else he could think of, but the woman remained surreal to Jessalyn.

Despite missing one parent, she hadn't grown up lacking.

But now her father had died of a heart attack—his sudden passing unexpected for a man in his forties—and Jessalyn found herself going through the motions. Numb. Numb. *So numb.*

Yes, she had friends in the seaside village of Piha, but they weren't her beloved father. They weren't the man who'd single-handedly parented her. The man who'd encouraged her to be herself.

She sniffed, a faint smile curving her lips at a memory. He'd raised an unrepentant tomboy who thrived on sport and art and, even worse—according to the local biddies—passed on his love of woodwork and carving. The truth—she'd tried ballet and hated it because her too-tall body stumbled around like a drunken giraffe, never in sync with the music. And the color pink—well, she'd learned it didn't stand up to muddy explorations of the creek or the local bush.

Aware of the clock ticking, she fumbled for a handkerchief and, coming up empty, knuckled away the tears still blurring her vision. She blinked until the words on the paper came into focus. A letter from the bank stating the mortgage payment on her father's house—now hers—was overdue. The bare basics—they understood Mr. Brown had died recently and held sympathy but they required payment by the end of the week.

Unbidden, her gaze ran over the polite words again. Perhaps she'd missed something—a ray of hope to show her a way out of her shock and confusion.

Dear Miss Brown,

We are sorry to hear of your father's recent passing and extend our sympathies at this time. Unfortunately, our records reveal the current mortgage payment of $2341.75 is still unpaid. We appreciate this is a difficult time and as such, we are willing to defer this payment until 22 January. If we do not receive the payment by this date, we will foreclose on the property at 23 Karaka Lane, Piha.

Yours faithfully,

Harry Standish
Bank Manager

Nope, nothing had changed since her first reading. A mortgage. When had this happened? Why hadn't her father told her? She and her father had discussed everything and anything, but not once had he mentioned a loan or the fact he'd signed away the house and land as security.

A glance at his latest bank statement reconfirmed her initial assessment. No insurance policy to make a claim on, and the funds in the business bank account fell short of the amount required to meet the payment. *Far short*. When his heart attack occurred, he'd had one big project underway, and he'd already received a hefty deposit for the bespoke bedroom suite. Jessalyn had banked the check herself. She flicked through several pages of bank statements. Although there were regular deposits, the outgoings far exceeded the income.

So where was the money? How had her father expected to meet this payment? As far as she'd known, the business was doing well with her father's creations—big and small—in high demand.

She ran her finger down a column of a bank statement, pausing to tap on a direct debit payment. Who was this Cameron Holdings her father was paying a considerable amount of money to every month? She'd never heard of them. A quick internet search revealed nothing to enlighten her, and she nibbled her bottom lip, at a loss as to her next action.

Jessalyn glanced at her watch. Secrets. It was painfully obvious her father had kept things from her, and she needed answers. *Today.* She had time for a quick search of her father's room before she'd promised to meet Danny. After their dinner, she'd start her shift at the local fish and chip shop.

She scrambled to her feet, did another quick swipe of her face and began a systematic examination of her father's belongings. Might as well bag his clothes and the other items she wanted to send to the hospice charity store. She retreated to the garage and collected half a dozen black rubbish bags.

Back in her father's bedroom, she started her quest by clearing the dresser drawers. She stuffed clothes into the bags and set aside papers and jewelry for later perusal. Surprisingly, it didn't take long to sort and pack her father's possessions. With the drawers empty, she attacked the wardrobe. She dragged clothes off hangers and after searching pockets, jammed the shirts, trousers, and jackets into the bags destined for the charity shop. Nothing she discovered during her search answered her many, many questions.

She scanned the room, her gaze falling on the king-size bed with its gray-and-ruby coverlet. Ah! Of course. Her father had preferred a minimalist approach and had added extra storage beneath the bed. She peeled back the covers and stripped the bed to reveal the concealed drawers.

The first drawer contained photo albums, and she set them aside for later. The second held bulky winter sweaters, and the third a selection of T-shirts. Jessalyn puffed out a burst of frustration as she peered at the now-empty wooden drawer. Surely, there was something in the house to offer answers.

"Dad, why all the secrets? Why didn't you tell me about the mortgage?" Her plaintive words echoed in the empty bedroom.

She shoved the drawer shut and stood, wincing at the stab of pain in her lower back. An old injury and one that niggled her when she became overtired. Too much bending and stooping. After a ginger stretch, she placed her hands in the small of her back and rose to her full height. It did nothing to rid her of the nagging ache pressing down on her body, her mind. Toting around boxes of frozen fries this evening might finish the job and cripple her when she couldn't afford to take a sickie.

The drawer dimensions grabbed her attention as she crouched to slide the third drawer shut. Since her father had taught her woodworking skills when she was young, she'd developed an eye for proportions. The interior was shallow compared to the depth of the drawer. Curious, she ignored the throbbing ache in her back and plonked her butt on the floor.

Ah! A clever button at the back—flush with the rest of the wood. The casual observer might miss the significance. Not her. She pressed on it until a sharp click sounded over her rapid breaths. A pocket of wood loosened, and when she lifted it, she discovered a square wooden box. Her father's favorite wood was kauri, although this had become increasingly rare and expensive. This box contained kauri, matai, and totara wood and bore exquisite workmanship, plus decorative carving on the middle panel.

Her fingers fumbled as she opened the box, and she gasped on seeing the key and the pendant inside. She had no idea what the key unlocked and set it aside. The pendant was old and reminded her of the jewelry the local Māori elders wore during special ceremonies. Round and made of bone. Likely whalebone if it truly was old. A craftsman had carved a greenstone or jade koru and somehow inset this into the face of the pendant. The round curling koru—symbolic of New Zealand's native fern—represented new beginnings, growth, and regeneration. This one was unusual with its inlay and unlike any others she'd seen.

She traced the stylized twist and a gentle warmth crept up her finger. Startled, she gasped again, but strangely, the tenseness in her shoulders from overexertion and grief drifted away, and the sharp edges of pain eased. She never lost contact with the greenstone as her finger made a return journey.

The alarm of her watch buzzed, letting her know it was time to prepare for her pre-work dinner with her friend Danny Ngataki. Jessalyn ran her fingers over the pendant face one final time before closing the box and returning the key and pendant to its original hiding place. She'd have plenty of time to ponder the pendant and her next steps during her shift. It didn't take concentration to fry baskets of battered fish and chunky fries. Before she slid the drawer shut, at the last minute, she grabbed several of the T-shirts she'd removed and stacked them inside. They'd done an excellent job of keeping the pendant concealed thus far so the hiding place should suffice for a bit longer.

Saturdays were busy at the *Cheeky Parrot* cafe and this one more so than usual. Jessalyn spotted Danny sitting at one of the outdoor tables.

"There she is," he said to the waitress, his tone one of satisfaction and relief.

Mrs. Merryford, the oldest waitress, lived opposite the lifesaving club. She turned and scowled, her black penciled eyebrows drawing together in displeasure at Danny taking up a table while others waited. It was the same scowl she gave the man in charge of the lifeguards whenever they partied loudly, late at night. Jessalyn had witnessed one or two of Mrs. Merryford's lectures and held a healthy respect for her temper.

"Mrs. Merryford, I'm sorry I'm late," Jessalyn said, determined to head off trouble. "I was clearing out Dad's room and lost track of time."

Not quite the truth but at least it made the stern lines on the waitress's face soften.

"How are you getting on, dear?" Mrs. Merryford asked as she handed over menus.

Jessalyn gulped hard, and luckily the waitress took that as answer enough.

"The specials' board is over there." Mrs. Merryford pointed at the blackboard on the wall. "Would you like something to drink?"

"We'll have two draft beers," Danny said, aiming for charm now that their table was secure. His thick black hair flopped over his face, obscuring his brown eyes. He was darker in complexion than Jessalyn since both of his parents bore Māori blood. The girls their age flocked to him, tossing their hair and flirting.

Yet ever since primary school, when they'd met at age five, she and Danny had been best friends. Despite the gossips' hints, there was nothing sexual between them.

"We might as well order. I'll have the rump steak with fries and Jessalyn will have the fish and chips."

"Right you are," Mrs. Merryford said as she reclaimed the menus. "There might be a wait."

Jessalyn opened her mouth to protest Danny's highhandedness at ordering for her and snapped it shut again. She'd enjoy the beer even if she preferred a glass of sparkling water, and the fish was always delicious, despite her recent craving for red meat. She'd hate to fight with Danny today. There was enough going on in her life without an argument about her best friend's arrogance.

"What have you been doing today?"

"I went to rugby sign-ups with my cousins."

"Already?" Jessalyn asked. "It's still the middle of summer."

"The Super Rugby competition starts this week," Danny pointed out. "Our coach wants us to win our division this year instead of coming second. For an hour, he lectured us on match fitness. He's given us individual training plans."

"Sounds serious."

"Anyone who slacks won't get picked for the team," Danny said. "There is a band playing at the pub tonight. Want to go?"

"I'm working an extra shift at the fish shop."

"What time do you finish?"

"I won't make the pub. I promised Gerry I'd close for him."

Danny leaned closer and ran his finger down her cheek. "There's a party at Martin's place afterward."

Jessalyn froze before she pulled from the contact. "Oh, no. I'm not going partying. Everyone will be stupid drunk while I'll be sober. I'm going straight home after work. I'm tired, and I haven't been sleeping."

Danny's eyes glowed with a strange light as he leaned closer. "Come to the party. Blow off your shift."

"No," Jessalyn said, incredulous at his suggestion. Gerry was counting on her. "I promised Gerry I'd work tonight. Besides, I need the money."

Danny shrugged. "You have your dad's house and business. You have more money than me."

Jessalyn gaped at him. Something was off with Danny lately, and she couldn't fathom the cause. "I—"

Mrs. Merryford arrived with their drinks.

Just as well. She loathed disagreements with Danny. He was her best friend—even if he did disappear with his cousins when it suited him. Yet given his recent behavior, she hated to confide her problems.

Instead, Jessalyn turned the conversation to juicy local gossip. The affair between the fire brigade chief and a summer visitor who stayed in one of the vacation homes lining the coast. Danny's cousins and the constant parade of women through their lives. The upcoming paddling competition.

Normally, Jessalyn entered with Danny as her partner, but this year he'd chosen to team up with a cousin. Yep, his recent behavior rankled her. This selfish side of Danny wasn't one she appreciated, and he'd hurt her with his rejection of a tradition they'd established as ten-year-old kids.

She hadn't spoken to him for three days.

That had been before her father's death, and when they'd discussed the matter, her father had told her sometimes young men didn't think. Instead of letting Danny boss her around, she could follow her inclinations. Her father's words had made her examine their friendship. Danny tended to lead their activities, but usually, they wanted the same path.

This year, she'd taken on more shifts with Gerry to save for a car. A depressing thought since her meager savings wouldn't come close to paying her father's debts.

Their meals arrived, and they ate them, in charity because they kept to their casual conversation and avoided contentious topics.

Jessalyn finished the last fry and set her knife and fork across her plate. She checked her watch. "I'd better leave or I'll be late." She opened her wallet and pulled out two twenties. "That should cover my share."

Danny picked up the notes and handed them back, a broad beam wreathing his lips. "Don't worry. I've got this."

She stared at him, a combination of shock and *what-the-what* bouncing around her brain. Money melted through Danny's fingers like a hokey-pokey ice cream on a summer's day. Often, she ended up paying their way.

She pressed her lips together and accepted back the money. "Thanks."

"Wait. Let me pay, and I'll walk you to work."

He bounded up and disappeared inside the café before her beleaguered brain snapped into gear. He what? She'd half expected him to join Hika Waaka, his older cousin, and the Johnson twins who'd sashayed into the café five minutes earlier.

Jessalyn rose, willing to wait for exactly two minutes, even though she couldn't believe Danny wanted to walk her to work rather than score a date with Elise Johnson.

She was wrong.

Danny jogged from the café, his brow wrinkled. On spotting her, he beamed his trademark broad grin, easing away from his worry and leaving her puzzled. *Weird*. What was wrong with Danny lately? His predictable behavior had turned on its head, and Jessalyn loathed the off-balance sensation.

She'd always counted on Danny and his predictability. The last three months—not so much.

He fell into step beside her. Jessalyn slid him a glance and caught him studying her. Was that calculation in his expression? No, this wasn't bizarre at all.

Jessalyn cleared her throat and tried to think of something to say, a problem she'd never experienced with Danny. She came up blank. Heck, they'd covered the local gossip. Thank goodness Piha was small, and they'd almost reached Gerry's fish and chip shop.

The blast of the frying food fragrance wafting from the open door had never been so opportune. At the end of her shift, her clothes and hair would stink, but right now, she welcomed an escape from Danny and his peculiar behavior.

"Are you sure you don't need me to pick you up after work?"

"What? No! Thank you," she added when his dark brows squeezed together in displeasure. The pain in her back had returned, but it had risen until it resided between her shoulder blades. All she wanted was to get through this shift and return home. She turned to face him properly, ready to demand an explanation and repeat her point of view on joining a party of drunken people.

But moving faster than his norm, Danny gripped her shoulders, drew her close with his masculine strength, and mashed his lips to hers.

Shock held her immobile for several seconds before anger gave her extra strength. She shoved him away and scrubbed the back of her hand over her mouth. "What is wrong with you?"

"I thought we were friends." Now he projected sullenness as if this was her fault.

"Not that kind of friend," Jessalyn snapped. "Go to your party. I've got work." She pushed past the red plastic strips guarding the door against swarms of flies.

"Hi, Jessalyn," Gerry said from his station behind the counter. His jet-black hair lay flat and limp against his head—a product of the steamy atmosphere—but his brown eyes held a curiosity that nudged into nosiness. "Did I see you and Danny kissing?"

"Yeah." She wrinkled her nose. "A brain fart or something. He's a friend. A brother. I don't know what he was thinking."

"Ouch." Gerry chuckled, his rich and throaty laughter pulling a wry grin from her.

Deciding she'd had enough of the topic, she retrieved her apron. "Do you want me to cook?"

"Please. Are you still okay to close for me tonight? I thought I'd leave after nine. Things should be manageable enough for one by then."

"Of course I'm sure," Jessalyn said, attempting to ignore the nagging pain between her shoulders. Somehow, she'd make it through her shift. The wages would come in handy to pay the bills. So many outstanding bills. Her father had fallen behind on the household accounts—the electricity and the water rates.

Two teenagers pushed past the plastic ribbons hanging from the door and strode to the counter. Jessalyn tied the apron around her waist and waited for the order. Minutes later, a family group entered, and she slid into her routine of battering fish and cooking burgers, toasting buns, and toting boxes of fries from the walk-in freezer.

The steady stream of customers kept her busy enough to forget her problems and Gerry surprised her when he told her it was nine-thirty.

"You go," she said when a lifeguard entered the shop. "I can cope now that the worst of the rush is over."

"I appreciate this, Jessalyn. It'll score points if I spend a few quiet hours with the wife."

"No problem. I'll take as many shifts as you can give me."

Gerry left, his amble ungainly because of his excess weight—he ate too much of his product—and she changed her routine, taking orders and payments plus working the fryers and grill.

The shop remained busy, and it was almost midnight before she cooked her final order and her stream of customers dwindled to nil. Exhausted, she closed the external door and turned the open sign to closed. The nagging pain between her shoulder blades had intensified, twinges darting up and down her spine. Waves of nausea spun through her belly.

Jessalyn trudged to the kitchen. She'd tidied as she worked, which made her final clean-up for the evening easier. She switched off the fryers and grills and placed the unused products in the fridge. By the time she'd almost finished the evening routine, the nausea swirling through her belly had become worse. She leaned against the central steel counter, her hands gripping the edges as she attempted to control her urge to vomit.

She swallowed her croak of distress. For a moment, she thought she'd be okay. She eased out a shuddering breath and drew in a fresh one. The layers of grease and lingering cooking smells caught in her throat. Her stomach convulsed, and acid roared up her gullet. A gagging sound escaped her, and she hung her head, barely able to stand, let alone make the journey to the restroom out the back.

The fish she'd eaten earlier...

She groaned and managed two shambling steps toward the restroom before the contents of her stomach rose up in a gush. Heat burned her throat, her mouth as she hunched in misery. Her stomach heaved and a spurt of flames exited her mouth. Shocked to the core, she cried out and surged to her feet. Her head struck the corner of the workbench, and pain reverberated through her skull. She fell and hit the floor.

She came to, groggy. Something trickled down her cheek, and she pushed herself to her hands and knees. Yellow and orange sparks danced over the fryers and the far wall. Smoke clogged the air.

Fire! The place was on fire.

If Jessalyn's body hadn't revolted, leaving her so wretched and weak, she might have shrieked. Instead, she gaped at the flames as they crawled over a patch of the oily counter. She gasped, light-headed, her stomach hardening. Clenching. The fire ran along the counter and expanded.

Nausea swept from her belly and up, up, up. She swallowed rapidly. Once. Twice. Three times. But it didn't stop. The heat built and built and built until nothing could contain it. Her mouth opened, and with a pained croak, another stream of flames spewed from her throat.

She fell back, the act leaving her drained. The blaze licked across the floor toward her, bright and capricious.

"Oh. Oh!" Jessalyn pushed upright with shaky limbs and teetered to the extinguisher. She pulled the pin and aimed the trigger at the growing conflagration. But the fire had reached the deep fryers. The orange blaze crackled and popped, exploding and growing. Smoke poured upward and the alarms wailed. The stream of foam from the extinguisher died to nothing.

The temperature of the fire grew as did the flames. She backed up and fumbled for her phone. Shaky fingers pushed the emergency number.

"Fire, police, or ambulance," a confident male voice asked.

"Fire!" Jessalyn cried. She rattled off the address and hung up. Retreat. It was the only option now. What had she done? How had this happened? She stumbled from the shop, her fingers trembling as she struggled with the lock on the door.

Outside, she dragged in huge drafts of air, reaction and shock racking her body.

The wail of a fire engine sounded in the distance, becoming steadily louder. The truck pulled up with a squeak of brakes and men piled out. Jessalyn huddled in misery while they dragged out hoses and attempted to tame the inferno. Smoke scented each breath while embers lifted into the air, the flames swelling with the evening breeze and engulfing the building.

The fire chief approached her. "What happened?"

"I don't know," Jessalyn wailed, aghast at the damage. "Something exploded while I was cleaning up after closing. I grabbed the extinguisher, but the fire spread so fast."

"Is that blood on your head? Do you need me to call an ambulance?"

"No. I'm fine. I'd better ring Gerry." Her throat worked, the lining tender from her vomiting. Flames. They had come from her. That's what her confused mind was telling her.

But no. That couldn't be right.

Every logical part of her brain told her that breathing fire was impossible.

Her fingers shook so much she took three attempts to ring Gerry. "Gerry, it's Jessalyn. I'm sorry, but you'd better come back to work. The shop caught on fire."

CHAPTER 2

Time For Plain Talking

One month later

The warehouse in Onehunga was the one place Manu Taniwha found privacy, away from the nagging concerns of his tribe. A place to escape the petty squabbles between the different families. A place to escape the brutal insults from his father who craved death and wanted Manu to execute him with the tribal sword. A place to escape the calls for him to resign as the leader.

A knot formed in his throat, and he swallowed hard to shift it. Tightness in his chest stuttered his breathing, then his lungs screamed for air and his traitorous body kicked back into gear.

In his mind, his taniwha sighed. His dragon had been doing that recently—tutting in disappointment and making Manu feel like an inadequate child. They no longer functioned together, his mother's death the impetus for pulling them apart.

But what sort of son kills his mother?

Manu shook his head hard, attempting to will aside the memories of his father's contempt. Samuel Taniwha refused to listen to Manu or Manu's two younger brothers Tane and Kahurangi.

The sole reason he'd used the sacred sword to behead his mother was because she'd been out of control and intent on murder. He'd had no choice. She'd accused Cassie of betraying Manu, then shifted to dragon and tried to slaughter his cousin Hone and Cassie, who was Hone's girlfriend, along with their friends Jack Sullivan and his mate Emma. Innocents. In doing so, the fallout would've created ripples for his entire tribe and the taniwha species.

He'd tried to talk to his mother, attempted to tell her he and Cassie were nothing more than friends who enjoyed each other's company. A waste of breath. Nothing he'd said had softened her or changed her mind. According to June Taniwha, those who deceived her son threatened her dynasty.

Then the unforgiveable had happened. The sacred sword—the one given by the gods to each tribal leader—had wrenched from his mother's dragon and burned into Manu's back. What should have been a week-long ceremony of happiness and celebration had occurred in the space of a blink.

This, combined with learning Hone was dating Cassie, had pushed his mother off the edge of sanity.

"And in breaking news, there is yet another fire burning in the bush above Piha Beach. A police spokesman confirmed this is the third fire to break out in the area. Although conditions are dry due to the lack of recent rain, Detective Webster stated they believe this most recent fire and the preceding ones are the work of an arsonist. He said—"

Again, Manu attempted to focus on the plans lying on the desk.

"Manu! Are you here?"

Manu turned at Hone's shout. Hone's friend and fellow private detective Jack stood with him. They were the only two people, apart from his brothers, he trusted with the location of his warehouse. Desperately requiring privacy, Manu had started spending nights here after his father and other tribal members had tracked him down to Hone's property in Red Hill, Papakura. Their goal: harassment.

No—they'd wanted to provoke him into losing his temper.

Manu issued a heavy sigh and tossed his pen aside. "Over here." It wasn't as if he was getting much design work done these days and not after his father's latest tirade this morning.

"How is the testing going on the stealth gadget?" Hone asked, setting a cooler bag on Manu's desk. His recent haircut had put a dent in his curls, and he gave off a contented vibe after his marriage to Cassie.

"It's not. What with all the stuff to do with the tribe and Dad's shenanigans, I'm not getting time to do anything for myself, let alone work on my inventions." Manu sighed inwardly. Hone and Jack were lucky. They'd both found true mates to stand at their sides. Not every taniwha was so blessed.

Jack placed a smaller cooler bag down beside Hone's. This one clinked.

"Cassie and Emma ordered us to track you down and make sure you eat dinner," Hone said. "They told us not to come home until we found you."

Manu frowned, sweeping his irritating, in-need-of-a-cut black hair away from his face. "I thought Emma is due to pop any day."

Jack shifted his broad shoulders in a shrug. "Emma pushed me out the door and informed me my hovering was making her nervous. She couldn't breathe, let alone think with me around. She informed me Cassie was coming over, and they both had me on speed dial if they required my presence."

Hone chuckled at Jack's uneasiness. "While we were searching for you, we discussed borrowing your stealth gadgets so Jack could hover over Emma in peace. Cassie sent food and a few beers. I think she is trying to placate everyone." As he spoke, he unzipped the smaller chiller bag and handed Manu a cold beer. After offering one to Jack, he opened the large bag.

This one held a bacon and egg pie—at least that's what Manu's taniwha senses told him—and filled rolls. Manu's stomach gurgled loudly enough for Hone and Jack to hear.

Hone tossed Manu a ham roll, and his taste buds kicked into a *feed-me* chant, echoing his stomach's complaints before Manu peeled away the plastic covering.

"There's a picnic table out the back," Manu said, indicating a door. "Might as well enjoy this food in comfort."

The men settled at the table with their food and beers. The faint tang of the sea floated to Manu, and he released his tense muscles, knowing with Hone and Jack, he could be himself.

Hone glanced at Jack before centering his gaze on Manu. "We're worried about you."

Manu didn't offer any empty words of pretense. "Taking over as the leader has been hell. I always knew this was what Mum wanted—to keep the tribal leadership in the family—but secretly I'd intended to continue with my inventions. I guess, I hoped the sacred sword would pick Tane or Kahurangi or even Haurahi, although I doubt he'd ever return to Auckland. Hell, the sword could've picked anyone in the tribe."

"It chose you," Jack said, his mien serious.

Manu laughed, the dark growl of amusement underscored with bitterness and frustration and every other black emotion roiling inside him. "I've tried to get rid of the bloody thing. I put on the stealth gadget, flew over the West Coast beaches, and dropped the sword in the Tasman Sea. Once I returned here and shifted back to human, I could feel my taniwha grasping the sword's hilt. This morning I tossed it into the crater lake on Mount Ruapehu. My sword didn't take to Lake Taupo or the Pacific Ocean either." Manu swallowed the last of his beer and set the bottle on the wooden tabletop with a thump. He stood and whipped off his trademark black T-shirt. With a fashion model swagger, he turned to present his back and show Hone and Jack his taniwha tattoo. "The sword is resting in my dragon's hand, right?"

"It's there," Hone agreed, then he laughed. "Your taniwha is giving me the finger."

Manu snorted. "That's directed at me rather than you. Damn sword is like a homing pigeon. I can't get rid of it so I continue to have these responsibilities for my ungrateful tribe. They're worse than a bunch of kindergarten kids."

Hone reached for the bacon and egg pie and cut three generous hunks. "Maybe you're having problems because you're reacting instead of acting. Set boundaries. Make rules. Clean house."

Jack dipped his head in agreement, his mouth full of pie. He swallowed. "Hone is right. Call a meeting and tell the tribe of your expectations. Enforce them."

Manu stared at his pie. "There is another problem. Everyone with single daughters is tossing them at me. They might not accept me as their leader, but as long as the sword remains with me, they view me as fair game. I don't want marriage."

Hone chuckled while Jack *tsk-tsked* at his whiny complaint of too many women.

"Not much has changed there," Jack said. "Before it was your mother tossing women at you."

Manu grimaced even as he steeled himself for the sharp pang of regret. He'd killed his own mother without hesitation. That made him a monster.

A bird arrowed overhead and settled in one of the three big totara trees still standing on the land surrounding his warehouse. It flapped its wings before calling in its distinctive hoot. *Morepork. Morepork.* It was a ruru, a native New Zealand owl.

Manu snorted because he could practically hear Jack's and Hone's thoughts. "A messenger from the underworld. I remember my grandmother telling us about the ruru. Their arrival outside a home meant there would be a death in the family. Her ancestors used to catch the bird and eat it, hoping to prolong their own lives."

Jack shook his head. "Some people believe they are guardians from the underworld, sent to help and advise. They can be a warning but also hold the power to protect."

"I vote for Jack's version of the story," Hone said. "My grandfather told me both versions when I used to visit with my parents. He still lives near a large native forest and would take me on evening walks to become one with nature. Besides, you only need to worry if the bird makes its *quee* call—the high-pitch screech. This one has called *morepork*. According to Granddad, that is an excellent sign. It says good news is on the way."

"I can do with all the protection and advantageous news I can get. Dad and his cronies are after my head." Pain arrowed through him at the mess he'd made of his familial relationships. At least Tane and Kahurangi supported him since they'd been there at the end. As had Jack and Hone. Haurahi, his youngest brother, wasn't speaking to him while his father blasted him with threats.

"Have the Waaka family approached you or attempted to take over the Auckland region?" Hone asked.

"Not yet, but my gut says it's coming. Nelson Waaka would love to rule over the Northland *and* the Auckland taniwha. He craves power. They're playing a game, waiting for us to tear ourselves apart and inflict enough internal damage to make their leadership coup certain of success," Manu said. "Tradition says the sacred sword goes to the strongest. At least that has happened in the past."

"Our point. You are an excellent leader and you're capable of guiding our tribe to great things." Hone handed out more beers. "But right now you're not leading. Grab your paddlers and make them row in time instead of letting the canoe bob around the sea like a floating stick."

"Fine in theory," Manu said. "But how do you expect me to manage that? They're a stubborn lot, and Dad isn't helping matters."

"Will he listen to Tane or Kahurangi?" Jack asked. "They

understand the situation and how your mother lost her marbles. Emma still has scars."

The owl hooted twice before gliding away on silent wings. Manu watched it fly until it melded with the evening sky, and he shuddered at how close Emma had come to death at his mother's hands.

"You're right." Manu shoved at his hair to clear his vision. "I disagreed with a lot of Mum's methods, but she kept everyone in line."

"It occurs to me you could use your stealth gadget to learn what is happening within the tribe. Get a handle on the weak spots. The hotheads. Your supporters," Hone said.

"That's intrusive," Manu objected, although his inventor mind rushed ahead, considering the opportunity to further test his stealth gadget.

"Think of it this way. What would your mother have done if she had the same opportunity to use your stealth invention?" Jack asked, cutting straight to the core.

"She wouldn't have hesitated," Manu said. "I'd hoped to do things differently."

Hone carved the last of the bacon and egg pie into three. "You can, but first, you have to exert control. Get to a place where you can talk to everyone, and they'll listen, even if they have issues with your possession of the sword. We were too young to notice what went down when your mother took over from her uncle, but Dad said she had difficulties getting the tribe behind her because she was a woman. She didn't stand for any crap from anyone. As her son, you know that."

"You could always hire George Taniwha and Sons to do the snooping for you," Jack said. "Does your invention make a taniwha invisible in human form?"

"Yes." A downside because this made his invention valuable to those who skirted or broke the law.

"Can our people sense our presence even though we're invisible?" Hone asked. "Have you tested that aspect of your invention?"

"Not yet. Getting the invisibility part right was more important," Manu said.

"We'll test it for you," Hone said.

"It might work," Manu agreed, the designer in him wanting his invention perfect in all aspects. "All right. Talk to Uncle George and make sure he approves of this scheme. Tane and Kahurangi will help." He hesitated before straightening his shoulders. Decisiveness—that's what he required. "I'll take a turn or two. As much as I dislike spying on my people, I have to do something. I hate the idea of the Waaka family sitting back and waiting to collect the spoils. Even if I can't reach Dad and his friends and make them understand, I might make a difference with the younger taniwha."

"Our work here is done," Hone said, not hiding his satisfaction.

He and Jack exchanged a high-five.

Manu frowned. "You came here to maneuver me into a decision. What if I'd said no or tossed you out on your butts?"

"You could try," Hone said with a wink at Jack. "Several problems with that. Our wives would protest if you messed up our pretty faces. Right now, everything sets off Emma and turns her into a Mama Bear. Secondly, you might best one of us, but two—not a hope. And thirdly, any reaction is better than this sullen ice-man front you've been showing us for the last six months."

"Tane said you're hanging out either at Hone's house in Red Hill or here and not seeing anyone if you can help it. What are you doing for sex?" Jack asked.

Manu understood what Jack meant. The moon controlled a taniwha, and if they didn't shift on a regular basis, only lots of sex enabled adults to hold their human forms. "Your spies have missed vital information," he said drily. "I'm flying most days since my stealth invention works well, and when I get sick of my own company, I put on a disguise and go into the central city. The pubs and restaurants at The Viaduct are ideal to find uncomplicated feminine company."

Jack gaped at him then grinned, and Manu returned the sentiment. There had been a time when Jack's expression never shifted from tough-guy surly. Emma had changed that, and it was an improvement.

"Full moon is an excellent time because most taniwha stay away from the city in case they lose control. I've found my restraint is better than ever if I can find a woman who attracts me. Women like my scowl and tattoos. When they see the bike that seals the deal. We go to a hotel, have mutual fun and pleasure then I leave while they get a paid night in swanky accommodation. Best of all, I'm not sleeping with a woman from the tribe who expects more. Win-win."

Hone shook his head. "I can't decide if I admire your strategy or feel sorry for you."

Manu shrugged. "I'm not doing anything different from every other single taniwha male. You both did the same in the past."

"You'll understand if you find a true mate," Jack answered for Hone. "Everything is different—better—when you have a woman who accepts you flaws and all, lying in bed beside you."

A phone buzzed, and Jack jumped. Manu bit back a laugh on seeing his friend's panic and the tremor in his hand.

"It's time," Cassie said, her voice easily audible with their acute hearing. "We're on our way to the hospital."

"I'll drive," Hone said, holding out his hand for Jack's vehicle keys. "Manu, we'll be back tomorrow for the stealth units. I'll talk to Dad tonight, but I'm certain he won't have any issues with this plan. He's worried and wants to help but hates to overstep. Cuz, we have your back."

"Hone, are you coming?" Jack snapped. "Emma is in labor!"

"We'll ring when there is news," Hone said, his amusement clear as he increased his strides to a jog. "We're gonna be uncles."

"No, you're not," Jack barked, sounding remarkably like the Jack before Emma.

"Honorable uncles," Hone said, their voices floating to Manu even though they'd disappeared around the front. "Uncle Hone and Uncle Manu. We're gonna teach your son or daughter to misbehave."

"Stop talking. Drive!"

Manu rolled his shoulders and stretched his hands above his head. The food and company had helped, his cousin's straight-talking making him think. Hone and Jack were right. His current style of leadership was a joke, and it was time to make changes.

A faint flutter of wings drew his attention to the totara trees. The ruru had returned. It settled briefly before taking off, doing a slow swoop over his head, and flying toward the inner city. When Manu didn't move, the owl repeated the same flight path. It was almost as if the ruru was tempting Manu to fly with him.

Not a bad idea. Manu strode to his safe and scanned his left hand to open the lock. With the stealth gadget strapped around his wrist, he disrobed before walking outside. The ruru sat in the tree.

Manu tapped a button on his gadget and shifted, letting his taniwha free. A blast of joy and happiness filled him, most of the emotion coming from his taniwha. He took off, flapping his wings and propelling his body into the air.

To his surprise, the ruru lifted off his branch and glided close to Manu. The way the bird turned its head told Manu it sensed his presence, despite his invisibility. The owl flew ahead of him, the bird's flight path taking him toward the business center of Auckland city. They soared past Cornwall Park and the dormant volcano cones of One Tree Hill and did a swoop over Mount Eden. The ruru appeared to prefer the areas where trees grew and zigzagged his way across the bright lights until he skirted The Viaduct and the port of Auckland.

Unconcerned with his destination, Manu kept pace with the darting ruru as the owl glided toward the Domain and the floodlit War Memorial Museum that crouched on top of the hill. Once they reached the Domain, the owl flapped in a lazy circle. It was almost as if the bird wanted him to see something.

With a mental shrug, Manu paid closer attention. He spotted several homeless people sleeping rough during the warmer summer weather. Two vehicles sat in the parking spaces nearest the museum. Their occupants lazed on blankets and ate a picnic dinner. His nostrils flared. Fried chicken and burgers. The men and women drank wine from paper cups, their laughter and happy chatter bringing a smile. A normal outing with clandestine drinking since the city powers prohibited alcohol in public areas. Close on the heels of his happy-for-you smile came envy.

This was something he could never have, especially not now.

If he exerted his leadership, the next step would be pressure to take a partner.

The ruru called—a shriek close to a *quee* but not quite.

Manu scanned the clump of trees below and caught the flicker of flames. As they flew on, he spotted several bare patches and sniffed the soot and ashes of a recent fire. The ruru did another slow circle over the area before winging in the direction of his warehouse.

At a loss to decipher what the bird wanted him to see, Manu gave a mental shrug and followed. The owl had taken a risk flying over the city and exposing itself to gulls. The least he could do was protect the ruru during the return flight.

CHAPTER 3

The Trespasser

I t was happening again! Jessalyn issued a pained cry, her gaze on the flames darting along the branch of a manuka tree. The fire spat and multiplied, feeding with ravenous hunger on the summer-dry branches.

"You!" a rough voice called.

Jessalyn moaned. Fear and panic at capture kicked in her flight instinct. She ran, her daypack filled with her remaining possessions. It *thud-thud-thudded* uncomfortably against her back with each step.

"Stop. Stop! He's over there!"

Masculine voices called, alerting others of her progress as she raced through the Domain. Her lungs burned, a stitch growing in her side. Her breaths sawed in her tender throat as she forced her weary body to greater speed.

Instinct—a whisper in her mind—told her to dart right, so she did. She sprinted past a wooden bungalow, one of the old ones built almost two hundred years ago by white settlers. Another bungalow of a similar age but painted a buttermilk cream sat next door. She raced past that one and several other buildings. Gradually, the age changed. Modern buildings. Shops. Offices. She slowed to listen for her pursuers and slowed yet again. She'd lost them. In the shadow of an exotic tree with flower-laden branches, she halted and bent at the waist to suck in air.

This was unsafe. *She* was dangerous, and it was a miracle she hadn't killed anyone yet. So far, she'd damaged property. Gerry's business. Part of the native bush surrounding Piha. Her father's garden shed.

She had no idea what was wrong with her, but this wasn't a problem fixable by a normal garden-variety doctor. People didn't go around willy-nilly spurting flames, setting trees and property alight. With no control over the fire, she never knew when an unfortunate sneeze or her dinner might produce flames. The one constant was her fire-breathing occurred in the evening.

So far, she'd avoided detection, but tonight had been a close thing. Maybe she should go back to Piha...

No! The authorities had already declared the fires the work of an arsonist. She'd made the news headlines. Jessalyn had told Danny she needed to sell the last of her father's wooden boxes at the Matakana Farmers' market. While it was true she urgently required money, she'd gone farther south and pedaled the boxes at a market in Onehunga. With no hope of meeting the mortgage payment, she'd sold her father's SUV. From the proceeds, she'd managed enough cash to pay almost four mortgage payments, and she'd deposited this money into her father's business account. A cushion to give her a chance to plan. Instead of returning home to Piha, she'd stayed in the city and found a job working in the kitchen of an upmarket pub in The Viaduct.

Things had been going well until she'd breathed fire again. Oh, and the lowlife who broken into her hostel room and taken possession of some of her belongings hadn't helped.

With her breathing almost normal again, Jessalyn scanned her surroundings for signs of her pursuers. But no shouts intruded into this quiet suburban street in Parnell. She eased from the shadows, straightened her daypack and made her way to the harbor. She'd promised to help with the stock count tonight. It wasn't as if the hostel was a haven now. It was time to find somewhere safer to live. Hopefully, someone had a copy of today's newspaper for her to scan, or failing that, she'd visit Auckland library and use their computers to do an online search.

The apartment in Onehunga, close to the train station, was

perfect. The two men searching for a flatmate were not. One glance at their sly blue eyes and her gut screamed danger. She'd told them she was looking at several places and departed with her skin crawling. Since leaving Piha, she'd learned the world was full of creeps, and she no longer wondered why women came into the pub where she worked in cackling groups. Easier to stay alive if you were part of a herd.

With nothing pressing to do, Jessalyn explored the area. She window-shopped and browsed in a secondhand bookstore, purchasing a cheap thriller and a battered copy of the history of the Onehunga area. She wandered past an old post office, now a trendy café busy with the evening trade, and inhaled. The tang of salt filled her lungs, and following instinct, she redirected her steps to the water.

Although it was almost eight, the passing groups of people and families on the well-lit street didn't give off threatening vibes. Her stomach released a hungry grumble, and she hesitated. She craved hot and spicy foods, but the spiciness caused extra flames.

A whiff of curry spices floated her way and soon an Indian restaurant came into sight. Her stomach rumbled anew. She held her breath and followed the deep-fat fryer scents of the fish and chip shop next door.

An overweight woman sprawled on a chair near the counter. A large greasy mark stained her apron at chest level, and her scowl told Jessalyn she wasn't keen on moving from her comfortable spot. She heaved upright with a heavy sigh. "What will it be?"

"A hamburger and fries."

"You want beetroot?"

"Yes, please." Jessalyn handed over a ten-dollar note and waited for her change.

"Hamburger with the works and fries," the woman hollered as she offered Jessalyn several coins.

"Hamburger works and fries," a young male called back, his voice cracking and soaring higher at the end of his sentence.

Jessalyn planted herself on a holey leather-covered bench and waited. A family arrived—a mother pushing a stroller with a baby plus a husband and a screaming toddler.

"Here," Jessalyn said to the mother. "Have a seat. My order won't be much longer."

The mother sank onto the seat with a grateful smile. "It's been a long afternoon, but hopefully Junior will sleep through the night. We've exhausted them with fresh air and exercise."

Jessalyn murmured polite agreement and did a bobblehead nod, despite her lack of experience with children. "Is there a nearby park where I could eat my dinner?"

"Yes, we've come from there. Turn left and follow the bike and walking path along the waterfront. You can't miss it. The park is a ten-minute walk, faster for you since you don't have children stopping to investigate every little thing. Or you can walk across the old Mangere Bridge toward Ambury Park. There's a small park that way too."

"Thanks." Jessalyn stood to accept her burger from the beefy woman at the counter.

Outside the takeaway shop, she hesitated as she recalled the woman's directions. She glanced left and right and picked left, eager to escape the delectable curry scent. Everything inside her churned. Her stomach. Her mind. Her thoughts. She bit her lip and scanned her surroundings. Nothing out of the ordinary.

Six steps later, she halted, whirled, and marched right.

The faint anxiety that had assailed her faded as she approached the old bridge, which now days was restricted to pedestrians, cyclists, and fishermen.

Jessalyn jerked her head in a silent greeting to two elderly men who dangled hand-lines over the edge of the bridge railing. Once she passed, they continued with their discussion on which team might win the Super Rugby competition this year. This area spoke to her. A pity the apartment hadn't worked out, but the creep factor from those two men... Yuck. No sense baiting trouble or making her life more difficult than it was now.

The water whooshed and slapped the shoreline with tiny waves, and the breeze tugged at her hair. In deference to the warm day and her job in a steamy kitchen, she'd tied her long hair into a knot at her nape. Now, she released the black locks and let the breeze stir the strands into disarray. With the turmoil in her life, the last thing she needed was to worry about her appearance.

Her mind slipped back to Danny. He'd attempted to kiss her a second time. She'd backed up and immediately scrubbed away the lingering contact. It wasn't as if she didn't enjoy a kiss or two or sex, but Danny's kisses repelled her. Wet, for one. Slobbery. Her actions had injured his feelings, and he'd stomped away in a huff. They hadn't spoken much before she'd left Piha.

Guilt sliced through her again, as it did every time her thoughts turned to Danny.

They'd been friends forever, yet at the end, the gap between them had never yawned wider. When she'd needed him most.

Jessalyn shoved Danny and her life in Piha—the fires—to the closet of her mind. The small park the woman had mentioned was a tiny sliver of green amongst the houses and other buildings. Despite the twilight, she was able to pick out one of the old, dormant volcanoes that studded the area. Unfamiliar with the suburb, she decided to visit the library soon and print out a map to orient herself.

She picked a spot on the ground near the waterfront and sat to eat her burger. After her walk, her food was lukewarm but her hungry belly didn't care. She bit into her burger, having difficulty getting her mouth around the meat patty and salad filling. Despite the slovenly appearance of the woman serving at the counter, the food was tasty and lettuce crunched as she bit down. A tiny moan escaped as the tang of relish, the sweetness of beetroot, and the caramelized meat combined. She swallowed and made herself pick up a fry. Lessons learned since arriving in Auckland. If she gobbled her food, she paid for it later. Her stomach turned acidic and soon fire surged up her throat.

Even though it was getting late, Jessalyn didn't hurry. Since a kind person had stolen most of her stuff and spare cash three days ago while she'd been at work, she'd had to leave the pay-by-day lodgings and sleep rough. Somewhere here in Onehunga was as good a place as any. The Domain had become too dangerous. If the weird flaming thing started again...

Jessalyn finished her meal and stood. She slapped dry grass off her jeans and wandered away from the shore toward the old volcano crater. A dog barked when she passed a house, and a woman spoke sharply, ordering the animal to desist. Jessalyn increased her pace, hurrying past since she hated to draw attention.

The sections ahead were bigger, and this part of the street seemed more manufacturing with warehouses and wire fences around boundaries. Somewhere ahead, a ruru called, and the faint anxiety that came from trying to decide where to sleep for the night eased. Jessalyn headed in the direction of the cries of the owl.

Morepork. Morepork.

She stopped in front of a lot that bore a rusted warehouse. The long grass and weeds around the building gave it a dilapidated appearance. The wire fence enclosing the lot fit right in with the rickety, iron-clad warehouse, although the shiny padlock on the gate told her someone owned the property and was serious in deterring intruders. She hesitated then darted down the side of the fence and squeezed through the first hole she discovered.

Her heart raced while she froze in her crouch and listened for signs her trespassing had been noticed. Not a dog barked. Not a voice hurled abuse. Instead, the ruru called from its perch high in a totara tree, and its call seemed welcoming.

Jessalyn found a spot where the grass grew tall enough to conceal her presence. Free from blackberry and other prickly weeds, the area would make a soft bed. She set the alarm on her watch to give herself time to catch the train to her job and made herself comfortable.

Restless, Manu tossed and turned on his narrow bed. After his long flight the previous night and the test flight for a newer version of his stealth gadget today, he should've fallen asleep. He stood and walked to the tiny kitchenette where he had the basics. Hot food, courtesy of an old microwave, a kettle, a fridge to keep milk and beer cold and a sink. A window above the sink allowed him to look over the rear of his property at the totara trees and the unkempt grass. The grass and weeds out the front were just as bad, but he'd found the neglected appearance kept away visitors.

He poured himself a glass of water and scanned the trees, wondering if he'd spot the ruru again. About to turn away, he glimpsed a spark of light in the long grass. As he stared at it, confused as to what it was, the bright spot grew larger.

Fire!

Manu raced outside via a side door, heedless of his nudity. With the lack of rain, if that fire spread, he might lose his warehouse. Damn. He could hardly beat out the flames with his hands. He sprinted back inside and grabbed a fire extinguisher. By the time he returned with the extinguisher in hand, the flames had spread.

He skidded to a halt as he noticed a woman, cursing and swearing as she thumped the flames with... Was that a T-shirt?

"Get out of my way," Manu snarled and pulled the pin on the extinguisher. He aimed at the base of the fire, terror racing through him. If this didn't work, he might lose everything.

The foam doused the flames and for a while, he thought he'd win, but the breeze picked up, breathing new life into the blaze.

Once the contents of the extinguisher finished, he cast it aside and raced for the hose.

"Make yourself useful," he ordered. "There are old sacks inside the door. Grab a pile and help me put out this fire."

Probably wasting his breath. He didn't bother waiting to see if the woman obeyed but turned on the water and ran out the hose. It was too short, but he aimed the flow at the surrounding grass. To his relief, the water doused some of the flames, and he relaxed once he realized he'd halted the spread.

The woman appeared, her black hair blowing around her face and obscuring her features. A stranger. What the hell did she think she was doing trespassing on his property? Hadn't the padlock told her he didn't welcome visitors?

She attacked the flames with the sacking while he continued to flood the area with water. Finally, the fire vanished and only charred grass and the delicate green fragrance coming from the woman remained.

Manu shook himself. What the hell? He stomped back to his warehouse, dragging the hose with him. After turning off the water, he coiled the hose, leaving it tidy for next time, and switched on the outer lights. He wanted illumination while he interrogated his intruder.

From the corner of his eye, he spotted the woman's stealthy retreat. "Where the hell are you going?"

For an instant, she froze then she bolted, darting toward a hole in his fence. Obviously, the spot where she'd entered his property. Manu sprinted after her and grabbed one kicking leg before she squeezed free. Fear and desperation gave her strength, but he was even more determined. He hauled her back and dragged her closer to his warehouse. She kicked but didn't shout or screech in the usual feminine manner. She didn't speak at all, just renewed her struggle.

Manu grasped both of her arms and shook her a little. "Stop fighting."

"You're naked." Her gaze darted down his torso, lingered on his groin, and skittered away with the speed of a frightened rabbit. Beneath her dark brows, her brown eyes were rounds, while her brown skin hinted at a combination of European and Māori ancestry. She stood tall, perhaps six inches less than his six-four height, and she was solid. Muscular rather than fat. The baggy jeans and burned T-shirt she'd donned didn't do her justice. Through the burn holes in the cotton, he glimpsed a flat stomach, and her breasts pushed against the fabric, hinting at their fullness.

Startled by the burst of heat in him, he sucked in a deep inhalation. A huge mistake. Her fresh green scent filled his lungs and stirred his taniwha from his usual sulk.

"Why are you on my property?"

"I wanted somewhere to sleep."

Truth.

"Why did you set the fire?"

"I didn't!"

This time her words held a crisp edge. *Lie.*

"Give me one reason why I shouldn't call the cops."

Her brown eyes widened. "No. Please don't do that. I—"

"Stop. If you're going to tell me you'll do anything in exchange for me turning a blind eye to this, don't go any further." He froze as her gaze slid to his groin again and cursed inwardly as his cock filled and lengthened.

He shoved her away but pinned her with a glower when she gathered herself to run in another escape attempt.

"Don't," he warned in a harsh growl.

"I-I'm not running. I'm gonna be sick." She made a hoarse

sound from deep in her throat and lurched to the right.

Manu glanced away, wanting to give her the illusion of privacy while every one of his senses focused on her. Instead of a vomit and stomach acid stench, ash, charcoal, and smoke filled his nostrils. His gaze whipped back to her, and he cursed. He grabbed one of the unused sacks he hadn't returned to his warehouse and beat at the flames that licked over the flattened grass. The woman made a croaking sound and spat another line of sparks. At least this one was on a patch damp from his firefighting efforts and the dry stalks sizzled but didn't catch.

Now, he watched her closely, and despite the soot and burned grass, he kept catching whiffs of her personal scent. It reminded him of standing in a patch of native bush, and he dragged her perfume deeper into his lungs. Underlying the fresh green was a hint of flowers and honey.

Nectar, his taniwha supplied helpfully. *I like it.*

Every muscle in Manu's body locked, his mind snapping and popping, so great was his shock. Beneath his tenseness, his beast quivered like an unruly puppy, ready to break his master's order to stay. Manu swallowed hard and cautiously sniffed. This time, he groaned faintly as he dragged in her scent. *Crap on a stick.* He closed his eyes as she barked out another croak. Once she stopped, he beat out the new fire.

"What is your name?" Manu understood his taniwha's stupid giddiness and excitement while he—the man—trembled as if he balanced on the edge of a cliff. One wrong move, and he'd free-fall. "Name."

She wiped her mouth and met his gaze with trepidation. "I don't know what is wrong with me."

"Name."

"Jessalyn McKenzie."

"Finished?"

She hesitated before releasing the tension in her shoulders.

Manu held out his hand, and caution slipped over her face before she grasped his fingers. He hauled her to her feet, so rattled by her scent and appearance he forgot to temper his strength. She bounced against his chest. Jessalyn grunted at the impact, and he steadied her with hands at her hips. A mistake because now her enticing scent flowed through his lungs. His mind groped to understand while his taniwha thumped out a victory haka.

This stranger... Jessalyn McKenzie was his mate. This woman was the one nature had determined his perfect match. He eased his grip on her hips and ignored her gasp and his swelling dick.

"How long have you been breathing fire?"

She blinked once, her dark lashes screening her brown eyes. Her swallow was audible, and anxiety shrouded her like the traditional feather cloak handed down through the generations in his family.

"Tell me." He snapped out the words, and she jumped.

His taniwha stirred beneath Manu's skin, and it was easy to discern his displeasure. He was scaring their mate.

"S-six weeks."

"The fires in the Domain?"

She gulped, her gaze darting to the battered runners on her feet. "Yes."

"Do you enjoy lighting fires?"

"No!" Her gaze snapped to him, and she tried to yank free. "Enjoy this? I have no control, and that's scary. There's something wrong with me, and it's not the kind of thing I can consult about with a doctor. They'd lock me up."

Manu frowned. He'd watched her poor control, but he'd assumed he'd scared her or made her nervous. But her lack of finesse was a problem. It was a matter of time before the cops caught her. He'd seen and listened to the media coverage—the speculation of a firebug lighting fires in the Domain. The press had interviewed several of the homeless people who slept rough in the nearby bush. He'd witnessed the glow of fires during his flight the previous evening.

An insidious thought crept through his brain, and his hands tightened at her hips. It had become obvious to him, she didn't know why she was breathing fire. And her control. She had none. She was a danger—to property, to herself, to the taniwha people.

Jessalyn McKenzie might be the woman destined as his mate, but if she didn't exert control on her taniwha, his people would fear for their safety and bay for her blood. He'd have no option but to execute her.

CHAPTER 4

Captured

The determination and hint of regret in the man's eyes scared her breathless. Jessalyn twisted her body, desperate to put space between them, so conscious was she of his naked state. The man was all muscle and grace, his shaggy black hair too long. He was taller than her, and his features settled into fierce and watchful, his eyes bulging and bringing to mind a Māori warrior. His brown eyes held an inner fire that was a little scary if she was honest.

"Come inside," he said, his husky voice causing gooseflesh to ripple over her skin. Something inside her, a small part of her weird mind, liked this man, approved of him despite the fact he was naked and sported an erection. While she was trying not to peek, it was difficult when the thing poked her every time he yanked her at the hips.

"You're a stranger." *And he knew she'd breathed fire.* What was he thinking? She couldn't read him. This time she allowed her gaze to drift past his muscled chest, over his rippling abs to strike his cock.

At least she'd been smart enough to give him a false surname. The name of her favorite All Black rugby player had popped into her mind, and she'd told the scary man without a blink.

Go her.

He laughed, the humor shifting his face from scary to sexy and charming. Then, he went impassive. "Inside. I'm not giving you an option. You can take a shower, and I'll find you a change of clothes."

Despite her trepidation, Jessalyn puffed out a breath and made direct eye contact to indicate acquiescence. He hadn't pounced, apart from when she'd run. He hadn't forced her to kiss or touch him. And he didn't give off the creep factor like the two men at the Onehunga flat.

Her fingers tingled, and she curled them to a fist to halt her treacherous urge to run them over his chest. She wanted—needed—to test his pectoral muscles and learn if his flesh was as hard and unforgiving as she expected. The urge—the craving left her knees weak, and they almost buckled when he released her and strode to a side door.

Given the opportunity to ogle, she stared with laser focus. Tight buttocks. Long legs. A tattoo of a dragon on his back. A fierce dragon holding a sword. She studied the lines, and as he stepped inside the door, she blinked. The dragon tattoo had not moved. It had *not* craned its elegant neck to better see her.

Curiosity had her straightening the daypack on her shoulders and following him. Whoever he was, because he hadn't told her his name when he'd demanded hers. She stepped inside the warehouse and a gasp escaped. The interior did *not* match the rusty exterior since it was sleek and modern and so neat she glanced down at her grubby shoes in trepidation. Her brain ticked over as she crept after him.

"If you're intending to knock me out and rob me, you should know I'm fast and much stronger than you," he said.

"Also bigheaded with eyes at the back of your head," she snapped.

He laughed and opened a cupboard. The dragon in his tattoo beamed toothy joy, his grip on the sword relaxing and making him wobble. Frowning, she refocused and shook her head. What the devil was wrong with her? Not only had she breathed fire, but her mind was conjuring impossible scenarios.

He turned and handed her a towel. "The shower is through there. I'll leave you a set of clean clothes outside the door. Are you hungry?"

"Yes." She was always starving these days but couldn't afford to eat as much as she wanted. Luckily, meals came as part of her job and that helped, but she'd dropped the extra weight she'd carried from indulging her sweet tooth.

"Coffee?"

"Do you have tea?"

"Yeah, I think so. Emma and Cassie have been drinking tea lately."

He turned away and disappeared through another inner door. Emma and Cassie? Did he have a wife and daughter? Her mind railed at the idea, and impatient with herself, she strode through the first door. She set her daypack right next to the shower cubicle where she could grab it if necessary. No way did she intend to lose the sole possessions she'd retained after the ransacking of her room.

The shower was no-frills basic, but the water was hot and she stepped under the pounding flow with gratitude. After leaving the hostel, she'd managed a quick flannel wash at work, but it wasn't the same as a shower. She helped herself to his soap and rubbed it over her skin to release a lemon fragrance. Jessalyn washed her hair too, sneaking a smidge of his shampoo. More of the citrus aroma filled the steamy shower. Aware of the passing time and her vulnerability in this naked state, she rushed through rinsing.

Once she'd dried herself, she cracked open the door. The clothing he'd promised sat in a neat pile on the spotless floor. She scooped them up and noted he'd included a pair of boxer shorts. Dressed in the black T-shirt and matching black sweatpants, she made quick work of rinsing her bra and panties and placing them on the towel rail to dry. Her T-shirt was only fit for the trash, but her jeans were still wearable.

With her daypack in hand, she went in search of the man. Hopefully, he'd donned clothes because staring at his naked body was doing peculiar things to her libido while her traitorous hands craved physical contact.

"I'm in here," he called.

The man had the hearing of a bat. She frowned and turned in that direction. To her relief and disappointment—bizarre, contrary emotions—he'd dressed in casual clothes. His feet were bare, and she found herself staring at them.

"I'm putting on a load of washing. I can toss your clothes in too."

"Thanks, I'll get them." She ripped her gaze off his long feet—who knew feet were sexy?—and retrieved her underwear along with her jeans and towel. "What is your name?" she asked on her return.

"Manu Taniwha," he said. "I've got beans on toast. That okay?"

She hovered, uneasy yet having few alternatives. Manu had already shown his strength and quick thinking. *No one knows where you are.* "Not helping," she muttered.

"What isn't helping?"

She scowled at him. "Your eavesdropping on private conversations."

"Often talk to yourself? It's a sign of madness, you know."

"As if I haven't already demonstrated I'm square in the middle of cuckoo land," she snapped. "Well, do you intend to feed me or not?"

Jessalyn groaned inwardly. She suffered from a broken filter too, or she'd never have offered him lip and rudeness. To her relief, he chuckled and strolled past her. She waited for a beat before following. Much safer since the unconventional inclination to lick his arm had her tongue tingling. Now, if she went ahead with the impulse and ran her tongue down his strong neck, that would truly paint her as abnormal.

"Take a seat," Manu said, gesturing at the small white table with two chairs.

"What is this place?" Everything was so clean, so neat. In contrast, her father's workshop was chaotic, but it was hard to keep the place spotless with wood shavings flying everywhere.

"If I work late, I stay the night."

Jessalyn scanned the area visible through the inner door as she placed her daypack between her feet. Her surroundings didn't give her a clue. "What do you do?"

He hesitated before saying, "I design equipment for manufacturers."

Which made her none the wiser.

He bustled around the tiny kitchen area, opening two cans of baked beans and dumping them in a bowl. After setting the microwave going, he pulled a toaster out of a cupboard and popped down four slices of bread. The man moved with grace and economy, taking mugs from a cupboard. It was like watching her own personal ballet performance. His body floated from toaster to kettle to microwave.

"Stop staring."

Jessalyn started. "You really have eyes in the back of your head."

"And excellent peripheral vision."

Unaccustomed heat surged into her cheeks. "Now you're staring."

"I'm wondering what to do with you."

"Nothing." Jessalyn bolted to her feet. "If you're not willing to share your info, I'll leave now, and you can forget you ever saw me."

He turned with a teapot and a bottle of milk in hand and set them on the table. "Sit."

It was an order, and Jessalyn's butt hit the chair again before she'd issued the command to her brain.

"Eat." He set a plate bearing a generous serving in front of her.

Smoky, savory beans and the aroma of hot buttered toast decided her. "I could eat before I leave."

A laugh escaped him as he joined her at the table. "My brothers sometimes stay here overnight. I put up one of their stretcher beds for you. Won't that be better than sleeping rough?"

"Who says I don't have a place?"

"My nose," he said, his brown eyes meeting hers.

Heat filled her face. She hadn't reeked that bad. Had she? "How do I know you won't try to rape me? I mean, who offers a stranger a bed for the night?"

"A decent one," Manu said in an even voice. "What kind of man would I be if I let you leave to light more fires?"

A different fear writhed through Jessalyn. "Are you turning me into the cops?"

"Not yet," he said.

Which meant he might change his mind. She picked up her mug of tea and sipped while trying to decide the best course of action. "All right." She'd agree with him, and once he'd fallen asleep, she'd sneak away.

"Don't creep out during the early hours of the morning. I'm a light sleeper and will hear you."

The bossy man was a mind reader too. What flaws didn't he have? "You can't keep me here. I have to work tomorrow."

His lips pressed together, and stupidly, she gaped at him, his sensual mouth. A shiver worked through her and this time heat flowed from her face, down her neck to sink into her breasts. The sensation made her nipples itch, and she struggled to remain still.

"I need my job," she added, her tone fierce to expel this unwanted warmth from her mind and body. An afterthought occurred, and she gave an experimental cough.

"No, you don't." He jumped to his feet, moving so quickly she found herself propelled halfway to the outer door before she registered a protest.

"No. Stop. I won't breathe fire."

He turned her to face him. His black brows squeezed together in doubt. "Are you sure?"

"You don't even seem surprised by me shooting fire like a flame thrower." She cocked her head. "Have you seen someone do this before? I don't do drugs. You can tell that, right?"

"Full of questions, aren't you, wee one?"

Jessalyn snorted. No one had ever categorized her as small before, but she supposed she was when compared to his height and breadth. "You're not behaving like most people would, given the crazy circumstances."

"I'm in shock," he said. "Either that or it was the beers I drank earlier with my friends."

"You have friends?" she retorted.

"Surprisingly, yes." His words emerged clipped, and the amusement melted from his face.

She'd irked him with that last comment. "Sorry."

"Eat your meal. Drink your tea. Let me think."

She snorted. "Can't you multitask?"

"No. I'm a male."

Jessalyn fell silent, letting him have the last word because that edgy heat had sprung to life again, frisking her body. Compelling her to squirm.

"What's wrong?"

She froze at the realization the wriggling hadn't been solely in her mind. "Nothing." In lieu of an explanation, because that would be mortifying, she concentrated on eating. The first mouthful of beans—ambrosia. She barely contained her moan of pleasure. Forcing herself not to shovel in the food or give him a greedy pig impression, she sipped her tea. Real tea.

"You use tea leaves."

"Is that a problem?" That impassive face again.

It was driving her crazy when she normally had no trouble reading people. She bet he was a hell of a poker player. "The tea is perfect."

"Cassie and Emma said it was the good stuff."

"Who are Cassie and Emma?" She eyed him, waiting, equal parts curious and jealous of these unknown women.

"Cassie is my cousin's wife. Emma is married to our friend."

Intense relief had her sipping more tea in case betraying words spurted free. In this case, she'd prefer to breathe fire rather than humiliate herself by expressing honesty. And her thoughts were kind of whacked. This man was holding her prisoner. He'd witnessed her breathing flames—starting a fire on his property, and he had done nothing except feed her. Unless...

"Did you call the cops while I was in the shower? Is this my last meal before I get locked up?" She spoke faster and faster until at the end, her words ran into each other. Breathless, she gasped for oxygen. "Did you—?"

Manu barked out an unexpected laugh that halted her tirade. "You're winding yourself up to a panic attack."

"What are you intending to do with me?"

His expression blanked, and apart from a brief golden flash in his eyes, she was none the wiser.

"I haven't decided yet."

"Oh. Well, it's normal for people to go around breathing fire. They do in all the superhero books I read. I watched a movie a few weeks ago." What was wrong with her? She didn't run off at the mouth as a rule. "Fire," she said. "Lots of thunderbolts and flame-throwing. You should keep that in mind. Just saying." Jessalyn forked beans into her mouth and chewed thoroughly. It seemed the best way to halt her chatter.

Manu finished his meal and stood. "I'll check on the washing."

"Okay." Jessalyn popped the last corner of toast into her mouth. The meal had hit the spot and settled her churning stomach. Next, she required a plan because now that *he* had learned she puked fire, he couldn't ignore his discovery. A sensible person would've called the cops already.

A yawn popped free. This fire-breathing act was exhausting.

"The stretcher bed is in the main area. I've left a sleeping bag on top for you, although I doubt you'll need it."

"Thanks." Another yawn strained her jaw. "I might grab some sleep now. What time is it, anyhow?"

He checked his phone. "9:45."

Nerves hovered in her gut again. The uncertainty gnawed at her. She'd get a few hours sleep and attempt to creep away once she'd recharged her batteries. The truth—if this were a movie, she'd be shouting at the character to escape. *Danger lurked ahead. Ignore those crazy yearnings to trust him, and whatever you do, don't like him!* He owed her nothing, and that was what she should expect. Nothing but trouble.

So now she had her plan.

Escape and worry about her mental state later because, really, outside of a comic strip or an associated movie, who'd ever heard of a woman who breathed fire? No such thing.

Reassured by her plan, she placed her daypack close to hand and stretched out to rest. Yeah, the fires were her imagination. She refused to dwell on the physical proof and the damage she'd caused because that way lay real nightmares.

Manu attempted to concentrate on the plans laid out on his desk, but every one of his senses remained attuned to the woman. His mate. The woman who didn't understand she was a dragon. Leader Manu understood what they required of him. A quick mercy killing for the greater good.

Manu, the man...

He dragged his hand through his hair. What the hell should he do with her? While the obvious thing would be to tell her, what if she had a brain fart and spouted off to the press? By starting fires everywhere, she'd already placed his people in danger. Taniwha law was clear on this. Humans were not ready to welcome others. They had a difficult enough time embracing different nationalities, let alone species with powers humans might conceive as dangerous.

His mother...

Manu did another hand-run through his hair. June Taniwha wouldn't have hesitated. On discovering Jessalyn, she would've acted to keep the tribe safe. Manu's taniwha whined like a buzz-saw and his disapproval echoed through his brain.

Jessalyn McKenzie was their mate—the exact fit for them.

It had been bad enough killing his mother. The repercussions were ongoing, causing turbulence amongst the tribe. Executing a mate and destroying his chance of future happiness would annihilate him.

He picked up his phone to call Hone and put it down again. Emma was having her baby, and Hone would be with Jack, keeping him calm. Instead, he rang his brother next to him in age. Tane's phone went to voicemail. He tried Kahurangi next. No reply. Looked as if he was on his own for tonight.

Unable to focus on work, he did an internet search. He typed in her name and the search came up with nothing. Was Jessalyn even her name? She hadn't hesitated when he'd demanded the detail. Something to remember. She might be his mate, but he couldn't trust her.

Reaching out to other tribes might be the next step, but he

hesitated to do this and leave himself open to nosy questions as to why he desired information on this woman. No, he'd speak to Hone in the morning. Aware of the passing time, he gave in to his desire to check on Jessalyn. He padded out of his cubicle office without turning on the lights. The stretcher bed was empty. He scowled. The woman had done a runner already. Then, the toilet flushed, and the tension leached from his shoulders. He retreated and watched her return to the stretcher bed. Another taniwha would be aware of his presence and sense he lurked in the office.

She gave off none of these vibes, merely turning on her side and falling back to sleep as evidenced by her even breathing.

Who was this woman?

Manu prowled into the separate cubicle he'd claimed as his makeshift bedroom. He peeled off his clothes and stretched out on the bed. With no fresh ideas about what to do with Jessalyn, he fell asleep.

Jessalyn wasn't sure of the time when she awoke, but pitch-black greeted her eyes. Cautiously, she sat up and blinked, hoping to accustom herself to the inky darkness. It helped a little. Fumbling, she located her shoes and slid them onto her feet. Commonsense had demanded she sleep in her clothes so she was ready to escape. With her daypack in hand, she crept across the warehouse to get to the side door.

Before she got there, she kicked something. A can? It skittered across the concrete floor, doing a *rat-a-tat* dance to announce its presence.

"Damn and blast," she whispered.

With her next step, she kicked another can. The lights switched on suddenly. Jessalyn blinked rapidly and scowled at the strategically placed cans sitting on the floor between her and freedom. An old-fashioned alarm system that had worked perfectly.

Manu appeared in naked splendor. He folded his beefy arms across his most splendid chest. Not that she was looking. His dark brows rose, making her imagine question marks and his eyes held a you-explain-this gleam. "Going somewhere?"

"To the restroom," she said promptly.

"It's that way. Did you get turned around in the dark?"

Jessalyn wheeled sharply and kicked at a can. *Ow, ow, ow!* She limped a few steps and ignored his laughter. "I have to go to work tomorrow. You can't keep me captive. My boss is expecting me on time. I'm a punctual and responsible employee."

"I'll drive you," he said. "Get some sleep. You don't want to spoil your excellent record."

She muttered a rude word, and the man chortled. An honest-to-goodness chortle that had her face flaming and her hands bunching to fists. Before the light switched off, she scanned the cans and memorized their placement.

"Don't even try to attempt a second escape. I'll be sleeping by the door. If you stumble into my bed, I'll assume you're extending an invitation."

Jessalyn's gaze darted to Manu, and it was hard to miss the satisfaction on his sensual lips. Her fingers itched to slap the grin right away, and his mouth stretched wider, the smile broader as if he'd plucked her thoughts straight from her mind.

She stomped to her bed and lay down, pulling her sleeping bag over her head even though it was too hot to sleep with a covering. Thankfully, the lights flickered out soon after, and she shoved the cover away, her mind stewing over how to escape this determined man.

Why hadn't he turned her in to the cops?

That was the question begging an answer. If she stood in his shoes and she'd found someone burning down her property, she'd act steamed. There'd been anger—yes—but Manu had assessed her with a thoroughness that had left her edgy and aware of her femininity.

What if...

What if he was a weirdo intent on keeping her locked up as a sex slave?

No. She pushed the thought aside as ludicrous since she didn't get the creep factor from him.

She'd bide her time and escape his clutches once he let down his guard. When she received her pay tomorrow, she'd buy medicine to settle her stomach and find somewhere else to stay. Her life would return to normal, and she could focus on saving enough money to keep paying the mortgage. This weird illness couldn't last for much longer.

She couldn't be that unlucky.

CHAPTER 5

The Investigation Begins

How did a woman get to Jessalyn's age and have no idea of her heritage? What had happened to her parents? Why hadn't they passed on the training essential to the survival of a modern-day taniwha? His father and mother and every taniwha kid of his acquaintance had received careful instruction. As they'd grown older, they'd had gatherings where the mature taniwha had taken a group each and given them training exercises. Dragons more at home in the water—Jack, for instance—had received knowledge specific to them. Other elders had taught Manu and Hone and other fire-breathers to control their fire. How had she missed the necessary training?

And worst of all, what was he going to do?

Teaching her now when it was obvious she considered herself human might backfire. Before he took this step, he needed to learn more. The woman's true name for a start. Every one of her human instincts would fight what he told her, which was part of the reason taniwha began their training at a young age.

You could take her to bed. Seduce her into obedience.

Manu froze at the sly suggestion from his taniwha. He swayed as blood rushed down his body to fill his cock. Heat roared through him as he clenched the battered countertop.

"Not happening," he growled.

At least not until he discovered the truth. The clueless woman was his mate, and if she didn't get her act together, he'd have to execute her to keep the rest of his tribe safe.

One woman versus the life of thousands. Not just his tribe, but the taniwha who lived in other regions of New Zealand.

Despite the rumbling growl from his taniwha, his human side accepted the reality. He was a monster for thinking this, but he couldn't risk many to save one.

The first time—the taking of his mother's life—had passed in a blur. He'd acted on instinct in self-defense. Still murder, according to his father, and Manu had never argued this point.

His phone sounded, and he answered as he filled the teapot with boiling water. "Yeah."

"Emma had twin girls," Hone said, laughter in his voice.

"Two?"

"Yeah, the doctors told Emma a while ago. She kept it a secret from Jack because the responsibility for one child was stressing him. Two might have shoved him over the edge." He paused a beat. "Twins. Wow, I hope Cassie never does that to me."

"They okay? Emma?"

Hone chuckled. "They're great. Jack is in shock, but you can see how proud and protective he will be. He's doing his hovering thing, and Emma is ready to deck him. She ordered him to go to work."

"I have a job for you. It's—" He paused as Jessalyn stomped toward him.

"You locked the door," she spat, hands planted on her curvy hips. "You can't keep me a prisoner."

"What's going on?" Hone asked. "Who is that?"

"I can't talk now, but if you'd swing around the workshop at ten, I can speak with you then."

"We'll be there," Hone said. "You're not in danger. Otherwise, you would've called us or your brothers earlier."

"Yeah," Manu said, wishing he could spill everything to Hone now. "See you at ten."

Jessalyn got right in his face, her brown eyes flickering to dragon. "Unlock the door."

"In a moment. Have a cup of tea."

"I need to get to the train station or I'll be late to work."

"I'll give you a lift," Manu said.

She shoved him again before blinking. Her hand dropped from his shoulder, and contrarily, he craved the intimacy of her touch again. Manu turned away, filled two mugs with milk, and added tea. He handed her one.

"You can stay here tonight."

"Most people would prefer to distance themselves from me. I-I'm a monster."

"Think about it, okay? You're safe here with me." How he squeezed those words out without choking, he had no idea. Her instinct for flight was an excellent one. "Drink your tea while I get your clothes from the drier." He skirted the frowning woman, leaving her alone in the kitchen. He ignored his erection and prayed she hadn't noticed. Things were bad enough now. Adding sex to the equation would act as a spark during a summer drought.

He retrieved her laundry and handed it to her. While she changed and drank her tea, he entered his office. He used his handprint and scanned his eye to open his safe, then pulled out one of his stealth units. He strapped it on his right wrist and re-locked the safe.

"Are you ready?" he called. "I can drive you to work now. You'll have to give me directions."

"I work at The Viaduct."

"No problem."

Five minutes later, they were on their way. Jessalyn sat in the passenger seat beside him, but her clasped hands told of her tension. The silence grew heavy and oppressive, and Manu wasn't sure how to ease the strain. Bottom-line, she was coming home with him tonight if he had to drag her over his shoulder and carry her there.

The traffic was lighter than he'd assumed, and they soon neared the inner city. The downtown area of the city was a construction zone with orange traffic cones and temporary fence barriers making stopping difficult. At this time of the morning, office and shop employees filled motor vehicles and buses and poured from Britomart train station. No one was going anywhere in a hurry.

"Where do you work?"

"You can drop me near the ferry terminal."

Manu didn't argue but pulled up in a waiting zone and let her scramble from the passenger seat. "What time should I collect you?"

"You don't have to worry. Thank you for last night." She slammed the door and hurried into the ferry terminal.

"Run, wee dragon," he whispered. "You won't escape me." Manu barked out a laugh, amused at his weird stalker vibe.

Manu found a place to park and checked both ways before he pushed a button on his stealth unit. Invisible, he locked his truck and followed in Jessalyn's footsteps. Cleverly—if he did say so himself—he'd washed her clothes with strong laundry soap, and he'd pick her scent from the crowd without trouble.

He dodged rushing humans, extra careful because while he could see them, they had no clue of his presence. A running man crashed into him from behind, sending them both flying. A grunt escaped Manu as he struck the ground, but he raised his wrist to save damage to his stealth unit. The man's expression had him laughing until Manu realized that was just as peculiar for the man as his unexplained fall.

After ascertaining the man was unharmed, Manu scrambled to his feet and sniffed to locate Jessalyn. *Ah, yes!* The pungent eucalyptus trail drew him to the left. This time, he took care to hug the wall of the building to avoid further incidents.

Jessalyn had walked through the ferry area and gone along the waterfront toward The Viaduct. Manu strode past the giant KZ1 yacht turned into a sculpture, and the New Zealand Maritime Museum, not yet open for the day. The briny tang of the sea filled his nostrils as he turned the corner. Two super yachts moored in front of him, the crew polishing the deck and shining brass.

The America's Cup tour company had a stand offering two or three-hour trips on the harbor in old America's Cup yachts. Farther on was a whale-watching boat and several other luxury vessels available for hire. To his left were restaurants, cocktail bars, and a pub. He continued following Jessalyn's scent.

The trail led to a rear door of the pub. Deciding to risk detection, he pushed open the door and entered. He discovered Jessalyn, busy at work in the kitchen, helping the chef with food preparation. At least, he presumed the man was a chef since he wore a tall white hat.

Manu listened to the conversation but learned nothing more about Jessalyn. The chef informed her and two other staff—a young male and an older woman—what he needed them to do, and each employee started their tasks.

Manu retreated and paused on spotting an office. It was empty with the door closed but not locked. He slipped inside, leaving the door ajar in case he needed to make a quick getaway. A roster, pinned on the wall, gave him no clues since it listed Christian names. The filing cabinets contained creditor invoices.

About to risk switching on the computer, he spotted an employee list with addresses and phone numbers in the top drawer of the desk.

Ah. Jessalyn Brown. Her address was a cheap hostel close to Queen Street. With a quick glance at the door, he pulled his phone from his pocket and snapped a photo. He'd just slipped the phone out of sight when the chef pushed through the door. He strode straight to the desk and grabbed the list of phone numbers from where Manu had placed it on the desk.

Manu eyed the door and waited.

The chef punched a number into the phone and snapped and snarled at a tardy employee. "Don't bother coming back." The chef slammed down the phone. "Bloody unreliable kids." He stomped from the office and headed back to the kitchen. "I need someone to work late. Volunteers." He scanned his staff.

"I can work late," Jessalyn said.

"Thank you," the chef said. "I need you to cover for Kelvin and finish at six. You can have an extra half-hour break."

"Yes, Chef," Jessalyn said and got back to work.

Satisfied with his sleuthing, Manu retreated and exited the pub. He'd drunk here a few times and found it a successful hunting ground for willing sexual partners. Outside the pub, he took a more direct route to where he'd left his truck. Pleased with yet another successful test of his stealth unit, he waited until he climbed into his vehicle before making himself visible again.

His phone rang before he arrived back at his workshop.

"Where are you?" Hone asked.

"I'm on my way now. I'm stopping at the supermarket to stock up on food. Give me another half an hour."

"Jack and I have paperwork to keep ourselves busy. I told Dad we were meeting with you. I mentioned you needed information to help with tribal decisions. Dad told us to make you our priority this week. He's concerned."

Hone and Jack, as well as his brothers, were worried about him. This made him realize he wasn't alone. "See you soon."

It was closer to an hour when Manu pulled up beside Hone's black work vehicle. Jack and Hone came out to meet him.

"Excellent timing. You can help me carry the groceries inside."

Hone goggled at the number of bags. "It's good to see you're intending to eat, but are you trying to send your taniwha into a sugar coma?"

"Long story," Manu said.

"You look happier," Jack said slowly.

Manu studied Jack. "You look like hell."

"This is how you look after you're up all night watching your wife give birth to babies. Not one but two girls." Jack shook his head as if he wasn't sure he was awake.

"He's been like this all morning," Hone said, humor digging into his face deep enough to leave a dimple. "Jack is right. You don't seem as stressed."

"Not true. Since you were here last night, I have an entirely new set of problems," Manu said, his gut twisting as he considered Jessalyn.

"What is that god-awful stench?" Jack asked.

"Eucalyptus-scented laundry powder," Manu said. "Cassie shopped for me and bought it without realizing we prefer products with no scent. As it happens, it came in handy."

They took two trips to carry the bags of groceries into the warehouse. Manu unpacked and put things away while he sorted through his thoughts.

"Last night after you left, I caught a woman lighting fires out the back. I believe she is the one responsible for setting fires in the Domain."

"What did you do?" Hone straightened from stacking

perishables into the fridge.

"Where is she?" Jack asked.

His cousin and friend exchanged a glance.

"Did you execute her?" Hone asked the question.

Manu's shoulders slumped. "She is my mate."

"What?"

"Who is she?" Jack demanded, appearing more alert now.

"She told me her name is Jessalyn McKenzie, but I discovered this morning her real name is Jessalyn Brown. I have learned nothing, apart from the fact she has no idea she is a taniwha and my dragon wants her. I should've acted straightaway, but I... I couldn't." He straightened and met Jack's and Hone's gazes this time. He saw no condemnation or judgment, so he continued. "I drove her to The Viaduct this morning and let her think she'd escaped me."

"You used a stealth unit and followed her. Hence the stinky laundry powder," Hone said.

Manu's brows shot upward. "Hence?"

"Cassie and Emma have me thinking the word too," Jack confessed. "What will you do?"

"I need info on Jessalyn Brown. She is working at the *Three Horseshoes*, the pub not far from the Maritime Museum. I figure she'll need to give them her IRD number to get a job, and they'd have details of previous employment, which might hint where she comes from. I didn't have a chance to rifle through the computer files this morning."

"Describe her for us," Jack said.

"I...um...took a photo of her. I'll send it to you both." Just thinking about Jessalyn made his skin itch. The distance between them was too great. He wanted her in his sight in case another taniwha tried to steal her.

The thought gave him pause. What was he? A barbarian?

Yep.

His taniwha's amusement sparked through him, and he must've had a strange expression because both Jack and Hone were grinning at him. "What?"

"Welcome to the club, cuz," Hone said.

"What if I have to..." He trailed off because he hated to think the words, let alone state them aloud.

"We'll help you train her," Hone said. "Can we tell Cassie and Emma? I know they're both human, but we have intelligent mates. They might help."

Manu saw the sense in Hone's suggestion. As women, they might get through to Jessalyn when he couldn't. "Just them. I'm not mentioning anything to Tane and Kahurangi yet. Hell, this is such a mess."

"Finding a mate will go a long way to appeasing the more traditional in our tribe," Jack said.

"And on the plus side, once you're mated, you won't get single taniwha women shoved at you," Hone added.

"Yeah, but if one whisper escapes about Jessalyn and her fires, the tribe will demand her death. She's a danger to all of us," Manu said.

"Jack and I were intending to start our spying this morning. Why don't we carry on with it? You've already visited the pub and know the layout. You could do the undercover work there. If you didn't find any paper records, they'll be on the computer. Most people have a password on their computer these days, and employers have employee numbers if more than one uses the same terminal. You'll need to stake out the office and wait until someone leaves the computer free to dive in and get the information we need. Have you tried an internet search?"

"I did last night, but she gave me a false name." Manu pulled out his phone and did a search, this time for Brown. "She has a social media page. Hell, she's from Piha. Waaka territory."

He lifted his head, his pulse racing with frustration and the urge to strike out at something or someone. His gaze landed on Hone.

Hone raised his hands in surrender and took half a step back. "No hitting my pretty face. Remember, Cassie will get upset. She won't send you any more food."

"Don't look at me," Jack added. "I'm a father. Two babies are expensive, so Emma needs me at full fitness."

Hone winked at Manu. "Two girls."

"Don't remind me. All I can think of is the boys who will chase my girls when they're older. I need another gun."

"What if this girl is a plant?" Hone asked.

Manu shrugged. "If the Waaka taniwha intended to send a spy, why not send someone with full power? That way they'd have a better chance to cause real friction."

"There is the alternative." Jack's brow furrowed as if he were deep in thought. "They sent her as a honey trap."

"No," Manu said. "She arrived dressed in worn jeans and a T-shirt. One of her shoes had a hole in it. Her scent said she'd been sleeping rough for a few days at least."

Hone nudged Jack with his elbow. "She's a dog."

"No, she is not," Manu snapped. "She is..." He trailed off on seeing his cousin's amusement.

Hone licked a finger on his right hand and marked an imaginary score.

"Don't give me a hard time. I helped you with Cassie," Manu said.

"I suspected you were trying to steal my girl," Hone corrected.

Manu diverted his mind from the rest of that story. It hadn't ended well. Not for him or his family.

"How are we going to work the Piha connection? It's not as if we can go around asking questions up there," Jack said.

"My suggestion," Hone said. "Investigate as much as we can down here. Once we get her full name and date of birth, we can apply for a birth certificate and learn her parents' names."

"Makes sense," Manu said. "Come to the office and I'll get you the stealth units. I need to build more, but I haven't had time with everything else going on."

Jack and Hone had both trialed the units for him, helping him with tests. He trusted them with his life and his invention, and that wasn't something he could say about many people. Apart from his two brothers, the list was short.

"We'll meet back here this evening," Hone said.

"You want to meet my girl," Manu said.

"Ah! You admit she is *your* mate. That's half the battle," Jack said.

"That isn't exactly the problem." Manu's phone rang before he could elaborate. "I'll see you later. I appreciate this."

"Don't worry," Hone said. "Dad will insist on sending a bill even if he gives you a discount."

Manu checked on his caller. "Hey, Tane. What's up?" He listened to his brother. "Crap. I'm on my way."

Half an hour later, he pulled up at the family property. A charred wood stink and smoke filled the air, and he cursed on seeing the remains of the garage to the right of the bungalow. He climbed out of his vehicle and scowled. From where he stood, he spotted his Ducati—or what was left of it.

He muttered a pithy and passionate curse. His father was out of control and he had not one clue how to deal with him. Manu paused at the front door of the house where he'd grown up and sucked in a deep breath to bolster his patience.

He strode inside. His brothers Tane and Kahurangi were in the kitchen with his father. The house was a mess with fast-food wrappers and beer cans strewn everywhere, discarded with no regard for cleanliness or hygiene. Given the squalor, it wouldn't surprise Manu to spot mice or worse, rats.

"What are you doing here?" his father shouted. "You're no longer welcome in my home." Alcohol fumes wafted from him and his still-black hair hung in greasy strands around his gaunt face. His bloodshot eyes snapped with belligerence. The once crisp white shirt carried the dirt and the food spills of days and his black trousers hung on his bony hips. His father had lost weight and his posture and demeanor was that of a much older man, given the taniwha race aged more slowly than humans.

Manu forced his expression to blank and ignored his father's taunts and insults. He'd had a lot of practice. Tane and Kahurangi offered him sympathetic glances but remained silent. They had no answers. He'd asked them for suggestions—a solution—months ago. If his father continued in this manner, he'd have no option but to pull out his sword.

"You murdered my mate." Samuel stood, his balance unsteady. Dragons handled alcohol well, and it was difficult to get a good buzz. His father had hit the spirits hard.

"I used my sword," Manu agreed.

Samuel blinked as if he hadn't expected him to agree.

"For once, put yourself in my shoes. How would you have

handled the situation? Tell me. Would you have let her murder Emma and Cassie? Innocent humans? Cassie didn't have a clue about the taniwha race. Ma broke the rules first by showing herself to a human. Then, she compounded it by trying to kill them. She intended to kill Hone, who'd done nothing wrong. Cassie was Hone's mate. She wasn't mine. Tell me, Samuel." Manu purposely ignored their family ties and embraced his position as leader—something he hadn't previously done with his father. A mistake he saw now. "Tell me what you would've done. I expect you to give me your action plan tomorrow morning. You can email it to me via our private message board, or you can ring me. Your choice."

He turned to his brothers, their expressions of approval lightening his mood. Pissed about his Ducati, he wanted to order his father to buy him a new bike and clean both the place and his person but didn't want to push his luck.

"Walk me out," he requested his brothers.

Outside, his shoulders slumped briefly before he straightened.

"Will that work, or am I wasting my breath?"

"Bro, you let rip with taniwha magic like Ma used to when she was pissed off. It rippled into the room. You haven't done that before." Tane beamed his approval, his beefy arms reaching around Manu in a man-hug before he stepped back.

Kahurangi lifted his brows and clapped Manu over the shoulder, his tattooed biceps rippling. "Impressive, bro."

"I'm tired of the crap from the tribe," Manu said. "I have other things to do with my time." His gaze went to the remains of the shed. "I can't believe Dad burned my Ducati. I loved that bike."

"It's insured. You can get another one with the insurance payout," Kahurangi said.

"Will you take care of that for me?" Manu asked. "I've got somewhere to be."

Tane cocked his head. "Something has changed with you."

Manu shrugged. "I decided to direct the canoe instead of letting everyone paddle when they got the urge."

"I don't suppose you can use the hocus-pocus on Dad again and get him to clean his mess and stop inviting his mates around," Kahurangi said.

"Have you guys sat him down and told him he's behaving like a two-year-old?" Manu asked.

Tane shook his head. "We've been tiptoeing around him the same way you have."

"It's time we stop that," Manu said. "Dad knows Ma was in the wrong."

"He'll never admit it," Tane said. "But we were witnesses. What Ma did was unethical. As much as I loved her, she was showing signs of instability. We'd all seen it, but none of us wanted to call her on her behavior. It's why the sword transferred to you, Manu."

"Tane is right," Kahurangi said. "Ma didn't give you an option. Her mind snapped, and she became a liability."

"Thanks. Do me a favor?"

"What do you need?" Kahurangi asked without hesitation.

"Circulate amongst the tribe. I want the gossip that's not reaching me. Keep your ears open for anything Waaka-related."

"Are you worried about a war with the taniwha from the north?" Tane asked.

"Our tribe has been in turmoil since I took over," Manu said bluntly. "It would be an ideal time for Nelson Waaka to make a move while we're fighting amongst ourselves." He didn't mention Jessalyn and his fears she might be a spy. "Where did Dad get the idea to set the shed on fire?"

"Probably listened to the news. Haven't you heard rumors of an arsonist in Auckland?" Kahurangi asked. "Dad has been drinking so much I doubt his idea was original."

Perhaps he should try his taniwha moves on Jessalyn and see if her dragon would listen and accept him as her leader. He muttered a curse. That should've been his first course of action. Too busy thinking with his dick.

"Manu?" Tane broke into his reverie.

Manu blinked and found both his brothers staring at him, their expressions odd. "What?"

"Where did you go?" Kahurangi asked, always the nosy one.

"None of your business," Manu retorted.

"You're more upbeat than you have been," Tane said. "Something has happened."

"Nope," Manu denied. "More of the same, but my pity-party was getting old." He checked his watch. "I have to go. Call me if you have problems with Dad." With that, he jogged to his truck and was soon on his way to the inner city.

Jessalyn chopped vegetables, washed and stacked dishes, and carried out the other tasks assigned to her by Chef. The mindless work allowed her thoughts to skip to Manu Taniwha. The taniwha was a mystical beast from Māori mythology and the perfect surname for the man who prowled and gave off predator vibes. Yet the weird thing was he hadn't truly scared her. Contrarily, he'd given her the illusion of safety, and she'd slept better than she had in days.

And the fire thing. He'd taken her breathing fire in his stride, which struck her as odd. He'd shaken her so much with his overpowering masculinity that her brain had become sluggish. Not great behavior.

She forced her mind to other matters, such as where she would stay tonight. No money. The fire thing. She sighed. She'd have to sleep rough again. There was no other alternative.

She glanced up and caught the door opening by itself. A slew of goosebumps slid across her forearms, and she paused in stacking the dishwasher. The door shut again, and she shook her head.

"Jessalyn!" Will, the bar manager, stomped into the kitchen. "We're slammed out there. Can you come and clear plates from the tables?"

Jessalyn glanced at the scowling chef.

"Can't one of your guys do it?" Chef demanded.

"We're short-staffed. One barman didn't turn up for work and there are two cruise ships in port today."

"We're short-staffed too," Chef stated, leading with his chin, but he jerked his head at Jessalyn. "Fifteen minutes then come back. We'll have dishes backing up by then."

Jessalyn welcomed the chance of a breather from the steamy kitchen. Out in the bar, customers stood in clusters. She cleared a table and assured the customer who claimed it that she'd be back to wipe up the spills.

Her nostrils quivered under the assault of many strong scents. Maybe it was hot outside, but the bombarding fragrances forced her to breathe through her mouth. Accustomed to waitressing since she'd done several stints at the café in Piha, she cleared tables, wiped tabletops, and ducked around stinky customers. By the time the bar's state satisfied the bar manager, half an hour had elapsed.

"Where have you been?" Chef roared on spotting her. "I said fifteen minutes. Peel these and chop them in julienne. We're running short of vegetables."

The younger of the kitchen helpers sent her a faint grimace of commiseration. He was busy preparing more salads while Chef allowed Elsa, who had been there forever, to cook steaks and grill fish and chicken.

Jessalyn got to work on the carrots. Feeling the weight of a stare, she glanced up. No one was paying any attention to her, too busy with their tasks and worried at facing the wrath of Chef to waste time gawking at her. Shrugging, she continued preparing carrots.

When six came around, Jessalyn's shoulders were sore from hefting heavy pots and clearing tables. The bar manager had commandeered her several times throughout the day.

She'd decided to find another park where she could sleep in privacy without other homeless people around. That might mean leaving the central city again, but she couldn't afford to let anyone catch her lighting fires. She headed for the restroom and washed her face. She changed her uniform shirt for a lighter T-shirt and made a mental plan to find somewhere to do her laundry.

Her hand hit the wooden box at the bottom of her daypack, and she couldn't resist opening it to gaze at the pendant nestled within. She stared at it, the sight relaxing her. Her forefinger stroked over the whorls of the koru. A vibration passed from the pendant and up her forearm. Startled, she jerked her hand away and gawked at the glowing pendant.

Voices outside had her snapping the wooden box shut and stuffing it out of sight. She hefted the daypack over one shoulder and left the pub via the employee entrance. Her entire body hummed and her mind darted to Manu. She swallowed, honesty urging her to admit to herself she found the man fascinating.

"Jessalyn."

Her head jerked up, and wariness clenched her muscles tight. "What are you doing here?"

"I thought I'd save you the train fare and pick you up since I was already in town."

"How did you know where to find me?"

"It wasn't difficult," Manu said and, to her frustration, didn't explain further.

Jessalyn planted her feet on the pavement. "I don't want to come with you."

"It's safer." His gaze drilled right through her, his expression saying everything she didn't want to hear.

"I'd be foolish to trust a stranger."

"I didn't call the cops last night. Come. I went shopping this morning. I have plenty of food."

Something in his voice throbbed, and she found herself moving toward him. It was the strangest sensation. She forced her legs to plant again, and her mind buzzed as if in protest. A tiny voice shouted inside her head. *Go!*

"Jessalyn." The no-nonsense tone of a man who expected obedience.

And damn if she didn't start walking again, trotting after him like a well-behaved pet.

CHAPTER 6

The Truth About Dragons

To Manu's relief, she followed him without making a scene and he led her past the row of moored luxury launches. He halted at the Kapiti ice cream shop. "Want an ice cream?"

From memory, eating often had helped with the control of his dragon. If he read Jessalyn correctly, she was short on funds and therefore not eating as she should.

"I'll have one cone with chocolate, salted caramel, and almonds and one with..." He turned expectantly toward Jessalyn who was studying the ice cream with avid interest.

"Nothing for me," she said. "I can't afford—"

Her gaze had gone to the gingernut side of the cabinet. "French vanilla," he said in a verbal prod. He'd bet French vanilla was the last flavor she wanted.

"Gingernut," she blurted before the woman behind the counter could roll the vanilla ice cream.

Manu smiled with quiet satisfaction and handed over a twenty-dollar note once the woman had rolled them an ice cream each.

"Let's go," Manu said. "With all the traffic cones and diversions everywhere, I decided to park in the Wynyard Quarter."

She licked her cone with obvious enjoyment. "Oh. I've wanted to explore this way but I never have enough time during a half-hour break."

"Well, now is your chance. This bridge is mechanical and a few times a day, they close it to pedestrians, lift the center, and allow the boats to leave or return to this part of the harbor. There are lots of restaurants over here." Manu continued in his guise of a travel guide. "See the rail tracks? They used to have a tram in use during the weekends. My friends recommend the restaurants in this area." Manu finished his ice cream, amused at himself. He hadn't talked half this much in the last six months, and he was steering close to prattle.

He steered Jessalyn in the direction of the car park while sneaking surreptitious glances in her direction. She wasn't his normal type. Whenever he dated—nah, *fucked* fit better, if he wanted honesty—he chose petite women. His brother Kahurangi swore he had a thing for blondes, but Manu considered himself an equal opportunity man with hair color. He preferred women who didn't douse themselves in artificial scents, ones who bore genuine smiles, and those who flirted and weren't shy about going after what they wanted.

Jessalyn Brown was none of these things. The woman was tall, and those who were uncharitable might call her chubby. While she carried extra weight, once she shifted, she'd burn through the calories, her fat becoming muscle. She had long black hair and a cautious nature, which given the circumstances, he didn't blame her for. She didn't trust him, and he admitted her lack of faith irked him. Stupid male pride.

Once they settled in his truck and were driving toward Onehunga, he started asking questions.

"When did this firebug thing start?"

Jessalyn shot him a quick glance, her eyes wide with panic. "What?" She pressed her lips together and stared straight through the windshield.

"I can't help you without details and background." He needed Leader Manu to appear, but Manu the man craved Jessalyn's trust and honesty.

"A while ago," she said after a lengthy silence.

"Before you arrived in Auckland?"

"I've always been in Auckland."

Manu sighed. "All right. Let's try this. What happens physically right before you breathe fire?"

"My stomach churns, and I get a pain between my shoulder blades that's almost like indigestion. Heat—it works up my throat until I have to open my mouth and release it."

"Interesting."

"Not what I'd call it," Jessalyn snapped. "I'm too scared to go to a doctor. I'm not stupid. A doctor wouldn't believe me, and then when he had proof of the fire bursting from me like some mythical dragon, he'd lock me up. The authorities would become involved, and they'd throw away the key." Her anger and fear throbbed in the truck's cab.

Manu sympathized with her. This unexpected arrival of a heritage she was unaware of must be confusing and terrifying. A part of him wanted to tell her, but there were gaps in his information. Thanks to his day of snooping, he had more knowledge.

"Do you have brothers or sisters?" he asked.

"No, I'm an only child. My mother died when I was two."

She never hesitated in her reply, and heartened, he continued in this vein.

"I have three brothers, all younger than me. Your father never remarried?"

"No. It was just the two of us. H-he died recently." She rushed out her final words, her voice thick and choked.

"I'm sorry." Manu reached over and clasped her fingers briefly, giving a comforting squeeze before returning his hand to the steering wheel. That was his probable answer to why she'd come to Auckland. "What was your favorite thing to do when you were a kid? Did you play with dolls and have tea parties?"

Her snort had him scanning her in surprise. "My dad was great. He bought me dolls, but I upset my friends' mothers when I started a trend for restyling my Barbie. I turned mine into an explorer and cut her hair."

Amusement flooded Manu on hearing the laughter in her voice. It was much better than the repressed tears.

"In my defense, I thought my doll's hair would grow back since mine kept growing. That's what I told my friends."

Manu chuckled. "I take it their mothers disabused them of this."

"Yeah, Dad received at least five phone calls from irate parents. He had to explain my doll's hair wouldn't grow back."

"Did you cry?"

"No, I liked my doll better in her explorer disguise. My best friend at school was a boy. Danny had toy trucks, and my doll and I had more fun playing with the trucks and going on adventures in the bush than we did at tea parties. As you can probably tell, I turned into a tomboy."

"What did your father think of that?"

"He went with my preferences, although, to be fair, he steered me to more feminine activities. I did ballet and learned how to cook. I can sew and knit if I really have to, but I prefer woodwork. My father was a trained carpenter although his real passion was making furniture. What did you do as a kid?"

"I grew up with lots of playmates. I had my three brothers and numerous cousins and friends. We played outside a lot and once we got older, we did team sports. Rugby during the winter and softball or cricket during the summer. We swam and learned to paddle canoes."

"Can you cook?"

"I can," Manu said. "Once I got older, I enjoyed the sciences. Cooking is simple chemistry. It's easy if you follow the steps."

"A lot of cooking is instinctive."

"Still chemistry," he stated as he pulled up at his warehouse. He used a remote to open the gate and drove through. Since he expected Jack and Hone to visit later, he left the entrance open. "You know how the elements will react together so you move on to the next step without too much extra thought."

"What are you cooking me for dinner tonight?"

No missing the faint challenge in her question. "I figured I'd wheel out the barbeque and do a beer chicken. I'm starving since I missed lunch, so I thought I'd do a few sausages first with French bread. Maybe I'll bake potatoes with the chicken, and you can make a salad so we balance the meat out with green stuff."

"I have no notion of what a beer chicken is, but it sounds good. I'm hungry too and I ate lunch."

During their dinner preparations, Manu kept up a steady stream of conversation. "My best friend is my cousin, Hone. Through Hone, I met our other friend Jack. Jack and his wife Emma have twin girls. Born last night, so I haven't seen them yet."

"Hone is married too."

"He is. Cassie and Emma were best friends growing up." He didn't mention Cassie was a renowned country singer in the United States and becoming more established in New Zealand now that her latest album had released. "I'm expecting Jack and Hone to drop by later tonight. That's why there is a lamb and a hippo riding in the back seat."

Jessalyn laughed. "I admit to curiosity about the huge soft toys but didn't like to ask. Danny has lots of cousins. My father was an only child so I don't have oodles of relations. Danny was related to most people in P—" She broke off before she revealed where she'd grown up, but he'd already learned she came from Piha from her employee record. As far as he knew, the facts on there seemed genuine, and this information gave him a better starting point for his investigation.

"Was your mother a lone child too?"

"Dad said she came from a small town up north. If she had relations, I've never met them. Ugh! You're sticking the beer can up the chicken's—"

"Cavity," Manu broke in before she could finish her sentence. "It might look rude, but I promise you, the meat will be moist and succulent once this bird is cooked." He carried it out to the barbecue. Earlier, he'd put on two potatoes to start roasting. Now, he positioned the chicken with its beer can stand and closed the hood to let it roast.

"Which parent does your Māori blood come from?" Manu was betting it was the long-dead mother.

"My mother."

"Did your father teach you about Māori mythology and customs?"

"No, everything I know, I learned from Danny and his relations and at school." She scowled and pressed her hand to her stomach.

"Is that the first warning signal?" He gestured at her midriff.

"Yes."

Her relaxed posture had faded in a blink and now she stood, slightly hunched, her palm pressed to her stomach.

"What do you normally do when you get to this stage?"

"Panic."

Her honesty wrenched a chuckle from him. "Have you tried eating?"

"No."

"Worth a try then," he said. "Earlier, you said you were hungry. The sausages won't take long to cook. I bought sliced ham. I'll make you a ham roll to eat right now."

While he made her a snack, he pondered this Danny and focused on tamping down the growl that built low in his throat. She'd known him since they were children and spoke of him with fondness. He had no right to the flash of jealousy. Yet, there it was, pawing and snorting like a bull, ready to charge.

Damn, he had so many questions for her, yet first, he needed to teach her to control her taniwha and keep her hidden from his tribe.

He handed over the filled roll. "Grab two beers from the fridge and sit outside. I'll be out there as soon as I sort out the sausages."

She tore off a bite of the bread and stuffed it in her mouth, nodding her agreement to his plan. While he prepared the sausages for the barbecue, his gaze went to her as she balanced her plate and pulled out two beers. Her clothes were baggy. The woman didn't dress to impress—that was for sure—yet she moved with confidence, and when she wasn't apprehensive about the appearance of her dragon, she stood tall.

A vehicle pulled up in front of his warehouse. Two vehicles. He listened carefully and scented the air before relaxing. Hone and Jack.

"Where are the photos of my newest tribe members?" he asked Jack.

Hone had followed Jack into his kitchen, and he rolled his eyes. "Now he's over the shock, he's gone gaga. His phone is full of photos."

"This is a fast trip," Jack said. "I'm visiting Emma. She and the twins are coming home tomorrow."

"Do they have names?"

"Not yet. We had a hard enough time agreeing on one name and now we have two babies, we're rethinking," Jack said.

"I got something for your girls," Manu said. "A toy each for the babies and a voucher for a cleaner for Emma. I know it's a boring gift, but I figured she'd be tired and could use the help. Cassie suggested it."

"Thanks," Jack said. "Cassie and Hone gave us a food-box delivery. Emma is thrilled with that."

"Grab a beer and come outside. I'll introduce you to Jessalyn." Manu picked up his plate of sausages and the buttered portions of French bread.

"Did you discover anything today?" Hone asked in a low voice.

"The basics. Name and address. I emailed a copy of her employee record to myself. I'll forward it to you later tonight. Investigate further but don't speak with anyone yet. I prefer to keep this on the down-low."

"She's pretty," Jack murmured an instant after they stepped outside.

Jessalyn seemed deep in thought and hadn't noticed their presence yet.

"Not your normal type," Hone added.

"No, but that doesn't make her any less my mate," Manu said. "Jessalyn, this is my cousin Hone Taniwha and our friend Jack Sullivan."

A wary expression darted over Jessalyn's face. It faded almost immediately, replaced by a friendly nothing-to-see-here smile, but Manu saw it, wondered at her thoughts, her instinctive fear. Was it because she sensed their taniwha, or was she shy meeting new people?

Manu checked his chicken and placed the sausages on the hot plate to cook. Hone and Jack joined Jessalyn at the picnic table while he watched the sausages. The heat of the day had dispersed, and the sun had dipped low on the horizon while he'd been preparing the food.

"Did the food help to settle your stomach?"

Jessalyn's wariness was clear this time. "Yes."

"That's good. Jack, are you going to show me baby photos?" Manu figured talk of babies might relax Jessalyn.

"Congratulations," Jessalyn said. "I hear you have twin daughters."

"Yeah." Jack flicked photos across his phone screen. He handed the phone to Jessalyn. "This is my favorite of Emma and the babies."

"What are their names?" Jessalyn asked.

"One and Two at the moment. Not that I can tell them apart," Jack confessed. "I don't think Emma can either, but she pretends she knows which is which."

The sausages were soon cooked, and Manu placed them on the table along with the bread.

"Where is the ketchup?" Jack asked.

"I'll get it," Jessalyn said.

As soon as she disappeared, Hone said, "I don't catch a whiff of taniwha on her."

"Me either," Jack agreed.

"I'm certain it's there. Today, I purchased two new fire extinguishers to replace the one I emptied last night. I gave her food to help settle her taniwha, but I don't think it will be enough because she's not eating at regular intervals."

He fell silent when Jessalyn returned with the ketchup. Her face had turned pale, and she had her hand cupped against her stomach.

"Jessalyn?"

"I don't—" She broke off to cough, and a spark shot from her mouth. It flared briefly before spluttering out from lack of fuel.

Hone and Jack set down their beers and jumped to their feet, both watchful.

Manu took the sauce bottle from her and set it down. He grasped both her hands and held them even though she tried to tug from his grip.

"I'll burn you," she protested, her voice deeper than normal.

"You won't hurt me," Manu promised, and as he uttered the words, he prayed they were true. "Try this. Instead of attempting to hold back the flames, put everything you have into it."

"But I'll start a fire." She kept darting glances at Hone and Jack.

"They're my family, and they won't hurt you," Manu said.

"They'll need to go through me first."

Hone edged closer. "Try what Manu said, sweetheart."

She blinked, a slow fluttering of long dark lashes over her panicked eyes. "Why is this happening? I'm a freak!"

"You're not a freak," Manu said.

"Should I show her?" Hone asked.

"That's the quickest way," Jack said, enforcing Hone's suggestion. "Her mind is battling what is happening because she doesn't believe."

Manu dipped his chin, decisive because the suggestion made sense. "It's dark and private enough here to avoid detection. Go ahead."

He stood close to Jessalyn, ready to grab her if she panicked or to put out any fires she might start while Hone removed his footwear and clothes.

"What is he doing?" Jessalyn demanded.

"Watch," Manu said.

"But he's taking off his clothes... W-what is he doing?" she whispered.

She crept closer to him, and on instinct, Manu looped his arms around her tense waist.

Hone's human body shimmered as it reshaped and scales rippled across his skin. Dragon shifts were typically fast and soon Hone towered over them—a red-and-black dragon.

"W-what just happened? How? Why aren't you surprised?"

Jessalyn trembled within his embrace, and Manu savored her proximity, the softness of her hair against his cheek and her scent filling his lungs. His taniwha purred, but his dragon's joy at having his mate so close remained muted.

"Hone, show her your fire," Jack said.

Hone's elegant head turned as his elongated gaze met Manu's. Manu gave a thumbs-up, and Hone inhaled once and blew the breath out with a stream of flames. He aimed his fire at the edge of the concrete area. When the flames died out, the concrete had turned black but Hone had enough control not to start a blaze.

Manu turned Jessalyn in his arms until he could see her face. "Do you understand now?"

Jessalyn's mouth dropped open as she gaped at Manu. His cousin had transformed into a freakin' dragon the size of a small house. Manu and their other friend—Jim? No, Jack. Neither of them had blinked at the unusual sight.

"Jessalyn?"

"No," she said, her reply automatic while her mind grappled with the big red-and-black dragon sitting before them. "I understand nothing."

She gawked at the not-so-mythical beast standing... No, the creature was slouching as if this entire situation bored him. This wasn't real. Convinced this was an elaborate joke at her expense, she stomped over to the dragon and slapped it on the shoulder.

Whoa! She followed this up with a quick pinch, but the creature's skin was hard and didn't give.

The dragon turned its big head toward her, and she could've sworn it wore a smirk. Its face held hints of black swirling within the red coloring while its torso was all crimson-red scales. Jessalyn already had firsthand knowledge of their hardness, but they were beautiful too and gleamed in the evening light. The dragon bore the same combination of red-and-black on its four legs. The creature's wings appeared to be red, but it was difficult to tell since they remained furled close to the dragon's torso. Two antler-type protuberances topped its angular head while sharp white teeth filled its great maw. The dragon's tail sat motionless on the ground but Jessalyn imagined it, too, could be used as a weapon.

When the red dragon bent its head to sniff her, Manu growled and stomped over to her and the dragon.

"Cut it out," he ordered.

The dragon grunted, and the sound reminded her of laughter, but he straightened and edged away. A weird glow radiated from the creature's scales, and before she could comment on the phenomenon, a naked Hone stood where the dragon had been seconds earlier.

"Eyes here," Manu ordered.

The heat of his touch on her shoulders zipped through her body and sank into parts she hadn't considered for months. Awareness of his masculinity followed—his height and breadth, his scent, and when she finally obeyed and raised her gaze to his face, his magnetic eyes snared her.

"Don't look at Hone."

His tone commanded, and she submitted even as the fact peeved her. How did he do that?

"You're a taniwha, Jessalyn," Manu said once he had her full attention.

His hands still clasped her and now it was easy to spot the concern in his expression.

"A taniwha? No." Jessalyn shook her head. She vacillated between outright panic and amazement. Impossible. She couldn't transform into a different shape. Her gaze slid to Hone, who now wore clothes. Impossible for her, she amended her thoughts. "No," she repeated, more certain this time.

"How do you explain the fire?" Manu pointed out.

She couldn't. She had no answers. True, although she'd seen the dragon, the creatures were fictional. But she had touched it...

No, impossible.

"You put something in my food."

Manu laughed as did his friend Jack.

"Can you do that?" she demanded of Jack.

"Yes, but I'm a different type of dragon, and I get trapped in my dragon for longer than Hone and Manu."

"You can do that too?" Jessalyn asked, frowning at Manu. In the words of the famous Mr. Spock—one of her father's favorites—this was not logical.

"Yes."

"No." Her mouth dropped open. She could hardly blame this situation on alcohol. "Prove it."

Hone chuckled and the more solemn Jack flashed a quick grin.

Manu gave a heavy sigh and removed his clothes with quick efficiency. So fast, she didn't have nearly long enough to peruse his impressive muscles.

He strode to a spot of clear ground. *Hmm-hmm.* Very sexy gluts and wow! The tattoo on his back was amazing. Before she'd finished her visual examination of the inked dragon, Manu turned and folded his arms over his impressive chest. The same weird glow emanated from his body and a gasp escaped her as he morphed into a large black dragon.

Spotting one dragon tonight told her there was something iffy in the food or drink, but two? Yep, she was quietly slipping toward insanity.

"Touch him," Hone said, his tone sly. "He'll like that."

Jessalyn didn't hesitate. She strode over to the black dragon. Manu. Okay, she admitted the existence of dragons. Insane or not, there was one standing right there. Manu lowered his head and sniffed her hair. A loud purr came from him an instant before he licked her cheek.

"Hey!" She took one giant step backward and rubbed her cheek. "Don't slobber."

A commotion behind Jessalyn had her turning to investigate. Hone and Jack were both laughing but trying hard not to do it openly.

"Can I touch him? Is it safe?"

"He touched you," Jack pointed out, and Hone sniggered.

The dragon—Manu—issued a grumpy growl. Jessalyn blinked. The Mr. Spock side of her mind lectured about impossibilities despite the evidence. She approached cautiously, eager to appease her curiosity.

This time, she patted the dragon's chest, where the scales were smaller and more pliable. She rubbed, and the dragon rumbled. The sound vibrated beneath her palm, and she smiled. She rounded the dragon and spied a big-arse sword clutched in its claw. Large red stones—rubies, perhaps—glittered on the scabbard.

Manu bent his head and nuzzled her hair, his warm breath tickling her neck and bringing a smile. His wings lifted and awed, she sidled closer, her hand trembling a fraction as she reached out to touch him.

"Wow," she whispered.

Manu licked her cheek again. In truth, he hadn't slobbered the first time, but he'd surprised her. Now, he made the move without haste, and his abrasive tongue tickled her.

"I don't slobber."

Jessalyn frowned.

"You're not hearing things, sweetheart. I can mind-speak while in

this form. Stand back with Hone and Jack. I'm going to shift, and I'd hate you to get hurt."

Speechless at this new development, Jessalyn hurried to join the other two men. Manu shifted and pulled on his jeans. Still shirtless, he approached them at a prowl. Jessalyn stared at his chest and studied the portion of his tattoo that curled around his side. The dragon's tail.

"I'm guessing your ability comes from your mother's side," Manu said.

Jessalyn shook her head since none of this made sense. But she *had* breathed fire, a tiny voice reminded her.

"I don't understand. Why didn't this happen earlier? Why now? My father never said a thing."

"Perhaps he didn't know," Jack offered.

"Or he might have watched you, and when you showed no sign of shifting, he decided not to mention the taniwha species," Manu said. "We have no way of knowing for sure."

"B-but what do I do now?" As she said the words, Jessalyn realized she hadn't blown more fire. During the previous times, once she'd started, the fire-breathing had carried on for an hour, sometimes closer to two. "I guess shock will do that," she muttered.

"What?" Manu asked.

"I've stopped vomiting out fire when normally I keep going for an hour or longer."

"You ate beforehand," Manu said.

"But I've eaten before. The first time this happened I'd had dinner out before I went to work."

The men frowned, their gazes seeming to conduct a silent conversation before they turned back to her.

"How long was it between when you ate dinner and when you breathed fire?" Jack asked.

Jessalyn frowned, thinking back. "Danny and I had dinner at the café, and I left to start work at six. It was after midnight by the time I closed up and finished cleaning ready for the following day."

"Too long between meals," Hone said.

Manu agreed. "You need to carry snacks. Chocolate bars and dried fruit. Eat as much meat as you can."

"That's easy for you to say. Chocolate is out of my financial reach, let alone meat. I get to eat at work, but my break times depend upon how busy we are."

"I'll make sure you have chocolate," Manu said.

Hone winked at her. "I'm sure you're allowed restroom breaks. Work out your timing and scoff a chocolate bar or two on the way there or back from the bathroom."

"That's fine while I'm staying here, but once I get a new place, I'll have a tight budget," Jessalyn said.

"You're not going anywhere," Manu said, his tone close to a growl.

"You can't stop me. As soon as I get paid, I'll have money for a hostel."

"And on that note, we're leaving," Hone said.

"You don't want to stay for dinner?" Manu asked.

"As much as I'm tempted, I promised Cassie, I'd be home before nine. Walk us out?"

"Jessalyn, wait there. I won't be long."

Manu's words were an order. A bad habit he'd need to unlearn. Danny had ordered her around too. She watched Manu stride away with his cousin and friend, her gaze going to the dragon tattoo on his back. The tattoo waved and blew her a kiss before Manu disappeared. A gasp escaped, and she clacked her teeth together, the sharp click a punctuation of her shock.

Curiouser and curiouser.

She sank onto the picnic table's bench seat and replayed her evening. Could they be telling the truth? Was she a taniwha? Part taniwha?

Her mind was still whirring when Manu returned almost ten minutes later.

"The chicken should be ready," he said and lifted the hood of the barbecue.

Jessalyn caught the decadent whiff of roast meat and groaned. "Charred flesh. Yum."

With easy dexterity, he portioned the chicken and placed it on a plate. "Jess, can you grab the butter, the salad, and a carton of sour cream from the fridge?"

Jessalyn stared at him, but he wasn't paying attention. He was removing baked potatoes from the barbecue and placing them on plates. Only her father had shortened her name. On the heels of this, two thoughts occurred. One: she missed her father so much, and right now she wished he were here so she could ask him pointed questions. And two: she didn't allow anyone else to shorten her name, but the urge to reprimand Manu never arrived.

By the time she returned with the requested items, Manu had the chicken, potatoes, plates, and cutlery set on the table.

"Sit. Eat," he said when she loitered, so off balance it was difficult to make sense of her jumbled thoughts. "We'll talk as soon as you have food in your stomach. Are you hungry?"

"Um, yes." Her belly agreed with a hearty rumble.

Manu and his friends were right about the snacking idea. She was constantly hungry these days, and if eating more meant she didn't breathe fire, she'd do it. Somehow. She didn't even care if she put on extra pounds as a result. In her mind, the trade-off was worth gaining weight.

She applied herself to her meal and ate several mouthfuls of the succulent chicken before she asked questions. "How do you control your fire? Did your parents teach you?"

"I guess they did, although my brothers, cousins, and friends were always visiting each other. I guess we absorbed the information from the tribe members during our play and gatherings."

"A tribe? How many of you are there?"

"A few thousand taniwha in the Auckland area," Manu said. "There are other taniwha tribes within New Zealand. Three in the North Island and two in the South."

Jessalyn crunched on a mouthful of salad. "Which tribe does Piha fit into?"

"Is that where you used to live?"

"Yes." Now that she'd learned about Manu and taniwha, it seemed stupid to keep secrets. If it wasn't for Manu, she might still be sleeping rough and placing herself and others in danger. "I still own a house there, although keeping up with the mortgage will challenge me."

"Piha is part of the Northern tribe run by the Waaka family."

"There are quite a few families with that surname who live in and around Piha."

Manu continued eating. He swallowed a bite of chicken. "Is your house sitting empty?"

"Yes. I had intended to return, but I decided on the spur of the moment to stay here and get a job." She shrugged. "A tiny voice at the back of my mind insisted this was a great idea."

Manu's gaze shifted from his meal to her. "What kind of voice?"

"I... Ah... I thought it was a gut instinct."

"It might have been your taniwha sending you the thought."

"Oh." Not a brilliant response, but it was the best she could come up with right now.

"You could rent your property. I'm guessing you get a lot of summer visitors to the area. You'd be able to ask for a decent rent. If you luck out, you might find someone who wants a long-term rental."

"Heck, that never occurred to me. That way, the rent would pay the mortgage and other expenses, and I might save again."

"Did your father not leave you any money when he died?"

"I helped Dad with his furniture making, and I thought he was making a decent living, but when I checked into his financials, I discovered he'd taken a mortgage over the house. He hadn't mentioned money problems or loan proceeds."

Sharing this with Manu lifted the emotional weight on her shoulders, leaving her lighter. Happier. His suggestion to rent the property offered her a solution.

"I'm glad you listened to your instinct to stay in Auckland. You said your mother and her people came from the north. Hone and Jack are both private investigators. They could help you learn more and perhaps fill the gaps in your family tree."

Jessalyn paused, a mouthful of potato halfway to her lips. Did she want to learn more? She waited, hoping for a sign. A gut instinct to kick into action.

Nothing happened.

"I guess. Can I think about it?"

"Sure. Back to your taniwha. We'll make sure you eat regularly. I can teach you breathing exercises—the ones they teach us as

113

children, and that might help your control. Most of all, you must learn to listen to your body. If you have any gut instincts, listen closely to them."

"How do I know if it's my taniwha or wishful thinking?"

Manu's eyes twinkled. "That's why I suggested you listen before you act."

"Will I change into a dragon like you and Hone?"

He shrugged. "No clue. I've never met a half-caste who showed signs of a taniwha. Most taniwha are closer to full Māori blood. Want to watch a movie after dinner?"

"Sure."

"Do you fly?"

"Yes," Manu said.

"How do you fly without people seeing you?"

"We've had hundreds of years to perfect our powers of concealment," Manu said.

"But it must be more difficult with modern technology," she persisted. People would notice enormous dragons flying through the sky. They couldn't fly too high or they'd run the risk of crashing into planes. Then there was the lower amount of oxygen at height.

"We have our own technology to aid us," Manu said.

His answer was evasive. It prodded her curiosity higher. She had so many questions.

"Do you have a hoard of treasure?"

Manu stared at her without blinking. "Yes."

"Where? Show me?"

Manu's expression cracked into a broad smirk. "Personally, I use a bank."

"Aw, no hoard?"

"During the last century, taniwha and other dragons kept precious stones and other tradeable items, but we've moved with the times. Most of us have bank accounts or land."

"That's disappointing."

"Sorry to burst your bubble. Eat." He shoved the platter of meat in her direction.

"Some dragon lore must be true. Do you sleep a lot?"

"No, although you will benefit if you take regular naps."

"You don't burn villages, toast small children with your fire or rape and pillage, and steal away with young maidens?"

"Sure," he said in an airy tone. "Every day before breakfast."

Jessalyn's lips quivered. "This I have to see. Will you take me with you tomorrow?"

Manu laughed outright and leaned over to tweak her nose. "Brat."

Jessalyn glanced down at her plate and allowed her smile to widen. He no longer resembled the grumpy man she'd first met, and she decided she'd come to like him. She thought she might trust him. A rare occurrence since she was slow to warm to people. This was a product of the teasing she'd received at school. She frowned.

"Did the people in Piha have knowledge of my background?"

"More than likely. They would've watched you closely as a child. It's what we'd do here. I'd say their close regard would've ceased once you showed no signs of shifting."

"The kids were always teasing me at school."

"Did you tell your father?"

Jessalyn thought back to a tearful discussion almost twenty years ago. "He showed me how to fight and told me to wait until I was out of school. He suggested I practice and bide my time. I punched one of Danny's older cousins and broke his nose. There was blood everywhere, although his nose healed straight. Danny's cousins never teased me after that. The girls kept teasing me because I was bigger than them and clumsy. A ballerina, I am not!"

"This Danny—is his surname Waaka?"

"No, his grandfather was white, although both his parents are of Māori descent. His surname is Ngataki. The cousin I hit was a Waaka."

Manu grinned at her, the bright smile making his eyes glow and the years fall away. He resembled an impish child. "You punched a Waaka in the nose. I've wanted to do that many a time."

"They are arrogant," she agreed. "They hold grudges too. Hika hasn't spoken to me since, not that I care. Hika Waaka is an ass."

Manu gave a loud bark of laughter, the depth of humor buried within making her stare. Manu Taniwha was a handsome dude, and he took after his surname.

"What's so funny?"

"If we're talking about the Hika Waaka I know, you punched the nose of the heir apparent. His father runs the tribe, and Hika is the taniwha who will likely take over from him."

CHAPTER 7

The Relic

When Jessalyn retired for the evening, she discovered a bag of clothes on her stretcher bed. Two pairs of jeans, a three-pack of plain T-shirts and underwear. In another package, she found a pair of runners and a six-pack of socks. Everything was the right size. She sat on the bed, sudden tears burning her eyes. She'd tried to keep clean and take care of her remaining clothes, but the constant washing had made the fabric thin. For Manu to do this without asking or making a big deal about her appearance meant so much. The man hardly knew her, but he treated her better than she deserved.

She made a silent vow to repay him.

Somehow.

She unpacked her daypack and placed her remaining clothes in piles to keep or discard. Her fingers grazed the wooden box she kept concealed at the bottom of her pack.

"Take it out."

Jessalyn started at the clear words ringing through her mind. The voice was feminine but sounded as young as a child.

Slowly, her fingers closed around the box, and she withdrew it. For some odd reason, her hand trembled.

"Open the box."

The voice again. Still childish but also determined and bossy.

Jessalyn opened the box since the pendant drew her. She'd refrained from looking at it often in case someone saw and stole it from her. Nothing city-dwellers did surprised her any longer—not after having her hostel room burgled.

Now, in light of what she'd seen and the things Manu had told her, she studied the pendant with greater interest. As she'd done in the past, she traced her forefinger over the whorls of the koru, the motion bringing comfort. New beginnings. Very apt for the current path of her life.

It was getting late. She sighed and traced the koru one last time. All of a sudden, the curls of the carving disappeared. Jessalyn jerked her hand away and watched in disbelief as the greenstone pattern reemerged from the bone. A fishhook.

She frowned, not one hundred percent certain of the meaning.

From memory, it had something to do with journeys and good luck. Jessalyn scowled at the pendant, unsure if she should touch it or not.

Finally, she gave into the deep yearning she was experiencing and caressed the pendant with the tip of a trembling finger. A faint warmth emanated from the fishhook, and a sense of satisfaction flashed through her.

"I should tell Manu. Show him," she whispered.

"No," the childish voice ordered, the strength of the compulsion rippling through her mind. *"It's our secret."*

"Wake up, sleepyhead."

Jessalyn forced her eyes open and blearily stared at him. "What's the time?"

"Seven-thirty. You have time for a shower before breakfast."

"Okay. Thanks." Her brain kicked into gear. "Manu?"

Manu paused in the doorway that led to the kitchenette. "Yeah?"

"Thanks for the clothes. I'll pay you back when I can."

"You're welcome. I don't expect you to pay me back."

"You should be careful," Jessalyn warned. "I might take advantage of you."

Manu stared at her for a moment before winking. "I wish you

would. I'm available anytime." And with that, he turned away and vanished.

Jessalyn blinked after him, her mouth wide with shock. Astonishment. Had he—? The thought was so fantastical, she stopped it before the notion fully formed. She was too tall and not especially memorable in the looks department.

Guys didn't want her in that way—apart from the captain of the rugby team, and now years later, she assumed Hika Waaka had made that happen since he was friends with the guy. He'd probably encouraged Maui to sleep with her. She'd had brief romantic adventures with summer visitors after deciding to steer clear of the local men.

"Jess! Don't go back to sleep," Manu called.

"I'm up," she shouted back.

To make her words truthful, she bounded out of bed, grabbed a change of clothes, and scurried to the bathroom. The entire time, her mind replayed Manu's words until she finally convinced herself they'd meant nothing.

Fully dressed and with her emotional armor in place, she marched into the kitchenette to join Manu.

"Can you pour the tea please?" he asked over his shoulder. He wore faded jeans and a tight black T-shirt. Once again, his feet were bare. Once again, she stared at them.

"Foot fetish." Weirdly, the voice in her head sounded a fraction older. Certainly more confident.

"I do not have a foot fetish," she snapped.

Manu turned a surprised face at her, a spatula in hand. "I'm pleased to hear it."

"I..." She stopped and inhaled. After blowing out the breath, she said, "I keep hearing a voice in my head. A young female voice."

"Your taniwha." He sounded pleased.

"I think the voices in my head—"

"She!" the voice corrected.

"She," Jessalyn said. "Has been there for a while, but I haven't realized because they've aligned with my own thoughts. This is so crazy. A higher being has plonked me in the midst of a bad dream."

"I'll answer your questions if I can. What time does your shift start today?"

"Ten. They want me to work until seven tonight."

"Excellent," Manu said. "I have time to grab personal details from you so Jack can start his investigation."

"What do you need?"

"Your father's full name. Your mother's too. We'll need a full copy of your birth certificate."

"Dad kept papers in a folder. I think I remember seeing it when I was going through his stuff. If you could wait until the weekend, I could go with you and sort out the rental."

"No," Manu said.

"No, don't return to Piha," her voice ordered.

Jessalyn frowned. "My taniwha loathes the idea."

"Why?" Manu asked, his gaze sharp.

"*Danger.*"

"It's dangerous," Jessalyn said. "I don't understand. If we share a mind, how can she know something I don't?"

"Our beasts are old souls. While we share the same body, we can think independently. We don't always agree with each other."

Jessalyn's brows rose. "That sounds like fun. Are you telling me my taniwha can stop me from moving my body from one side of a room to another?"

"It's usually the bigger life-changing moments."

"This is going to take some getting used to. Part of me wants to return to Piha, but I have an underlying fear. Almost like a premonition."

"A suggestion," Manu said. "How much stuff is left in the house?"

"A few of my clothes plus the furniture. I'd cleared out Dad's room. His business papers are there in folders. I packed up a lot of stuff from the house and sold it at the market. I'll keep my clothes, the business papers, and the tools in Dad's workshed. Everything else can stay in the house."

"Would it be all right if Hone and his wife Cassie went up to clear the house? If anyone asks, they can say they're renting it for the month."

"Will they mind?"

"Hone suggested it when I mentioned you had decided to rent

your property."

"Okay." Jessalyn set two mugs of tea on the tiny table. "Do you have a paper and pen? I'll write down what I know of my father's family and the things he told me about my mother."

"Add the address for your property too. I'll get Jack to do a property search. That might turn up something. Do you have a picture of your mother?"

"Dad had a painting of her. It's on the wall of his bedroom. I guess I'd better keep that too."

Manu placed a plate with bacon, eggs, and fried bread in front of her. Her stomach rumbled, and he laughed. "Eat your breakfast while I call Hone to give him instructions."

"What is the hurry? Eating more seems to help my control."

"For now," Manu said, his tone foreboding. "There is one thing I haven't mentioned about the taniwha species. Once a taniwha enters his or her late teens, the moon controls them. As the full moon approaches, it exerts a pull on us. There are two ways to deal with this problem. We can either shift, which isn't always practical in these modern times, or appease our taniwha with sex. Lots of sex," he said with his attention focused on her.

"You're kidding." Was he making up stories to scare her? Her gaze did a quick up-and-down scan, and she shivered. No. No. *Definitely not.*

"Ask Jack and Hone if you don't believe me."

Okaaay, perhaps he was speaking the truth.

"I can't ask them about sex." Jessalyn ignored the girlish chortle echoing through her mind. "If this is true, why haven't I...er...?" She hesitated, trying to find the words she needed. Huh. No matter how she phrased this, it would be embarrassing. "Why haven't I become hot and bothered every full moon? Wait, will I try to throw myself at every man I see?"

"No, of course not. You'll still be aware and capable of giving your consent. It's not rape. Do you understand? You always have the option of saying no, and from what I've heard, some of the single taniwha women lock themselves in their rooms with a vibrator."

Jessalyn wrinkled her nose. "That's reassuring."

"I'm assuming the moon hasn't affected you because your taniwha has been sleeping. Now that she is waking, you should prepare."

"I can't shift," Jessalyn whispered.

"No." His gaze was watchful, his expression unreadable.

Jessalyn turned the options over in her mind and came up with one. "So you're telling me I'll turn into a sex addict?" Her words arrived at a screech, and they echoed for long moments afterward.

"I'm here for you."

If he hadn't cracked a smile, she might've managed more control. Instead, she jumped to her feet and advanced on him, temper a ball of heat in her gut.

"I like him," the crazy voice said, and Jessalyn's eyelashes

fluttered without her permission. Fluttered!

Her temper ratcheted up another notch, and she pounded her fist into Manu's chest. White flashed before her eyes until she blinked hard enough to focus. Manu's arms wrapped around her, and her entire body softened, fitting her curves to his muscles. *It softened.* Then somehow, without having a clue how it happened, their lips met in a fiery kiss that reverberated heat through her from her head to the tip of her toes.

Jessalyn clung to the edges of her sanity and forced instructions through her brain. Stop. *Stop!* She wrenched away and scuttled back two giant steps.

"Why did you kiss me?" she yelled.

"Because you fluttered your lashes at me and puckered your lips."

"I did not."

"You did."

"I didn't mean to," Jessalyn cried. "Am I going to go around planting kisses on every strange man I meet?"

"Knock-knock!" a feminine voice called. "Is it safe for me and Hone to come in?"

"*Please.* Someone needs to save me from myself," Jessalyn muttered.

Manu grinned and her hands fisted. The urge to strike him again pummeled her mind, but it wasn't right to hit others. Her father had explained that to her when he'd taught her to fight. Only in extenuating circumstances, he'd told her. She was to use her words before her fists.

"Stand next to Hone," Manu said. "See if you get the urge to kiss him."

"But that's his wife," Jessalyn said.

"If there's any kissing going on with Hone, I'd rather see it than have you do it behind my back," the woman said. "I'm Cassie, by the way. You must be Jessalyn."

The woman wasn't what she'd expected since she had distinct curves and was pretty in a girl-next-door kind of way.

"Hello," Jessalyn said. "Ah, is it all right if I stand by your husband?"

"Please." Cassie gestured, her interest bright and curious.

Jessalyn studied the woman for a beat longer before rounding the table to stand beside Hone. She gazed at him, and he returned her regard with clear interest. When the urge to kiss him remained absent, the tension released from Jessalyn's shoulders. Until Hone leaned closer and sniffed her.

"Hone," Cassie chided.

Jessalyn jerked away and stomped back to her half-eaten breakfast. "What is amiss with you men? The men in Piha beat their chests a lot, but they didn't go around sniffing me. I *did* have a shower this morning."

"Well?" Manu asked.

"I get a faint whiff of taniwha," Hone said. "It wasn't there last night."

"She is making herself heard. Jess is aware of her now."

"I'm right here," Jessalyn snapped. "I hate this. Cassie, you're not a taniwha, are you? I think Manu told me you're a human. You're lucky. This breathing fire and kissing without my permission is most disconcerting. And that's the polite description for the out-of-control sensation."

"It must be difficult," Cassie said. "Especially if you knew nothing of this part of your heritage. But at least there is one plus to come from this."

"I can't think of one," Jessalyn muttered.

"You're helping Manu," Cassie said. "You've given him purpose."

Jessalyn shot him an aggrieved scowl. "I don't enjoy being anyone's project."

Manu blinked. Cassie was right. Since Jess's arrival, his moods weren't as dark, but it would be all for naught if he couldn't aid her to control her dragon. Although the additional food and their presence had helped her last night, it was obvious her taniwha was stretching and testing her power. There'd be times when Jess had no way of remaining in charge. This coming full moon would test them all. Shoving aside his uneasiness, he forced a confident smile.

"Eat your breakfast," he said to Jess. "Can we have the keys to your house?"

"Yes. Are you going today?"

"The sooner, the better. I've decided to go with Hone and Cassie. Jack will try to trace your mother from the information you've given me."

"Is it all right to waltz into the Waaka's territory?" Jess asked after swallowing a mouthful of egg. "I get the impression they mightn't welcome your presence."

"No problem," Manu said. "We'll use sneakiness."

"How—?"

"Don't worry. Eat your breakfast."

"Bossy much?" Jessalyn mumbled into her plate, but Manu's quiet laugh told her his hearing was exceptional.

Manu strode over to Hone, and they spoke together in low voices.

"Hone, do you want coffee?" Cassie asked.

"You'll have to put on the coffeemaker. I made tea this morning since Jess prefers it to coffee."

"He's sexy. Mine."

The voice was so loud and clear, Jessalyn jumped and her fork flew from her left hand and clattered to the floor.

"Something wrong?" Manu asked.

"No, just clumsy," Jessalyn muttered, heat filling her cheeks.

Cassie bustled around the kitchen and started the coffee before pulling out the other chair at the table and joining Jessalyn. "I saw that. You were staring at Manu's backside."

"Mine." The word was a shout inside her head, and a growl emerged from her mouth as she started to speak. She clacked her teeth together.

"Jessalyn is growling at me," Cassie said cheerfully.

Manu and Hone broke off their conversation to focus on her.

Cassie beamed. "I mentioned Manu's backside."

An identical growl broke from Hone, and Manu frowned. "Cut that out. Cassie is your mate. She loves you. You know that, dickhead."

Cassie winked at her and did a creditable job of copying Hone's growl. "Don't call my husband a dickhead."

Manu rolled his eyes. "Cute comedy act. The pair of you need to knock it off."

"Payback," Hone stated.

"Yeah. Yeah. Jess, you're welcome to stare at me. Touching me will help to control your dragon."

"Is he telling the truth, or does he want me to cop a feel?" Jessalyn asked Hone.

"He's saying it how it is. Your taniwha is possessive of him, perhaps because he's helping you."

"You've stayed with me for two nights, and I haven't put a toe out of line," Manu said, his tone pissed. "You're safe with me." He checked his watch. "We'd better get moving. We'll drop you off at work on the way. Are there neighbors who might wonder what is going on?"

"No, the properties on my road aren't close together. Mature native trees surround the houses," Jessalyn said. "When you get there, you won't see my nearest neighbor. The only way anyone will learn of your presence is if they're watching my place."

"Hone and I should be able to load your father's tools and the other personal stuff in my truck then. We should sense if there are other dragons nearby," Manu said.

"But won't they sense you too?" Cassie asked.

"Yes, we'll play things by ear. Jess, do you have your stash of chocolate bars and fruit?"

"Yes, Manu."

"Excellent."

Manu drove and when they reached The Viaduct area, he pulled into one of the residential streets on the Wynyard Quarter side. "Won't be long," he said to Hone.

He climbed from the vehicle and opened the door for her. Bemused, she exited and slipped her daypack over one shoulder.

Manu crowded her against the side of his truck and tucked a lock of her hair behind her ear. The voice inside her purred while Jessalyn concentrated on locking her knees to support her weight instead of leaning on the vehicle.

A confident man-comfortable-in-his-skin smile curved his lips and brightened his eyes. "I'm going to kiss you, Jess. If you don't want me to, tell me now."

"I—" She broke off and swallowed the lie she'd intended to spout. The truth—she *did* want his kiss.

"I'll take that as a yes."

His lips met hers seconds later, and any argument she'd intended to marshal fell by the wayside. His lips were soft yet bold, his touch pushing a roar of desire through her body. Unbidden, her hands lifted to his shoulders, and she sank into his embrace. It was Manu who pulled back, pausing to press his forehead against hers before he stepped away.

Jessalyn stared at him, gaped at his intimate yet charming grin and shook her head. "I'd better hurry or I'll be late."

He stepped closer again and ran the backs of his fingers over her cheek. "I'll be here to pick you up after work. I'll meet you at the rear door."

"You don't have to babysit me."

"I'm helping because I want to, not because I have to," he said. "Remember that." With a wave, he climbed back into his vehicle and drove away.

"What are you thinking, Jessalyn? You don't need a man to complicate your life." Jessalyn headed toward the pub where she worked. "Your life is already complicated enough."

A woman wearing a smart black business suit sent Jessalyn a strange look and detoured around her.

With a wry smile, Jessalyn entered the pub via the rear entrance. "And things are worse than you admitted because you're hearing voices in your head *and* talking to yourself."

"Does Jessalyn know she's your true mate?" Hone asked.

"Her taniwha knows," Manu said. "Every time Jess checks me out her taniwha shouts *mine, mine, mine*. She's broadcasting and doesn't realize it. I'm giving Jess time to catch up because all of this is new to her."

"Is that why you haven't moved Jessalyn into Hone's place in Red Hill?" Cassie asked.

"Dad and the others hassle me there. I'd prefer to keep them away from Jessalyn. If I can keep her a secret until we train her to manage her taniwha, so much the better."

"You're lucky you kept your ownership of the warehouse a secret," Hone said. "It's a wonder the tribe hasn't tracked you down there."

Manu shrugged. "It's far enough away from Papakura that no one has considered the location. I've been leaving my vehicle here and flying across the estuary if I have to conduct business. My stealth units are ready for market, but I'm reluctant to release them at present, given the drama within our tribe."

"What are you working on now?" Hone asked.

"An addition to the stealth units to mask the taniwha scent.

We'll be trialing it today when we enter Waaka territory."

"How bad could this get if they discover you and Hone?" Cassie asked.

"A challenge to the death at worst," Hone said, his tone grim.

"And best-case scenario?" Cassie asked.

"An old-fashioned whopping," Manu said. "But don't worry. Hone and I will have the upper hand. We'll be invisible, and even if my latest tweaks for scent don't work, the foreign aroma will confuse anyone who notices because they won't see us."

"Reassuring," Cassie said with a roll of her eyes.

Once they left the metropolis of Auckland and turned onto the road leading to Piha and the surf beach it was famous for, the traffic grew lighter.

"We're lucky it's Thursday and not the weekend," Hone said.

"Yeah, that's why I wanted to come today rather than wait," Manu said. "I'm hoping most people will be at work rather than paying attention."

Manu's phone rang, and he answered it with his hands-free unit. "Manu speaking."

"Are you alone?" Jack's voice.

"I'm with Hone and Cassie. We're going to Piha now. Have you got something for me?"

"I have more information regarding Jessalyn's mother. She's a direct descendant of one of the families from the first canoe. Her maiden name was Kupe."

"They allowed her to marry a white man?" Hone asked.

"Not exactly," Manu said, rifling through the family history and the knowledge of his people. "She didn't have a true mate so her family arranged a marriage with a Waaka."

"That's right," Jack said. "I found a copy of the engagement notice. They meant her to marry Ngahoe Waaka, Nelson's older brother. I couldn't find a notice of marriage."

"Is her marriage to Brown close to the date of the engagement? Didn't Ngahoe die?"

"Yes, he was decapitated in a freak accident at work. Humarie was twenty-one when she married Brown. Reading between the lines, I believe the marriage was against her family's wishes. They still intended for her to marry into the Waaka family. She died when she was twenty-four. According to the newspaper story I dug up, they never found her body. They declared her legally dead at a later date," Jack said.

"I wonder if her relations tried to get custody of Jessalyn," Hone said. "Twenty-odd years ago, a man alone would've had difficulty raising a daughter on his own."

"I'd say not." Manu glimpsed the sea as he slowed for a tractor turning into a paddock. "Jessalyn didn't mention relations. She told me both her parents were lone children. My guess is Humarie's tribe didn't ask for Jessalyn because of her white blood. To their mind, she would never shift to taniwha and was therefore below their notice."

"Here's another question," Jack said. "Doesn't the oldest female in the Kupe line have guardianship of the relic?"

Manu swore. "I believe it left the family once and went to a Waaka male. Mum told us it reverted to the Kupe family."

"What's the relic?" Cassie asked. "*Ooh!* What a great view. The waves look tiny from here."

"The surfers are out in force," Hone said. "And those waves are bigger than they appear."

Manu took a moment to appreciate the panorama of ocean, white waves, and Lion Rock, the silent giant sentinel that looked over the sandy beach. He pulled over at the next outlook point. The ocean always exerted a pull over him, and he never tired of skimming the waves in his dragon form. "Cassie, can you drive from here? Hone and I will go invisible."

"Sure," Cassie said and exited his truck.

Once Cassie sat behind the wheel and he and Hone activated the stealth units, they continued their journey to Piha.

"Tell me about this relic," Cassie said.

"The stories say an old taniwha—one known for his bravery, cunning, and prophecies—guided the first canoe to the land of the long white cloud. When that well-respected taniwha died, the tribe kept his jawbone because they thought it contained power. According to the taniwha's wishes, and because of his friendship with a young Kupe maiden, they declared the Kupe family guardians charged with keeping the relic safe.

"The Kupe's prospered, and other tribes declared their interest in keeping the relic so they, too, could grow rich from the magic of this well-respected taniwha. Tribes fought over the relic. Our tribe went to war with the North and returned with our tails between our legs. As far as I know, the Kupe family only once relinquished their hold on the guardianship. They recovered the relic, and it passed down through the females of the family."

"Why the female line?" Cassie asked. "Why not the male side?"

"The original taniwha trusted and respected the Kupe maiden. He stated his wishes to the tribe and promised dire consequences if anything different happened. For generations, the people adhered to his request, but after a while, jealousy entered the equation," Manu said.

"I don't understand. If the Kupe family came from the north, wouldn't they be part of the Waaka tribe?"

"No, the family followed the taniwha's edicts to the letter. They classed them as independent of the tribe. They declared the holder of the relic a tohunga. That's an expert in his or her chosen field," Manu explained before Cassie could ask. "Powerful tohunga are a law unto themselves. Their rules said no matter who the holder of the relic is or who they marry, the relic will always return to the Kupe family."

"So where is the relic now?" Cassie asked. "If Jessalyn's mother died, who inherited the taniwha's jawbone?"

"I don't recall," Manu said. "My info came from Mum. She

wanted us to understand our history."

"Where did the taniwha species come from?" Cassie asked.

"We're related to the Asian and Chinese dragons," Hone said. "Like most groups of settlers, our ancestors were looking for a better life."

"This stuff is interesting," Cassie said. "But both you and Jack have mated with Europeans. Does that mean our children will never have taniwha powers? And is that why some of your people turn up their noses at us?"

"Their loss," Hone said. "My taniwha chose you. Remember that, sweetheart, when our people are acting like idiots. When we have children, I will love them regardless."

"Honestly, Cassie, I don't think anyone knows for certain what determines if a man or woman can shift. There are documented cases where a taniwha of full blood has never shifted. It's rare, but it has happened. Times have changed since Jessalyn's parents wed, and it's obvious Jess has a taniwha," Manu said.

"Fascinating. If Jessalyn is your mate, and she accepts you, it might appease the more vocal tribe members who are causing trouble." Cassie peered at a road sign and signaled a right turn toward the main beach and the township.

"And if Jessalyn's taniwha takes control and refuses to obey her, Manu will have a different problem. He'll have to execute her," Hone said.

Cassie gasped. "Is that true?"

"Unfortunately," Manu said, the truth as unpalatable as when he'd taken his mother's life. "You want the next right."

"I hope those kids don't think I'm crazy talking to myself," Cassie said as she drove past a group of teenagers and took the next right.

Trees screened Jessalyn's property, and Manu relaxed at the privacy around the house. This should be a quick job—in and out with no complications.

A Wrinkle Or Two

"**C**assie, I don't think we need to worry, but we'll take precautions. Open the doors for us and pretend you're getting something out of the truck," Manu said.

"Sure thing." Cassie climbed out of his truck. She opened the rear door and clapped her hand to her forehead. "Ugh!"

Leaving the rear door open, she returned to the driver's door. For a few seconds, she peered through the window then stomped around the hood, muttering to herself.

Manu grinned, entertained by her antics. He slipped from the passenger seat once she opened it for him. "We're both out," he whispered. "The keys to the house are in the console."

Cassie retrieved the keys and her handbag and shut all the vehicle doors. She strode up a narrow concrete path and approached the door.

"Someone has broken the lock," Manu murmured.

"I'll check around the back," Hone said. "Don't move, Cassie. Okay, I'm out of your way now."

"Open the door, Cassie," Manu said. "Then stand aside. Let me enter first."

He entered the house cautiously and checked the small kitchen, an adjoining dining room, a lounge, and two bedrooms. Cupboards and drawers hung open with the contents strewn over the floor.

"Cassie," he called. "You can come inside. There's no one here."

Cassie stepped over the threshold and closed the door after her. "Opportunists or thieves looking for something in particular?"

"Call the local cops," Manu said. "Tell them you've rented the property and arrived to find someone has trashed the place. Say you don't know if anything is missing and you can't contact the owner because they've gone overseas."

The front door opened and closed.

"Hone?"

"Yeah," his cousin said.

"Ah! I can scent taniwha now. I need to make more adjustments to my screener," Manu said. "Have they broken into the shed?"

"The padlock is still on the door," Hone said. "It doesn't appear busted."

"While Cassie is waiting for the cops to arrive, we might as well load the contents of the shed. We should hear their vehicle coming before they see items floating through the air."

Hone chuckled. "I hadn't thought of that."

Manu grabbed the keys and found the one to open the padlock. He unlocked the door, fumbled for a light and stepped inside.

A low whistle came from behind him. "Lot of money sunk into these tools."

Manu surveyed the different pieces of equipment. "It should all fit in my vehicle."

A police car arrived, and he and Hone ceased working while they listened to the sole policeman who'd arrived from the Waitakere Police Station.

"I'll do a report," the tall, thin man said. His watchful eyes scanned the items on the floors as he did his walk-through. "But that's the best I can do. We don't get a lot of trouble around here, but empty houses and kids with too much time on their hands are a recipe for disaster."

Cassie patted her upper chest and stared up at the policeman. "Is it safe here?"

"We haven't had other reports of disturbances in the area. I'd make yourself known to your new neighbors and watch out for each other. I'm sorry, but that's the best advice I can offer."

Cassie accepted the copy of the report he handed her. "Thank you for coming, Officer."

Once the policeman left, Cassie cleared the mess from the floors while searching for business papers and anything else likely to aid their investigation. Manu and Hone finished clearing the shed and joined her inside the house.

"Who are you?" a male voice demanded.

Manu froze. They were in the kitchen, checking drawers and restoring tossed items to cupboards.

"What are you doing in Jessalyn's house?"

Cassie turned to the new arrival. She approached the tall Māori man with a pleasant, polite, yet cool smile. "I'm Cassie," she said. "I'm moving in here."

Taniwha. Manu scowled at the man.

"Where's Jessalyn?"

"Jessalyn?" Cassie frowned. "Oh! You must mean the owner. I've never met her, but the agency said she was going overseas. I'm renting the property." Cassie's frown deepened. "Although someone has broken in and ransacked the house. I might change my mind."

"Jessalyn is letting the place?"

"Look, I don't mean to be rude, but who are you?" Cassie asked.

"I'm Danny. Her boyfriend." He inhaled, and his eyes widened. He leaned nearer and sniffed her.

Boyfriend? Manu's hands curled to fists. What the fuck?

Cassie drew a sharp breath and took a huge step back. "Did you sniff me? No!" She lifted her hands as if to ward him off.

"I—sorry," Danny said. "Do you have the number for the rental agency?"

Cassie rattled off Jack's cell number, and Manu hustled into the lounge, where he could pull out his phone and text Jack to expect a call from Danny.

Danny left as suddenly as he'd arrived.

Manu returned to the kitchen. "I'll follow him. Hopefully, I'll learn who broke into Jess's house."

"We're almost done," Hone said. "We'll finish up here and wait for you. Call if you need me to rescue your butt."

Manu growled, and both Hone and Cassie laughed.

"Must work on my leadership skills," he mumbled before he left the house at a jog.

Danny's scent was easy enough to pick up, and he trailed the young man to the beach and the Surf Lifesaving Club. This Danny wasn't much younger than Manu, but with responsibility for the tribe weighing down his shoulders, Manu felt immeasurably older.

At the doorway to the clubhouse, he hesitated. Danny was a taniwha, and Manu figured he'd gone to meet with other dragons. Hopefully, his scent would get lost with the others.

Manu entered the open room and spotted ranch sliders leading out to a big balcony overlooking the ocean—an excellent escape route if he required one.

Danny had joined a group of Māori men over the far side of

the room. They spoke in hushed voices, but he recognized none of them. He'd need to do his research and match Waaka names to faces. It might come in handy at a later date.

"...and she said Jessalyn had gone overseas," Danny reported. "I have the rental agency number. The woman knew nothing else. Weird thing, though. I swear I caught a hint of taniwha." He grunted. "I sniffed her, and she jumped a mile. The woman threatened to call the cops, so I backed off."

"Fuck, Danny. If you'd done a better job of romancing the pakeha, we'd have access to everything. That relic must be there somewhere. Grandma said she sensed a magical wave before Jessalyn left, and she read of changes in the stars. She's never wrong," the man said. "I knew I should've asked her out instead of leaving it to you."

"She would've laughed in your face," Danny retorted. "You and the rest of your friends treated her like she was shit on the bottom of your shoes. At least I got close to her and followed Grandma's instructions."

The bastard had used Jess. Manu inhaled and fought his snarling taniwha. He battled his own indignation on Jess's behalf.

"We'll get Allen to visit the woman once she has moved in. He's the closest neighbor so she shouldn't get suspicious. That way we can check to see if her story changes," the one who appeared to be the leader said.

When their talk turned to the upcoming rugby season and the

latest rescue from one of the dangerous Piha rips, Manu left.

The grandmother was obviously a tohunga who read the stars or foretold the future. Manu's tribe didn't have a future-reader.

When he arrived back at the house, Cassie and Hone had gone through every room and packed anything personal in his truck. They'd also included the folders of business and personal papers for Jack to go through while Jack and Emma adapted to life with two new babies.

Manu recounted what he'd heard. "They were using Jessalyn in the hope they'd find the relic. None of them—not even Danny, her so-called boyfriend—has any respect for her."

"Because she couldn't shift?" Cassie asked.

"That's my guess. And because her mother had married a white man," Manu said.

"This worries me," Cassie said. "Please explain again why no one in your tribe protested at Jack and Hone marrying pakeha women."

"It's simple, sweetheart," Hone said, blinking into sight. He curled his arms around his wife. "Both of our taniwha claimed you and our human sides fell in love. Jack and I live to make you and Emma happy."

"But wouldn't Jessalyn's parents have done the same?" she asked.

"We don't know," Manu said. "The issue of the broken engagement clouds the truth. That and the fact Humarie died not long afterward."

"Jessalyn's father never remarried," Cassie pointed out.

"I doubt we'll ever learn the truth," Hone said. "Both of her parents are dead, and there is no one to ask."

"Let's do one more search for anything out of the ordinary," Manu said. "Hone, you'd better blink out again in case we're being watched."

An hour later, they locked the house and left Piha. Back in Auckland, they dropped off the paperwork they'd discovered with Jack.

"Ah," Jack said. "I'm glad you're here. I dug into the details surrounding the death of Jessalyn's mother since I was waiting for more information. This newsletter article has the main details."

Manu accepted the A4 sheet of paper and started reading.

Wednesday, 3 October 1998

After exhaustive searches by volunteers, police, and the Coastguard, Humarie Brown, a resident of Piha, remains missing. A keen fisherman, Mrs. Brown was last seen carrying her baby daughter, Jessalyn and her fishing gear. Locals assume she was on her way to her favorite fishing spot.

When Mr. Brown arrived home from a business trip to Auckland to find the house empty, he rang around his neighbors before he and several others went looking for his wife. He found his daughter, wrapped in a warm blanket, and his wife's fishing tackle but there was no sign of his wife.

Police found blood on the rockface and assume Mrs. Brown either fell or a rogue wave surprised her.

We have called the search off because of bad weather.

"I found another article in the local paper. Authorities declared her legally dead seven years later," Jack said.

Emma and Cassie arrived in the lounge, each carrying a baby. Both babies had black hair. Despite his fear of having two girls, Jack's love for his children and wife was glaringly obvious, and envy flooded Manu, taking him by surprise.

"Here," Emma said. "Hold this one for me."

Manu found the bundle thrust into his arms. The baby eyed him, and he returned her interest. He stroked her silky cheek and pondered his and Jessalyn's children—if they had any. He smiled inwardly at his thoughts, the idea sinking into his heart. Somehow, he had to help Jess gain control of her taniwha. He'd accept no other outcome because if he didn't, his future looked long and bleak.

Jessalyn left the pub at ten minutes after seven, exhausted after another busy day. The snacks throughout the day had helped, but now her stomach lurched at the myriad scents that assailed her. Perfume. Food. Unwashed bodies. Petrol fumes. The brine of the sea. Fear sped through her. What if Manu wasn't here? Could she hold it together?

She scanned the people around the exit. Her fear notched up to panic. *Come on, Jessalyn. Breathe through your mouth.*

"Jess," a voice came from her right. "Sorry, I'm late."

"My stomach is churning," Jess whispered. "Too many contrasting scents. They're bombarding me."

"Here." Manu slipped his arm around her midriff and handed her a package wrapped in silver foil. "Your hands are shaking. Let me."

Manu unwrapped the package to reveal a doner kebab.

"Thanks." Jessalyn bit into the pita bread and groaned at the savory meat and the blast of hummus and garlic.

"Did you eat your snacks?"

"Yes. Everything was normal until I came outside. I'm used to the kitchen odors. What is wrong with me? I've never had this problem. And is it customary for my taniwha to go silent? She chattered up a storm this morning, but she has gone quiet."

"She'll be resting. Your taniwha senses are kicking in, and all of this is hard on her, too."

That made sense. "You always smell everything?"

"Yes," Manu said. "We learn to screen out most or at least cope better. How are your audible senses?"

Now that he'd mentioned it, her hearing had improved. As had her eyesight.

"My theory is that everything is happening fast and your human body is having trouble keeping up with the changes. That's why you're having difficulties with control. We'll keep going with lots of food and rest. How would you feel about a real bed tonight? A hot bath?"

"Yes."

"I hoped you'd say that," Manu said. "Let's go."

"How did things go in Piha?" She savored the heat of Manu's arm around her waist as they ambled toward the Wynyard Quarter. Her stomach had settled after the food, and she continued to nibble on the snack Manu had brought her.

"Someone broke into your house. Cassie called the cops so the break-in is on record."

"Crap, is there much damage? Dad let the insurance lapse, and I can't afford to fix stuff."

"It looked as if they were searching for something. It's difficult to know if they took anything or not."

"I had nothing valuable... My father's tools?" Her stomach

hollowed at the thought of losing this last tie to him.

"They didn't break into the shed. I have all your tools at the warehouse. We cleaned out the cupboards and drawers, so you can ring a rental agency and list it when you're ready."

Relief poured through her. "Thanks. I'll do that tomorrow. There is a real estate place in Waitakere. I'll use them since they won't voice the nosy questions the people at Piha Real Estate will ask."

"Makes sense. We had a visitor while we were there. Danny turned up and demanded to know where you were. He said he was your boyfriend."

"He is not!" Jessalyn's brows drew together. "What did you tell him?"

"He didn't see me or Hone. Cassie handled him perfectly and told him you were going overseas. Don't worry. He has no idea of your location. How did you get on with Danny's friends and relations? By the way, they're all taniwha."

"Really?"

He nodded.

"I didn't like them, and they returned the sentiment. Danny was the only one who ever hung out with me, although his behavior turned weird at the end." Jessalyn took another bite of her kebab.

"Did he sniff you? He did that to Cassie. Of course, she knew what he was doing, but she behaved outraged."

"Worse," Jessalyn said. "He kissed me. Twice. It came out of the blue, and I haven't spoken to him much since."

Manu's arm tightened around her waist. "What did you do?"

"I wiped it off. His kiss was slobbery." Indignation filled her at the memory. "It was so random."

"You didn't wipe off my kiss."

Jessalyn shot him a sideways glance. "Bighead."

Manu grinned. "Eat your kebab. Jack printed the newspaper stories about your mother. Have you seen them?"

"No. Dad gave me the basics, her interests, et cetera. I'd like to read the story."

"I'll get it for you later. How was work today?"

"Busy. I'm tired."

"A bath will hit the spot then."

By the time they reached Manu's truck, Jessalyn's stomach had settled and breathing through her mouth filtered out the pungent scents.

The traffic leaving the city was much lighter, and it didn't take long to drive down the Southern Motorway. Manu took the Papakura turnoff and once they'd reached suburban streets, he pulled over.

"Jess, I want you to drive. I'll give you directions. And, I'm going to trust you with a big secret. Please don't let me down and blab this to everyone you meet."

"Ah, okay?"

They swapped seats, and Jessalyn stared at Manu, wondering at the obvious battle taking place within him. A frown furrowed his brow, and his eyes glittered. Now that she'd learned more about taniwha, she understood this was a glimpse of his dragon.

When he remained silent, still struggling with whatever he wanted to tell her, she said, "You and your friends are helping me. I'm loyal to my friends."

"Except if they behave strangely and offer sloppy kisses."

"Your kisses are a one hundred percent improvement." On replaying her words through her mind, she blushed. Maybe she should keep a closer watch on what she admitted instead of blurting out stuff.

"I haven't had complaints."

"Bighead," she said and tried hard not to crack a smile. The man didn't need encouragement.

"Mine. Mine!"

"Oh, good gravy," Jessalyn muttered. "Stop already."

"Are you talking to your taniwha?"

"Excellent. He didn't hear," Jessalyn said with a quick glance at Manu. Her mouth widened on seeing the quiver of his lips, and she groaned. "You did hear. How do I stop her enthusiasm? She's not making any sense. I have no idea what she's blathering about. You were going to give me directions?"

Manu touched a button on the watch on his wrist. The next instant he was gone. Jessalyn blinked once. Twice. Then, she flung out her arm.

"Hey, woman. Watch where you're putting that fist."

Jessalyn gasped. "You're still there. How did you do that?"

"When I'm not dealing with tribe business, my passion is inventing things. I've designed a stealth gadget to make me invisible when I'm in my human or dragon forms. We're heading to Red Hill. Stay on this road until you get to the next set of traffic lights."

Jessalyn pulled onto the road and followed Manu's instructions. "I can't believe you're there. If you weren't speaking I'd assume the passenger seat was empty."

"Other taniwha sense my presence. I'm working on that angle and haven't quite got it right."

"So if a taniwha wears your watch thingie, they can fly around Auckland and no one notices them?" Jessalyn asked as Manu directed her to pull into a driveway.

"That's right. Good. My father and his friends have gone home to their beds. We should have a peaceful night."

"Why is your father staking out your house?"

Manu sighed. "Long story. Basically, after my mother died, the leadership of the tribe passed to me. My dad doesn't approve. Some of my tribe agree with him."

Jessalyn studied him and instinct told her there was more to the story. But she didn't push. It was none of her business. "This is a nice place."

"It belongs to Hone, and he's letting me rent it from him."

"But you spend most of your time at the warehouse. Is that where you do your work?"

"It is."

"You work alone."

"If I need help with anything my two middle brothers step up or I can ask Hone and Jack. Hone's father is always around too. You'll like Uncle George. He's my father's brother. Do you fancy lasagna for dinner? There is one in the freezer."

"Sounds good." Jessalyn climbed out of the truck. "I can't believe I grew up among taniwha and never noticed a thing. There is so much to learn." She croaked and slapped a hand over her stomach. "I'm going to breathe fire."

"Quick." An invisible hand grasped hers and tugged her around the house. "Hone has a fire pit near the deck."

Jessalyn hiccupped and a spark shot out. She lifted her free hand to her mouth, and her second hiccup-induced spark burned her palm. It hurt but far better that than setting the house on fire.

"Here," Manu said.

But she'd already spied the pit, and she bent over, her shoulders racking with the force of her hiccups.

"Try this," Manu said, off to her right. "Instead of fighting the urge, embrace it. It's safe here. See how big a flare you can breathe out. A dragon can spout fire for several hours if they need to, but they pace themselves."

"It's strange speaking to you while you're invisible. You—" She broke off, heat swirling in her stomach, growing bigger and hotter. This time, instead of panicking, she inhaled and the faint sense of nausea she always experienced retreated. Encouraged, she repeated her breath until she could bear the heat no longer. She inhaled—a deep, long breath—and expelled it while aiming her face toward the fire pit.

A fiery spurt of flame shot from her mouth, so big it startled her. With no fuel to grow, the fire flared and died to a flicker before vanishing.

"You did it." Manu sounded thrilled with her accomplishment. "Do you need a repeat, or is your stomach settled now?"

"I'm good. I think."

"Come inside, so I can become visible again," he murmured. "I'll open the garage and get you to park my truck inside."

As Jessalyn followed him, the moon caught her attention. A half-moon, it sat low in the sky.

"*Pretty,*" her taniwha crooned. "*I like it.*"

Jessalyn took a final glance before returning to the truck. She hadn't liked the way her taniwha had almost purred at the moon, especially since the copious amounts of sex discussion.

"Something wrong?" Manu's voice came from the garage.

She jumped. "My taniwha was staring at the moon and praising it. It made me remember what you said this morning."

"Don't worry too much. You're not alone, and we'll help you. You have nothing to fear."

Jessalyn climbed into the truck, and once Manu opened the garage door for her, she parked the vehicle. The door came down behind them and a light flicked on, telling her she hadn't run Manu over during the maneuver.

It was all right for him to tell her not to worry, but this was all new for her. How could she not worry?

Manu materialized. "I'll put the lasagna in the oven. Come on inside. Do you want a beer?"

"A cold drink sounds perfect. My throat is tender. Does fire-blowing make your throat sore?"

"No, I think because I've used my fire since I was young. I don't do it in human form like you either."

Jessalyn accepted the bottle of beer Manu handed her. "If you blew fire from a young age, how come you didn't get in trouble or draw attention at school?"

"I did get in trouble, and our teachers were very strict in what we could and couldn't do. We have our own school, and the teachers would threaten to send us to June for punishment. My mother," he added. "Believe me, my brothers and I soon learned our punishments were always worse than the other boys and girls who misbehaved. All of my brothers were bright enough to realize misbehavior had to occur when no one in authority might witness our transgressions."

"Isn't the moon pretty? I'm all tingly inside."

Jessalyn spluttered out a mouthful of beer. "That wasn't me!"

"Behave," Manu said in a deeper than normal voice.

"But I didn't say—" Jessalyn broke off when Manu placed a finger against his lips in a sign for silence.

"Are you listening?"

"Yes, sexy."

Manu rolled his eyes. "Behave." He spoke sternly.

Thankfully, the loud voice in her head—the one that shouted for Manu's entertainment—fell silent.

"We're not sure what the burglar wanted. There was no damage. They'd dumped things on the floor as if they were looking for something. It wouldn't surprise me if they break into your shed next."

Had they wanted the pendant? "Do you think—?"

"No," her taniwha said, her tone sharp and bossy. *"Wait. Don't tell him yet."* She spoke in an *inside* voice—the way to explain Manu's lack of reaction. Her taniwha had spoken only to her, which meant...

"Do I think what?" Manu asked.

"Perhaps they found what they wanted."

Manu shrugged. "Who knows? I'll give you a quick tour. Kitchen. The pantry, in case you get hungry. You'll find biscuits and chocolate bars. You've seen the lounge and the deck already. The fire pit is ready if you need it. The garden is private so no worries with spying neighbors."

He led the way along a royal-blue runner. The natural wood

flooring showed on each side of the carpet. Two bedrooms. "I use one as a home gym. And this is my bedroom. This room has an en suite, and there is another bathroom through that door."

"Where will I sleep?"

"You can take my bed," Manu said.

"Where will you sleep?"

"The couch is comfortable. I've gone to sleep there while watching the telly."

"We could share his bed," her inner voice said helpfully.

"No!"

Manu's brows rose, his lips curling into a quizzical smile. "No, what?"

"Uh, nothing. Can you hear my taniwha now?"

"Not everything."

Jessalyn speared him with a skeptical gaze. "Are you sure you're telling me the truth?"

Manu's quick grin sent her pulse racing. "I am."

The oven buzzer interrupted their conversation, and Jessalyn followed Manu to the kitchen. A tantalizing spicy tomato, cheese, and meat fragrance drifted on the air, and her stomach gave a loud rumble.

She held her belly, heat rising in her cheeks. "I can't believe I'm eating so much food."

"Don't worry." Manu set the lasagna on a trivet he'd placed on the table earlier. "Sit. Sit."

Jessalyn hoovered up the lasagna. It was mouthwateringly delicious, and she savored every morsel.

It was kind of nice, sitting in a home and eating dinner with someone who wasn't her father. This was different from eating a meal in the warehouse.

"What did you do during the evening when you lived at home in Piha?" Manu asked.

"Often, I'd help my father with his bespoke furniture pieces. It's part of why I wanted to keep Dad's tools and equipment. I enjoy working with wood and thought I might continue making the carved boxes Dad used to sell at the Auckland markets. They're smaller pieces and take less time to make."

"How often did your father make the trip to the markets in Auckland?"

"Once a month."

"Did you ever go with him?"

"When I was young, Dad left me with a babysitter. I offered to go with him once I was older, but Dad told me he enjoyed selling on his own. Our discussion was kind of uncomfortable, actually. I got the impression he used that time alone to entertain a lady. After that, I never asked again. I started working at the fish shop on Friday nights and the weekends."

Manu nodded. "Do you know which markets your father used to sell at?"

"All different ones. There is a heap of markets in Auckland.

When Dad got enough stock, he'd look at what was on and book a stall at whichever one he thought would work best."

"Do you want to watch another movie?"

"Sure."

"An action movie?"

"Perfect." Relaxing in this way, without having fire-related stress—well, it seemed as if she hadn't slowed down since her father's death. Thanks to Manu, she had a plan of sorts. It made all the difference.

The action movie entertained and enthralled her until it came to the steamy love scenes. She blinked at the sudden expanse of flesh, her mind steering down the same driveway. Once the thought entered her head, it refused to leave. That tiny, annoying voice spoke up with an opinion. Of course, she had one.

"We should practice this stuff with Manu. I'd enjoy that."

No. Jessalyn sent the thought back in the firm and decisive manner her father had used on her when she was trying to wheedle permission.

Somewhere, in the depths of her brain, her fledgling taniwha must've ferreted out her past process and utilized her experience.

"Please. Please. Please!"

Stop shouting.

"Pleeeease!"

"Something wrong?" Manu asked.

"No! Nothing." Now that her dragon had started this kerfuffle,

Jessalyn couldn't focus on the action on the screen. She squirmed on the couch, her limbs twitchy. Squeezing her knees together heightened her arousal. Heat crawled across her skin. She shifted positions. Nothing helped to ease her growing arousal.

Jessalyn glanced out the terrace windows, her gaze alighting on the half-moon. Mesmerized, she gawked at the pale celestial body. For some reason that made everything worse. Manu's presence beside her, plus the movie and the moon in her direct vision, combined to set her on edge.

"Touch Manu. Pleeease!"

Jessalyn leaped to her feet. "I...ah...I think I'll go to bed now."

Manu paused the movie and stood. "The sheets are clean. Do you have everything you need?"

A splutter escaped Jessalyn before she could control the blast of black humor. "Yes. Yes! I'll be fine. Good night."

"Jess! What time are you starting work tomorrow?"

"Ten."

"All right. See you in the morning."

Jessalyn practically ran to the master bedroom. She shut the door behind her. It slammed, and she winced.

"Get a grip, Jessalyn," she muttered.

A quick shower later, her body still twitched and toweling dry increased the sensitivity of her breasts, her skin. Everything.

Jessalyn hung up the damp towel and padded from the en suite to the bedroom naked. She flopped onto the bed and closed her eyes. Even breaths. *Even breaths.*

"I want sex," her voice whispered. Her taniwha sounded a little desperate, and Jessalyn got it. She also no longer sounded childlike but more like a female with goals.

Every inch of her skin tingled while her pussy pulsed with urgency.

Jessalyn muttered a soft curse and parted her legs. The cooler air hitting her folds forced a groan of pleasure from her. She stroked herself. The return journey of her finger had her moaning.

Then, a knock sounded on her door.

"Jess, is everything all right?"

CHAPTER 9

The Power Of The Moon

Manu tapped again as his dragon growled. Worried when Jess didn't answer, he stepped over the threshold.

Jess was stretched out on his bed, naked, her hand buried between her legs. Manu understood even before her first shriek.

"Get out!"

Her cheeks were red, and her eyes glittered. Was that her taniwha he'd glimpsed? Manu took another step closer, mesmerized by the way her irises flashed golden.

"Manu, what are you doing?"

He sat on the corner of the bed but kept his hands clenched in his lap. "Is it your taniwha?"

Jess made a choked sound and tried to scramble under the covers. "Ever since we discussed what happens to dragons during the full moon, the voice in my head has droned on and on about how pretty the moon is. Then the movie. Those love scenes. And you—your scent."

A sob of despair emerged from her, and it twisted his gut. He'd known his taniwha since childhood, and he and his beast mostly worked together. This was new for Jess, and her frustration was obvious.

Manu swallowed, her decadent scent and distress tugging at his control. This was his mate. Every part of him wanted to declare it to the world, but Jess had enough to deal with now. She didn't need him adding to her burdens.

"Would you let me touch you?" The words burst from him, and he would've recalled them, except the flare of her eyes and her throaty groan hinted she might welcome his touch. She hadn't ordered him to leave for the last two minutes. "I'll keep my clothes on and use my fingers and mouth."

His dick twitched as if to refute his promise. Manu dug his fingers into the duvet cover and waited.

When she merely stared at him, his shoulders slumped. "I'll go." He stood and was halfway to the door when she spoke.

"No, don't leave. I—you—please touch me. I ache so bad."

Manu exhaled his relief before turning back to her with hopefully a pleasant but impassive expression. "You're certain?"

"Yes." She beckoned him closer.

Manu cautiously sat on the bed again, this time nearer to her.

"Come closer." Her voice was strained.

"Yes?"

Jess struck, grabbed his head—no, his ears—and gripped hard enough to force their faces together.

"You will touch me, but so help me, if you tell anyone, I will cut off your balls, crush them, and use them as fertilizer on the first public garden I find. Do you understand?"

Manu struggled to keep up. "I never gossip."

The truth. She didn't understand. Not yet. Learning these different facets of her personality, her strength and her tomboy ways fascinated him. He'd never taken the time to get to know a woman this way. Mostly, he charmed them out of their panties, bedded them, and left. Everything with Jess was different.

Her grip on his ears remained firm. "That's what the captain of the first fifteen told me when I gave him my virginity, then he boasted to his rugby mates, and they told their girlfriends. Pretty soon everyone in Piha knew I was a rotten lay."

"The bastard!" Manu wanted to hunt down the moron and flatten him. "I am not him."

"No, but I'm making sure you don't tell your cousin or friends."

They'd already know where his mind was headed since he hadn't shown this attention to any other woman.

"I will not discuss anything that happens in this bedroom with anyone but you," he promised, holding her gaze for the entire time.

"All right." She shuddered and released him. Her right hand smoothed down his cheek, the stroke tender and no longer aggressive.

It was a surrender, and Manu wanted to howl at the moon like a dumb wolf.

Now she'd given him permission, he allowed himself to study her body. Her clothes—looser than necessary—screened the beauty of her sleek muscles. Her breasts were large, her nipples a deep rose rather than the brownish color more common to those with Māori blood. He brushed one taut nub, and a noticeable shudder worked down her torso.

Her waist nipped inward—surprisingly small—then flared out to hips, perfect for a man to grip as he loved his woman. Manu let his hand drift downward, skimming one breast, her rib cage, her hip. She stirred restlessly, her body silently pleading for more.

Manu wanted to record this moment in his memory to pull out as he grew older. It was her scent that propelled him onward. Rich and heady with a hint of spicy green and musk. He parted her legs farther and fit his body in the V between.

"Please hurry," she urged.

He kissed an inner thigh, reveling in the silkiness of her skin and the fragrance of the body-wash he used in his shower. He traced his fingers over her intimate flesh, a barely there skim of her cleft. A low moan accompanied the slight lift of her hips.

"Manu." She shifted her lower body from side-to-side, restless in her quest for his fingers and mouth.

Manu gave into his craving to taste her and ran his tongue along her folds. She hissed, and he wanted to howl in concert. Both he and his taniwha could feast on her for hours. She was wet and ready for a cock. His cock. But building trust with her was important. While other taniwha in the past might have captured their mate and spirited her away to a private, confined place until she acquiesced, this was a modern age. He might be on the bossy side, but he needed Jess to claim him as he claimed her.

When she shuddered against his tongue, he sensed how close she was, her desperation. Manu licked around her swollen clit and inserted a finger into her channel. It slid inside her with ease, her swollen tissues hugging his digit. Manu added another finger and curled them, searching for the patch of flesh that would please her most. He sucked gently at her clit, gradually giving her more. As he kissed and caressed, he stroked her internally.

Her body strained and shuddered, her breaths coming in harsh pants.

Manu continued loving her with his mouth and fingers until her body tensed. She climaxed two seconds later, her pussy pulsing around his two fingers, clenching and releasing rhythmically while he eased up on his contact with her clit.

Gradually, she relaxed, and he withdrew his fingers. He rose up the bed and viewed her expression. Her eyes were closed, her features as tension-free as her body. He kissed her, and her arms curled around his neck as she returned his smooch.

"Are you okay?" he whispered as their lips parted.

"Touch my breasts," she murmured, her voice dreamy.

"My pleasure, sweetheart." He shaped one breast with his hands, finishing with the nipple squeezed between his fingers.

Her murmur of approval had him repeating the move on her other breast then he used his mouth.

"Manu," she whispered. "Make me come again."

Manu groaned since his jeans held his dick in a strangled position. After a deep breath, he pushed aside his own needs and focused on his mate. Her need was greater, and he'd tend her as long as she required.

"It will be my pleasure."

And he loved her long into the night.

Jessalyn woke to the ring of a phone. Warm and relaxed, she stretched then froze when she realized another body inhabited the bed with her.

Her eyes popped open, and she turned her head.

"Bloody phone," Manu grumbled. "Whoever is calling me will get an earful."

He rolled out of bed, giving her a flash of a naked back. The tattooed dragon on the man's back brandished his sword and blew her a kiss. Her gaze lowered, and she was almost disappointed when she struck a pair of black boxer-briefs.

"Yes," Manu barked. "This had better be good."

He froze as the person on the other end of the call spoke. The masculine rumble reached her, but she couldn't decipher the actual words. Manu turned to face her, giving her the front view. It was just as perfect as the back. A broad chest with no body hair, olive skin, and muscles that told her he did plenty of physical activity to counteract his inventor work. Probably his flying.

The thought gave her pause. Would he take her flying if she asked? She doubted she'd ever fly, but she could ride on his back. Not one human would witness their flight if she could wear one of his inventions.

"All right," Manu said. "Find the address, and we'll visit tonight once Jess finishes work. Good job, Jack." He hung up and sat on the bed beside her. His expression turned tender as he smoothed the hair from her face. "I have news about your father."

Jessalyn sat up, grabbing the sheet to cover her naked breasts. She'd pleaded with him to get her off, and he had. Several times without asking anything in return. "What news?"

"Jack has been checking the records we took from your house. He discovered where the money received from the bank went." Manu paused.

His uncharacteristic indecisiveness warned her of something momentous about to happen. Every muscle in her body clenched. "Tell me."

"To a Karen Baker. Jack checked the birth records again this morning. Your father has two other children with this Karen Baker. A boy and a girl."

It took a while for the information to sink in since it made little sense. "Dad had other children?"

"Yes, Jack is positive. Your father is listed on their birth certificates."

"Why wouldn't he tell me? Why would he keep this a secret?"

"I don't know, sweetheart. Jack is working on finding an address."

"None of this makes sense. Wait, will this Karen Baker even know Dad is dead? I didn't put a notice in the *Herald*."

"Hard to know. Once Jack has the details, we'll visit this woman. Maybe she'll help answer your questions."

Thankfully, work kept her busy, but her thoughts never strayed far from her father.

Why?

That question rattled through her brain for the entire day. She wiped away the worst of the greasy cooking odor with fragrance-infused wet-wipes and exchanged her clothes for a clean set in the employee's washroom. A pair of new jeans, an older but tidy blouse from her own wardrobe, and sports shoes, also courtesy of Manu.

At the last moment, she opened the wooden box and pulled out the pendant. Her finger traced the shape of the greenstone fishhook set into the bone, and the churning of her stomach settled. On impulse, she slipped the stout string over her head and tucked the pendant under her blouse. After making certain the mystery key remained safe, she returned the wooden box to her daypack.

With jerky movements, she shoved her clothes on top and went outside to wait for Manu. By the time Manu picked her up, her shock at learning of a second family had shifted to anger.

She had a half-brother and half-sister somewhere in Auckland, and her father hadn't bothered to tell her. Why hadn't he blended his families? She hadn't known her mother since she'd died when Jessalyn was two. Instead, her father had visited his second family while leaving her with the babysitter in Piha.

"Have you found an address?" Her first words on entering Manu's truck.

"Are you sure you want to do this?"

Jessalyn gazed at him in surprise. "Wouldn't you be curious to meet your father's secret family?"

"He kept them hidden for a reason."

Her incredulity turned to her father's motivation in keeping quiet. "The logical excuse is that it was against the law. I need answers, Manu."

"I understand," he said. "But what if the answers make everything worse?"

"You said Jack traced the money to this woman. Dad didn't expect to die. He must've had a plan, but he's left me a mess. The why of it is killing me."

"Let's go then," Manu said.

"Where do they live?"

"Howick, overlooking the sea."

"How do you know that?"

"I recognize the address, and I took a flight over this afternoon."

The topic of flight distracted her a fraction. "I wish I could fly. What does it feel like?"

"It's my favorite thing. I love the wind in my face and soaring on the breeze, the salty brine of the sea. It's difficult to explain. Have you flown in a small plane?"

"We went on a school trip to Australia when I was ten. That was fun, but it was an Air New Zealand 747."

"Flying in dragon form is better."

"Would you take me flying one day? I could ride on your back, couldn't I?"

Manu frowned. "I've never carried another while flying. I suppose it's possible."

"Will you think about it?"

"Perhaps."

Jessalyn fell silent and let Manu navigate the streets and refer to his GPS. Almost half an hour later, they pulled up outside a wooden bungalow. It was an older house and the mature trees reflected this. Garden-beds full of bright yellow pansies and purple petunias bordered a footpath that led to the front door.

"It's not too late to change your mind."

Jessalyn shook her head. "I have to learn why Dad kept this family a secret from me. He mentioned nothing in his will."

"I'll come with you."

"Thanks."

Her stomach churned as she made her way up the decorative path. She applied the brass lion-knocker to the door and waited with Manu standing nearby.

A teenager answered, and Jessalyn gasped at seeing him. The male—somewhere in his late teens—was the masculine version of her with brown eyes and skin of the same shade. His black hair flopped into his eyes, and he shoved it aside to peer at her.

Jessalyn swallowed, fearful her knees would fail to support her, and she'd face-plant on the verandah in front of her newly discovered brother. Half-brother.

"Hello," she croaked.

The boy stared at her, his black brows drawing together. "Mum," he called.

Footsteps approached, and she again swallowed, her stomach churning in tandem with her racing heart.

The door opened wider, and an older Māori woman appeared. She wore office clothes: black trousers and a pale violet blouse. Her long black hair—shot through with silver—sat atop her head in an elegant updo. Her brown eyes widened on seeing Jessalyn before her features hardened.

"Oh, Jessalyn. What have you done?" Anger coated the woman's words. She yanked her son back and attempted to shut the door in Jessalyn's face.

"No," Manu snapped, and he used brute force to push his way inside. "It's obvious you don't want Jessalyn here, but don't you think you owe her an explanation?"

CHAPTER 10

The Past Rears Its Head

"B-but you're dead."

Manu's grasp of her hand was the sole thing keeping Jessalyn grounded. Her chest had tightened, and she struggled to breathe past her shock and confusion. The lies. The betrayal. She shook her head, then released a forceful breath.

This woman was her mother.

Her real mother.

She'd been alive all this time, and her father had lied to her.

Everything she'd believed...

"Why?" Jessalyn growled as she battled with disbelief and hurt. Rage.

Humarie Brown or Karen Baker—whatever name her mother went by—scowled. "Why are you here? Where is James?"

"He's dead. A heart attack almost two months ago."

Jessalyn glimpsed a pained wince, a faint dropping of the perfect posture, but it was brief and fleeting before her mother collected her emotions and abruptly gestured them into a room to their right. A formal reception room with gleaming surfaces and pristine furniture. A foreign mint tang married with the fragrance from the bunch of lavender sitting in a vase on an oak sideboard. Jessalyn's practiced eye took in the expensive piece of furniture before her gaze flittered to her mother. No, the woman who'd given birth to her.

She'd never been a mother to Jessalyn.

Her brother had silently retreated, and Jessalyn didn't blame him. Part of her wanted to flee, to escape the hovering storm about to break over her head.

As if he sensed her mindset, Manu reached for her hand again, twined their fingers in silent support, and drew her to a two-seater.

Her mother—Karen—strode over to a single seat, her heels quick and somehow impatient on the wooden flooring.

The rapid clicks—before her mother reached the thick Persian rug and her footsteps silenced—and the blast of angry rejection had Jessalyn tensing further and sitting straighter.

Then Karen sat, her posture perfect again, her attitude still unwelcoming. "Why are you here? And why did you bring *him* with you?"

Did Karen even care about her?

Jessalyn swallowed while she sensed rather than saw the growing tension in Manu. "Dad died, and the finances..." Saying this suddenly seemed disloyal to the parent who had loved and supported her for all these years. "I came to Auckland to sell his vehicle and remaining stock, and on impulse, I stayed."

Her mother didn't reply but turned her cold gaze to Manu. "How did you become involved with Manu Taniwha?"

"You know Manu?" Jessalyn asked.

Karen's attention zeroed back in on her. "I know of him. He killed his mother."

Jessalyn let out an involuntary gasp before risking a glance at Manu. No longer the tender man of the previous evening, he'd reverted to the angry stranger she'd first met in Onehunga. She waited for him to defend himself, to snap and snarl at her mother.

No! This woman had never been her mother. Never. Never. *Never.* This was the woman who'd given birth to her.

"Nothing to say?" Karen taunted.

Manu wasn't a murderer. She'd seen and experienced his compassion, watched the way he'd held one of Jack's babies. She'd ask him for explanations once they left this house.

"Why did you leave me alone on the clifftop? Why did Dad lie and pretend you were dead all this time? You have two other children. *I have a brother and a sister.*"

Karen jumped to her feet. "You will stay away from them and forget their existence. I didn't make this sacrifice for you to expose us and place me and my children in danger."

What about me? Jessalyn swallowed hard and battled her tears.

"How are you in danger?" Manu spoke for the first time, his voice lower and more rumbly than normal. Insistent.

Karen's mouth twisted. "Don't bother. That taniwha power won't work on me."

"You know about dragons?" Jessalyn asked.

"Taniwha," Karen snapped. "I am a Kupe. Of course, I know." Her eyes narrowed, and she darted to Jessalyn. Her cool fingers plucked on the string around Jessalyn's neck, and she pulled out the pendant. "Oh, child."

Unexpected sorrow filled her voice, a complete turnabout to her initial reception.

Manu's hand tightened on hers, drawing her attention. "Jess, where did you get that?"

"I found it in the house when I was packing up Dad's things. Dad had hidden it in a secret compartment. The proportions were off in the drawer. That's how I noticed."

Karen laughed, the sound melodic. Genuine—the sort of laugh that spoke of parental amusement. "I told your father he shouldn't have taught you to work with wood."

A strange emotional hunger burst free in Jessalyn as she toyed with the cord on her pendant. Weirdly, she craved approval from this woman. This absent parent who'd left her and walked away without a second thought.

She closed her eyes and swallowed hard. The lump in her throat refused to shift. The knowledge of her rejection had tremors quaking her body. The knowledge she had siblings who would never know their older sister if this woman had her way. The knowledge this woman held secrets she didn't want told, didn't intend to share. She didn't give a damn about the consequences for Jessalyn.

Tears continued to build behind her eyes, the pressure forceful. Yet again, Jessalyn fought to hold her composure. She refused to crack, to show any more of her pain, her vulnerability to this stern woman.

"Is that the relic?" Manu asked in a strange voice.

"Yes," Karen said with a sigh of resignation. "Jessalyn, do you have a taniwha?"

Jessalyn traced the whorls of the greenstone in the pendant, her gaze on Karen, her voice silent.

A strange expression crossed the woman's face. "My parents told me the relic remains with the chosen until his or her death, but I had a plan. I forced my taniwha to sleep and gave the relic to James. He told me he'd destroyed it. I never realized he'd kept it all this time."

Karen seemed to drift into the past, remembrance curving her lips, then she gathered herself, and an icy persona slid into place.

"The relic accepts you. I should've guessed since you liked to touch it when you were a baby. It glowed when you played with it. You must go. I and my children will travel to Australia. Once I sell the house, we will not be returning."

"Why?" The rejection sent her reeling, pummeled her mind, and left her lungs struggling for oxygen.

"The Waaka family cannot know of their existence. They must not learn I am still alive," Karen said.

"Did they threaten you?" Manu asked.

"They weren't happy when James and I ran off and married. The tribe was even more concerned when we had a half-breed child, and they threatened to kill James and Jessalyn. Their threats forced James and me to fashion a plan." She shrugged, the silk-clad shoulder gesture elegant and indifferent. "I died, and the problem resolved itself. You'll be in danger now," Karen continued, her tone lacking sympathy. "As will my son and daughter, simply because you're all of my blood. Taniwha have an uncanny way of sensing the relic."

"I didn't perceive it," Manu said. "Why?"

Karen frowned. "You should have."

They turned their attention to her, their expressions full of questions. Jessalyn tugged at her T-shirt, avoiding their gazes. "The pendant was in a wooden box. A carved box I assumed Dad made. I haven't worn it before. This is the first time."

"Ah! James discovered a way to shield the power. It will be the lining or the material. If I were you, I'd return the relic back to the box and bury it in a deep hole where no one will ever find it. The legend behind the relic creates trouble."

"The legend?" Manu asked.

"No more. You must go. You've placed us in danger by coming here. Go and never return."

Jessalyn flinched and closed her fingers over the pendant. Without another word, she stood on shaky legs and tottered toward the door. She refused to outstay her welcome. Her thoughts leap-frogged each other, collided, scrambled into mental soup.

Rejection.

Her legs synced with her brain. Her steps lengthened. *Flee.* She had to leave before she howled.

No. Jessalyn forced her shoulders to straighten. She forced her steps to slow. She forced her chin to raise and spun to face the woman who had given birth to her. "Thank you for speaking with us."

"Good girl. Don't let her know she has upset you." The words filled her mind. Manu's words. She hadn't realized mental communication was possible, although they had spoken when he'd shifted to his taniwha.

Jessalyn marched to the door with Manu and Karen at her back. Questions still ricocheted around her mind—pinballs in a gaming machine. Faster and faster, they whirled. Questions about Karen, her siblings. Questions about Manu, the Waaka family. So many questions.

Outside, one final issue occurred to Jessalyn. Karen had almost shut the door when Jessalyn darted back.

"Wait. Please."

The door stopped closing. "What?"

"I found a key in the box with the pendant. Do you have any idea what it might be for?"

"Describe it."

"It's silver and has a number on it. 712."

"James kept a locker at the storage place in Botany. He left tools there."

Jessalyn's gaze met her mother's, and for a fleeting second, she thought Karen might say more. Instead, the woman's expression grew icier, the slamming of the wooden door cutting their connection.

"Come on, Jess. We'd better go," Manu said.

He was right, but she still hesitated, her mind crying out for the comfort of a mother.

The lost years.

A car pulled up, and a young girl of around fifteen jumped out. Still wearing a school uniform, she waved to her friends and skipped toward Jessalyn. When she spotted Jessalyn, her steps slowed.

The door opened behind them. "Rachel, good. You're home.

Dinner is almost ready."

Her sister edged past her, and seconds later, the door shut.

The final rejection.

Manu took Jess's arm and propelled her to his truck. Her face was pale, and she trembled, upset. Hell, anyone would be distraught to discover the parent they'd believed dead was healthy and very alive. Add to that the lies from her father, his continued marriage to Humarie, and the news of two siblings, and it was a wonder she wasn't pitching a fit.

Jess sat in the passenger seat, unmoving. Manu reached over and clicked her seatbelt into position. He started his truck and pulled away from the house.

"Did you kill your mother?"

"Yes," Manu said, his heart stuttering at the confession. While he'd done the right thing, saving many, his act still stunk of betrayal. It was why he suffered his father's abuse.

"Why aren't you in jail?"

She didn't sound frightened, merely curious. Didn't mean his explanation wouldn't break the fragile trust he'd carved out with her to date.

He moistened his dry mouth with a hasty swallow. "My mother led our tribe and held the sacred sword. Toward the end, she became unstable. She fixated on me and my two middle brothers marrying and having children. My mother lost the plot when

Hone paid attention to Cassie since she thought Cassie was the perfect woman for me. She flew to Clevedon, where Cassie and Hone now live, and attempted to kill them for their betrayal.

"Cassie and I were never more than friends, but Ma refused to listen. Emma still bears the burn scars from my mother's attack. Along with the attempted murder, she risked outing us to humans by flying in her dragon form. Our tribe has a sacred sword, and it chooses which taniwha it resides with. The chosen one leads the tribe. The sword transferred to me that morning." He risked a glance at Jess before turning his attention back to the road. "I had no option. Ma wouldn't back down. She refused to listen. Not even Dad could talk sense into her." Manu paused, the knife-edge of pain still sharp and pointy. Debilitating. "I beheaded her to save Jack and Emma. Hone and Cassie. Humans spotted her, and the police turned up, but I burned her body before they arrived. Do you understand?"

Half a year seemed to pass while he waited for her reply. It was important she understood—this impossible dilemma and his struggle since the act.

"You sacrificed one person to save many," she said finally. "I get it. In Karen's mind, she did the same. Manu, what happens if I can't control my taniwha?"

He flinched, his hands clenching the steering wheel to still his taniwha's silent roar of protest.

"You'd execute me?"

"It's my job. Sweetheart." His voice cracked, and he coughed to clear his throat, the excess emotion screwing up his speech. "I'd never do this willingly. Even thinking it upsets my taniwha, but I bear the sword and have a responsibility to my people."

"It's late. Will this storage place still be open? I have the key with me."

Changing the subject. Manu didn't blame her. "We'll drive to Papakura via Botany. If the relic is as powerful as Karen indicated, you'd better return it to the box and hope it didn't set off alarms with the Waaka tribe."

She scowled. "Every part of me, every instinct, is screeching to wear it. Having the skin contact soothes my stress."

"From what I've heard—snippets picked up over the years—your mother running away with another man still aggrieves the Waakas. They'll be wanting to put that right, and if you don't hand over the relic, they'll take you any way they can. Kicking and screaming if need be. Dead would be better, and that's the likely outcome, given you can't shift."

Her posture went rigid. "Why do the Waaka family want the relic so much?"

"All I have is hearsay since this happened hundreds of years ago. No one is still alive to back this up one way or the other. The relic is a part of the jawbone of the original taniwha. He chose a Kupe—someone in your mother's line—to receive the relic after he died. This decision upset the other tribes, so he used the last of his magic to bespell the relic. The pendant chooses its favored candidate, much like the sacred sword of my tribe. A Waaka man wore the pendant for a short time. He fell in love with a beautiful maiden from the Kupe family. After their marriage ceremony, the pendant showed a preference for his wife. I think—and this is my opinion—the Waaka family are hoping if they marry into the family, the pendant will return to them."

"And with my mother, they were willing to commit murder and force her to marry into the tribe," Jess said.

"Yes," Manu said simply. "It looks as if the storage place is closed."

"Is this the only one in the area?"

"I'm not sure. We'll do an internet search."

Jess fondled the pendant. "Why aren't you after the pendant?"

Manu stopped at a set of traffic lights and caught the distrust that flickered across her face.

"Do you want the pendant too?"

"Use your brain, Jess." A honk from the car behind forced his concentration back on the road. "I didn't know you had the pendant. I learned about it at the same time as your mother."

"She's not my mother," Jess spat. "She's the woman who gave birth to me and discarded me."

"Jess, she wanted to save you and your father. She's right. The Waaka tribe would've killed you both without a second thought. It's a matter of prestige."

"What about the other tribes? There must be more than two."

"Stories handed down say warriors from other tribes attempted to woo the Kupe maiden. She married a southern warrior on the condition they stayed in the north with her people. The pendant stayed with the women in her line until it passed—briefly—to a Waaka. Legend says he abused his power, which is why the pendant returned to the Kupe line."

"What powers does the relic give the holder? I have it in my possession, and nothing has happened."

"Legend says the holder is a peacemaker, or they can go to the opposite spectrum and create war to make peace from the resulting chaos. It's said the relic allows the holder to put taniwha to rest. If your siblings or your mother had a taniwha, I couldn't sense them."

"Do you think she did that to my taniwha?"

"Your father was of European blood. I'm not sure if your taniwha is weak because of the diluted blood and your contact with the pendant is giving you power or if your mother did her magic and forced your dragon to sleep. You'll have to ask her."

"You heard her. She wants nothing to do with me."

"Perhaps she'll change her mind."

As they neared the outskirts of Papakura, Manu pulled over. "Would you mind driving again? I'd prefer to remain under the radar at the Red Hill property."

Without replying, Jess got out of his truck and rounded the

hood, ready to trade places. Once he'd settled in the passenger seat, he pressed a button on his stealth gadget. Jess still hadn't taken off the pendant, but he hated to harp on about the relic.

It was too late anyway. If the magic in the relic was as strong as the legends indicated, members of the Waaka tribe had likely already arrived in Auckland or were making plans to launch an attack.

They'd want the relic and would lay claim by force if necessary.

CHAPTER 11

An Intimate Encounter

O nce she arrived at Manu's house, she exited the truck and opened the garage.

"Who are you?" an elderly man demanded.

Jessalyn started at his abrupt appearance. He walked toward her, limping a fraction as he left the deep shadows cast by a pohutukawa tree.

"Well?"

"I am Jessalyn Brown. I'm staying here."

"Where is Manu?"

"Who?"

"My son."

"I don't know any Manu. I'm a friend of Cassie's, and she suggested I stay here." Manu's father was tall, but his shoulders slumped and fatigue emanated from him. A surreptitious sniff told her he was a taniwha, which she knew already, but discerning this herself meant her own dragon was growing in skill set.

"You're lying, girl. I catch a trace of him on you."

Jessalyn shrugged. "Believe what you want. Doesn't make it true."

"You're driving his truck."

"Is it? Cassie lent me the truck for the few days I'm here. She said her friend wouldn't mind."

"You're lying."

Anger flared in Jessalyn. People kept bossing her around, accusing her of things she hadn't done, and she was tired of it. "Go away. I don't know your son."

Manu's father leaned closer and inhaled. He shook his head. "There is something wrong with your scent."

Jessalyn grabbed her phone from her pocket and brandished it like a weapon. "I'm calling the police."

"I'm going." He stomped down the driveway and disappeared. A few minutes later, a car started, the engine discernable for three or four beats before it faded.

"Thanks," Manu said. "Dad wants me to kill him so he can rejoin my mother. I refused, of course, and he's harassing me. He's hoping to prod my temper and snap my control."

"That's terrible. I-I'll meet you inside." The truth—she needed a moment away from Manu. So much info churning through her mind. Her mother. His mother's death. Manu admitting he'd kill Jessalyn if she failed to control her taniwha. At present, she was too numb to panic about something that might happen.

As she climbed into the truck to park it in the garage, the moon peeked from behind a bank of clouds. Immediately, her taniwha stirred, her contented purr echoing through Jessalyn's mind.

"Well, hello," Jessalyn said, not even trying to hide her sarcasm. "You couldn't help me while my mother was on the attack?"

"She made me sleep. I had no wish to anger her," her taniwha pushed the words through Jessalyn's mind.

"Understood. She scared me too."

"You were horrible to Manu. I like him."

"Can you confirm what she told me?"

"I was asleep."

Jessalyn maneuvered the vehicle into position and switched off the ignition. What the hell did she do now?

"You should have sex," the taniwha said, her tone firmly in sly territory. *"That way Manu will know you've forgiven him."*

Jessalyn snorted and, after closing the garage door, stomped inside, purposely not sending her gaze skyward to the moon again. She would not imagine sexual hijinks with Manu Taniwha.

She would not.

Her life was complicated enough without adding sex to the

equation and with the man who might execute her at that.

"How do I shut up my taniwha?" she demanded after following a rattling noise to the kitchen.

"Do you want a beer?"

"As long as the alcohol doesn't lessen my control. My taniwha is adamant I should sleep with you tonight."

Manu's eyes glowed with a blaze of gold before returning to their normal brown, but he didn't smile or make a smartarse comment. Instead, the silence stretched unbearably long. Jessalyn nibbled on her bottom lip and chided herself for not censoring her words.

Manu closed the space between them and took her hands in his. They stood, hands clasped while Jessalyn's heart raced. Thankfully, her taniwha remained quiet rather than splitting her concentration.

"There is nothing I'd enjoy more than having you share my bed, but I'm not going to drag you there. Given everything we've learned today, you need to decide if you trust me. Sleep in the spare room if you have the slightest hesitation. It won't take me long to reassemble the bed for you."

Not what she'd expected, yet she should have if she'd considered the matter instead of focusing on her own problems. All along, Manu had behaved with generosity and decency. He hadn't taken advantage and had gone out of his way to help her. Yes, he'd admitted her mother—Karen—had spoken the truth when she'd accused him of killing his mother. He'd explained the facts, and despite her newness to the taniwha world, she understood the difficult position he'd found himself in because of his parent. Then, there was Jessalyn's inability to control her fire. If she didn't correct this, he'd take her life too...

She swallowed hard, promising herself to follow every bit of advice regarding taniwha.

She had to remember. Not everything was black or white or a lie.

Apart from her life.

Her mother had deserted her when she was a baby.

Her parents had lied to her.

Her life was one big fabrication.

Manu separated their hands, and if her lack of response disappointed him, he didn't show his displeasure. He walked to the fridge and pulled out a bottle of beer. "Here, take this and sit outside on the deck. I'll have dinner ready in half an hour."

Jessalyn took the beer but remained in place. "I should cook dinner."

"You can cook on your day off. When is that?"

"Monday and Tuesday."

"Cook our dinner on Monday."

Jessalyn drifted outside and dropped onto a seat at a wooden table. The garden was larger than she'd expected. Along with the fire pit, there was a barbecue area and a spa pool, currently covered. The wind played a musical song in the large trees while in the distance, the lights of Papakura and the suburbs closer to central

Auckland twinkled—a myriad of tiny stars.

"Pretty moon."

"I wondered when you'd decide to press your case," Jessalyn murmured.

"You should be inside with Manu. We like Manu."

"We do," Jessalyn said, not bothering to argue because her taniwha spoke the truth. Despite everything she'd learned since arriving in Auckland, Manu had stood at her side and offered advice. If it wasn't for him, she'd never have learned of her siblings, the lies and half-truths regarding her background. The man had honor and integrity. He'd executed his own mother to save many, and now that she'd learned this, it was easy to see the act gnawed at him.

"He'll kill us if you can't control our fire."

"Thank you for the reminder," Jessalyn snapped.

"He would not do this lightly. He tries to aid us."

The abbreviated truth. The real truth held many nuances.

Jessalyn frowned and sipped her beer straight from the bottle. "He might turn on us, yet you want to have sex with him."

"Manu and his taniwha are strong and powerful, yet they have a kind heart. We need them."

Also a fact.

"And I believe the sex would be spectacular. I wish to make beautiful music with his taniwha."

"Ugh!" Jessalyn groaned. "That was the line the rugby captain used on me, apart from the taniwha part. Are you trying to make me crazy?"

"We will make adorable babies with them."

"What? No! No babies," Jessalyn spluttered and pictured images of icy lakes and snow. White-clad mountain ranges. But despite her attempt to cool her taniwha's jets, sensual heat roared through her body, frisking her breasts and settling in a volcanic ball low in her belly. She made the mistake of casting her glance skyward, and the moon snagged her attention.

"Pretty. So pretty. I want sex now."

"No!" Jessalyn leaped to her feet, appalled at the surge of lust that almost took her out at the knees. But the truth was she craved Manu's touch, his comfort, and the incredible pleasure she already knew their physical contact would bring.

Jessalyn sucked in a deep breath, admitting her needs are going some way to decrease her panic. The rich scents of plants, flowers, the steak Manu had dropped on the griddle, and the foreign drift of curry spices from nearby filled her lungs.

In the kitchen, Manu was singing, and this small show of happiness bolstered her confidence.

"If you stop pushing me, I'll think about it, but I'm not on birth control. What if Manu doesn't have condoms?"

"We will make beautiful babies together."

Jessalyn snorted, half-surprised, and the rest shocked. "Not happening. I'm having enough trouble with my life and you. The last thing I want is to inflict this relic on an innocent child."

"Times change. Your mother ran from the Waaka. We do not have to follow in her footsteps."

"What do you mean?"

Her taniwha sniffed. *"We do not have to do anything. The relic chooses us. We make the rules."*

"I don't want to throw my weight around. I want a normal life."

"Isn't that what your mother and father wanted? Why they made the decisions they did. You should think of a way to use the relic to create peace instead of conflict. I can help you."

"I wouldn't know where to start."

"Sex clears the head."

An exasperated laugh escaped Jessalyn. "You're impossible."

"One of us has to keep her eye on the prize."

"Yeah. Yeah. Beautiful babies. I've got it."

"Do you want children?" Manu spoke from behind her.

Jessalyn jumped and struck her knee on the table edge. She briskly rubbed her ouchie. "I hadn't considered it. I mean, it's not a thought that has entered my mind."

"Until now," her taniwha chirped. *"Beeeeatiful babies."*

"Go back to sleep," Jessalyn muttered.

"Talking to yourself is a sign of madness," Manu said, his lips twitching a fraction.

"Huh! I'm on the road to Madness and have stopped at Cuckoo Boulevard to view the sights."

Manu grinned. "What's the verdict on the sleeping arrangements? I'm waiting for the potatoes to cook. I can make the bed in the spare room now."

Without warning, heat roared through her body, relighting sensual fires she'd put out while driving the conversation. "Quiet in the cheap seats," she snapped.

Manu's grin grew wider. In the kitchen, a timer went off. "The potatoes are done. Dinner won't be long."

"Do it. Do it. Do it!"

"I wonder what spell Karen used to quieten her taniwha and to send my cheeky one to sleep?"

"You wouldn't."

"Let me drive our body, and we'll enjoy our existence better."

"I don't feel well."

Jessalyn's stomach clenched and tightened further in a painful spasm. Pressure forced her to gulp, and she released her next breath along with a loud burp. A blast of heat—ten miles away from sensual and exciting—ripped from her stomach and forged up her throat. She let out a pained croak, rose, and stumbled to the fire pit.

Crap, she wasn't gonna make it. She leaped down the three steps leading from the deck and skidded on her knees across the gravel.

"Jess?"

Jessalyn didn't acknowledge him. Instead, she put every thought and bit of power she possessed into manipulating her actions.

This uncontrollable fire—it was her unruly taniwha having a tantrum. The realization gave her unexpected strength and clarified everything.

"I don't want to breathe fire right now," she gritted out.

Manu reached her side, his trepidation written on his features. He leaned in, his hand on her shoulder, helping her to ground herself and gain strength. She mentally willed the fire down, pushing the heat back to the pit of her belly. Once the fire obeyed her resolve, she imagined a fireproof cage and blockaded off the combustible force.

Certain of her control now, she pushed to her knees and stood. "Okay?"

"Yes," Jessalyn said, her steps toward the deck confident. While part of her wanted to do a happy dance and shout *take that!* to her taniwha, she restrained the impulse. Whether she liked it or not, they were a team, but the leadership role was not up for grabs. Her taniwha needed to understand this.

"Well done, Jess." Pride at her achievement shone in his features. "Dinner is ready. I thought we'd eat out here."

"I'd like that." While she'd fled the moon the previous evening, tonight she was enjoying the gentle glow and the faint tug of something she needed to do. Manu disappeared inside, and she reclaimed her seat.

Sex or fly.

That wasn't even a question.

A thought occurred, and Jessalyn stood again. With long strides, she reached the steps and jogged down to the fire pit. She sucked in a breath and mentally released the barrier she'd placed around her fire. This time, instead of resisting and fighting, she embraced the heat, intent on forcing it free. Within seconds, the fiery energy roared up her throat, and she directed the blast. The flames flared bright and intoxicating for long seconds until her supply dwindled to almost nothing.

In her mind, she built the barricade again, closing off the remaining sparks. Her body returned to normal, and she straightened in quiet confidence. She'd controlled her fire. It was all her. She'd made that happen, and she'd made the flames cease on her timetable.

She strutted up the stairs, thrilled with her discovery. She *could* do this. Manu wouldn't need to execute her if she continued in this vein.

Manu set a plate before her and she breathed in the delicious scent, starving on the heels of her victory.

"I'm so hungry I could inhale this steak."

"I've got garlic bread." Manu set his plate opposite her and returned inside. He was soon back with a platter. "Mum used to make this. It's a family favorite."

Jessalyn could almost taste his anguish along with her forkful of fluffy potato. She swallowed and reached out in silent commiseration, squeezing his forearm.

Manu sat, but he didn't eat.

"What's wrong?"

"Not sure how to help you with your fire problem. I mean, as much as I love having you here, you can't spend the rest of your nights confined to places that have fire pits."

"I can control it. That last time, I made the fire start. I can manipulate it, Manu." Jessalyn lifted her hand for a high-five.

Manu didn't reciprocate. "Explain."

"The fire is my taniwha showing her displeasure. It's like a...a dragon tantrum. Once I realized that, I painted a mental barrier around the fire and closed it off. Then, I wondered if I could force fire by reversing the process, and I did. That's what you saw. Cool, huh? I'm hoping I have a handle on the fire-breathing dragon stuff now." Jessalyn cut a piece of steak and moaned in pleasure as the juices coated the interior of her mouth.

"Jess, I've never met a taniwha who can breathe fire while they're in human form."

Jessalyn froze with her fork halfway to her mouth. "Never?"

"There are no myths or legends of fire-breathing people."

"Oh. That's not good."

"Does your throat hurt?"

"Not now. At first, it used to get tender, but now, all I experience is the heat. The fire doesn't burn."

"You might not handle your fire next time."

"This is not a fluke. My theory is that the fire happened because my taniwha wanted payback. She was angry at being forced to sleep for all those years."

"You speak about her as if she is a different entity sharing your body. My taniwha and I are one."

And once again, she was different. Jessalyn turned over Manu's words in her mind. "You were aware of your birthright from childhood. You and your taniwha grew together and blended into one. I know little of my background, and my—Karen—did something to make my taniwha snooze. We haven't had years together to learn each other. That's why our thoughts are so different."

The aromatic garlic bread enticed Jessalyn, and she reached for a slice.

Manu helped himself too. He bit down, and butter glistened on his lips before he licked it away. "What did you and your taniwha disagree about to make her react so strongly?"

"She wants sex and babies. In that order."

"What do you want?" Manu asked, caution ringing in his tone.

"Fun sex and friendship."

"Sounds fine."

"Excellent," she said and bit down on the bread. "This is delicious. The entire meal is great. I'm not sure I can meet these standards. Condoms?"

A piece of garlic bread shot across the table, and Manu coughed twice and thumped his chest. "Woman, you could wait until a man finishes his mouthful."

"Where is the fun in that?"

"You're as ornery as your taniwha."

Jessalyn sighed and pushed away her empty plate. "It's a coping method. I divert attention from what is bothering me."

"What is the main thing that's upsetting you?"

"The taniwha thing. When I was a child, I wanted to fit in like the other children, but I couldn't because I differed from the other little girls. Once I realized that, I played with the boys, but I didn't fit there either. And now, when I'm an adult, I feel as if I'm on the outside looking in again, except the stakes are higher."

"You could take each day as it comes and put trust in the fact tomorrow will take care of itself."

"Yeah." Jessalyn picked up another piece of the oozing buttery goodness that was Manu's garlic bread. "I've been doing that, but after seeing my—Karen—the future is looming big and scary." She ate the piece of bread and wiped her fingers on a napkin. After a brief hesitation, she plucked the pendant from under her shirt and ran her right thumb over the jade pattern inset in the bone. She closed her eyes and focused, the answer coming to her. "I'd better put the relic away in its box for the moment. I'm tired. Let's do the dishes and go to bed."

Later, in Manu's bedroom, Jessalyn put the pendant in safekeeping before stripping. Naked, she slipped between the sheets.

Manu finished in the en suite and halted on seeing her in his bed. No, it was the bare shoulders that stopped him rather than her presence. Although the condom question should've given him a hint.

"I thought you were tired."

She winked. "Not that bad. Strip."

Manu's eyes widened before a slow grin spread across his face. He lifted his T-shirt over his head. She sighed at the broad expanse of muscles. Already barefooted, he removed his jeans and underwear. Ah! Thick, masculine thighs and an erection in working order. Perfect eye candy. Perfect everything.

He slid between the sheets and turned out the light. The lack of illumination didn't bother Jessalyn since the moonglow crept through the window. She inched across the mattress, her fingers tingling and ready to touch and test all that male beauty.

"It's a good thing we both ate your garlic bread." Bother. She didn't want him to get a hint of her nerves, yet the second she opened her mouth, babble jumped free.

But Manu laughed and met her halfway.

"One day at a time," she whispered and wrapped herself around his body before lifting her face for his kiss.

Their first kiss was tentative as if Manu expected her to change her mind. Little did he know. This—she—was a sure thing tonight. She pressed her breasts against his chest and tangled her legs with his. The captain of the first fifteen had been a boy as had her casual summer lovers. Manu was solid and very masculine. A man in his prime.

A purr rattled from her throat, yet she couldn't blame her taniwha.

Manu lifted his head and, obviously reassured by whatever he saw in her expression, he rolled her onto her back. Seconds later, he'd trapped Jessalyn between him and the mattress. Her pulse raced a little faster while her senses worked overtime. His heady masculine scent full of citrus and the outdoors thrilled her even as her gaze ranged over bulging biceps and enticing pectoral muscles. So much temptation, and right now, all hers.

"Last chance," he whispered next to her ear.

The heat of his breath raised a shiver. No way was she foregoing this chance to enjoy herself.

"I'm not changing my mind," Jessalyn said and her firm voice obviously amused him. He issued a charming and toe-curling smile, one he'd never displayed before. She gawked, mesmerized and smitten.

"Thank Maui and all the Māori gods." His brown eyes glowed golden, and she sighed in appreciation.

It made her wonder how a carefree Manu might behave—a taniwha less burdened by responsibility. She returned his smile with one of her own and cupped his face. The prickle of stubble beneath her fingertips had her testing more of his jaw, exploring.

Manu leaned nearer, his intent clear. Her mouth met his

halfway, and she sank into the caress. She opened to him, and their tongues tangled, their kiss rapidly morphing to hot and heavy.

Jessalyn moaned, her body undulating against him. Skin and exquisite friction. She needed more of him touching her. *Everywhere.* She ran her hands over his back and lower to cup his muscular buttocks. His tattoo burned beneath her fingertips, and curiosity filled her mind with questions. Later.

Now they were touching, urgency filled her, and her heart thundered. His swollen erection nestled between her thighs, warm and promising. Her fingers tightened on his butt in silent demand.

"We have all night, sweetheart." He nipped her jawline, the hint of pain shooting straight to her pussy. Her summer lovers had warmed her passion in slow increments. Her first-fifteen lover—not so much. Manu stood on a different level, and already, she ached for him to fill her.

Manu's fingers drifted down her neck, and his hand settled on her breast. He tugged on her nipple and grazed her jawline again with his teeth.

"Yes." Jessalyn moved her hips against him, silently urging him to give her more. Nah, hints were for the birds. Now she had him naked and paying attention to her as a woman, she craved speed and immediate satisfaction. "Please. I need... I feel empty. Fix it, please."

"My pace." Manu trailed kisses along her neck and moved farther down the bed.

Jessalyn attempted to twist her body to free herself, to exert some control. Manu laughed and easily restrained her.

"You intrigued me from the moment I saw you. I fancied a taste of your sweet mouth." He pressed a kiss to her lips. "I suffered from a craving to touch you here." He cupped his hand around one breast. "And I desperately wanted to slide my cock into your pussy and revel in your heat, your arousal until we both burned."

"Yes, please." A violent spasm of pleasure rippled through her at his words. "Not stopping any of that." Her hands laced in his hair, and she tugged hard enough to gain his attention.

In retribution, he rocked against her, his cock leaving a wet smear on her thigh. A low growl vibrated in his throat, and she leaned down to recapture his mouth. Their tongues twirled together in a sensual dance, and she stirred restlessly, rubbing against his harder body.

"Please, Manu," she urged. "We can do the slow build next time."

Manu pulled from her touch and reached over to open a bedside drawer. He pulled out a strip of condoms and slapped them on the nightstand. But instead of rolling on a condom and getting down to business, he returned to her side, his expression hinting at an alternative plan.

"Before we fuck, I want to taste you again."

Manu held himself in check, but she thought a few cheeky comments might persuade him to move faster.

Before she could protest his plan for a leisurely loving, he distracted her with a combination of hands and mouth. His tongue traced her nipple before pulling back to blow on the crest. He pinched her other nipple and diverted her from the nip of pain with the slide of fingers across her hip. Without waiting for his request, she widened her legs, the blast of air against her hot, needy flesh bringing a growl from deep in her throat.

His fingers stroked her, circled her clit, and caressed her achy flesh while his tongue teased her rigid nipples. He bit and nibbled and licked. He massaged and rubbed, pushing her rapidly toward a climax.

"Manu," she gasped.

Her body swooped and soared, trembling on the cusp of great pleasure. One more swish of his finger sent her flying, surging headfirst into orgasm. She shuddered and groaned, her hands grabbing Manu's shoulders as an anchor.

He lapped at her, prolonging the pleasure until she could take no more. The instant she pushed instead of clung, he lifted his head and grinned at her—boyish and full of charm.

"Ready for round two?" he asked.

"Bring it." After coming so hard, repeating the act might be difficult, but she still wanted to experience him filling her, surrounding her with his strength.

Manu's eyes glowed, and he kissed her with a tenderness she'd never experienced. She closed her eyes and clung, wanting more of this man's generous heart.

Manu parted their mouths, and she presumed he was reaching for a condom. The rip of foil confirmed her assumption.

When she'd anticipated he'd hurry, she was wrong. He kissed her slowly and thoroughly, building her passion again. He touched her with purpose, exploring her body and learning what touches and pressure she enjoyed most.

Only then did he part her legs and notch his shaft to her entrance. With a nudge, he pushed deeper until he could go no further, that first stroke so perfect, she sighed in bliss.

"Okay?" he asked, his gentle hands smoothing locks of hair from her face.

"Wonderful."

"Hold on," he warned. "This next bit is gonna be fast."

His firm, rapid strokes pushed her into another zone. Each slide of his cock hit her in the perfect spot, driving her high when she thought another orgasm was impossible.

Jessalyn kissed his shoulder and nibbled his neck, wanting to leave her mark. He grunted when her teeth dug deep into his biceps but the rhythm of his strokes never ceased. If anything, his hips moved faster and with more purpose.

"Feels good, Jess. Your sweet pussy clutching my dick. I can't imagine anything better."

His dirty talking thrilled her, but she'd need to practice alone before she returned the chatter.

"Aw, Jess. Can't hold on much longer. You close?"

"Go," she whispered, her fingers plucking at his flat nipple.

He cursed under his breath, a pithiness she didn't catch but his desire, his desperation was clear.

He surged deep, his stroke strumming her clit. With his next thrust, she fell into more pleasure—this time gentle but still sweet and exquisite. Satisfying.

"Aw, Jess," he whispered, his breath hot against her ear. He joined their lips and kissed her with passion, his tongue duplicating the motions of his cock. One more stroke. A second. A third decidedly deeper, harder thrust, and his big body shuddered. He stilled, buried deep within her, and she held him tight.

Long moments later, he pulled free, and she mourned the loss, the weight of him. He kissed her—a slow, drugging kiss of passion—before he raised his head.

"That was incredible," he said and snatched another quick kiss. *"He-haw!"*

Jessalyn blinked while Manu gaped before his chortle escaped. Heat sneaked into her cheeks, and she was fiercely glad of her darker skin tones, which hid the worst of her embarrassment.

"I guess you heard that, huh? My taniwha."

"Yep."

"I never hear your taniwha."

Manu stood and casually removed the condom. He walked into the en suite and returned. "I've had longer to forge a relationship.

My dragon's aware that in order to keep us both alive, we have to remain hidden. Your taniwha will learn. Speak firmly to her."

"Huh! Did you hear that Ms. Taniwha?"

"I'm in a sexual stupor. Don't ruin my perfect mood."

A snort escaped Jessalyn.

Manu's expression turned quizzical. "Did I miss something?"

She rolled her eyes. "My taniwha approves of the sex and wishes for time alone to process."

Manu's broad smile sent her pulse rate skittering. "That will give us time to cuddle and recharge," he said. "Because I agree with your taniwha. He-haw!"

CHAPTER 12

Danny Causes Chaos

Manu parked in the Wynyard Quarter at ten the next morning. Today she lingered instead of escaping as she had in the past and leaned toward Manu to offer her mouth for a kiss. Instead of the quick meeting of lips she'd intended, their mouths clung, and the slow dance of tongues had her primed for another round of glorious sex.

Unwillingly, she pulled back. "Hold that thought. See you later."

"I'll pick you up, and we'll go straight to Botany to find your father's storage locker. Jack said he'll have a list for me later today."

"Thanks." Jessalyn slipped from the vehicle. With a wave, she jogged from Wynyard Quarter toward the restaurants and the walking bridge that crossed to The Viaduct. A ring of an alarm and the flash of lights slowed her steps. Perfect. A launch or yacht was leaving the enclosed part of the harbor and required the bridge to lift in order to pass.

She glanced at her phone. She'd already cut it fine time-wise. Now she'd be officially late. Jessalyn scanned the surrounding people. Most wore impatience, equally impressed at the delay. Auckland. Everyone was always in a hurry. To pass the time, she made up stories about the people standing around her. The couple in business clothes—black suits and the smart white contrast—they were work colleagues, and the defined space between them hinted at an affair, especially since she intercepted their heated glance.

That man over there in the navy-blue hoody and faded jeans—Jessalyn stared harder, but the man darted out of sight. She frowned. He reminded her of Danny, but that couldn't be right.

The bridge lowered, and the restless pedestrians surged forward once the barrier arm lifted. Jessalyn glanced over her shoulder but didn't spot the man again. She pushed aside her unease and lengthened her stride. The sooner she reached the pub, the quicker she'd face Chef's wrath and move on with her day.

"Sorry, I'm late." The words burst from her on seeing a scowling chef. "My friend always drops me at Wynyard Quarter because of the road work along Quay Street. They lifted the bridge to let two launches through and I had to wait."

"We have two work groups in the function room today," Chef snapped, ignoring her tardiness excuse. "One at twelve and the other at five-thirty. I need these onions chopped." He gestured at a huge pile of red onions. "As soon as that's completed, I want you to chop the ingredients for our range of salads."

"Yes, Chef." Jessalyn hid her groan at the onion assignment. She'd bawl for sure. While most places used pre-cut onions, Chef preferred fresh ingredients. She got to work, glad for Chef's knife-skills training. The man might be a bad-tempered tyrant, but he passed on his expertise to those who wished to learn.

While she chopped the onions, she planned the meal she intended to cook for Manu. Roast beef and all the trimmings. Chef had taught her to make Yorkshire puddings and told her she'd done an excellent job, even if he'd stinted his praise.

With the onions done, Jessalyn washed her hands thoroughly before she collected a tissue to wipe her streaming eyes. Aware of Chef's testy mood, she moved on to salad preparation.

"Jessalyn." A barmaid appeared in the kitchen. "There's a guy wanting you out front. Says he's your boyfriend."

"Manu?"

"I've no idea what his name is," she said and flounced out.

Jessalyn wondered why Manu hadn't sent a text. She'd confided about her irascible boss. She glanced warily at Chef.

"Finish the salad prep, and you can take ten."

A quarter of an hour later, Jessalyn left the kitchen and took the employee door to the bar. Two steps into the bar, she came to an abrupt halt.

Danny.

Crap, what was she going to do? She didn't want to talk to anyone from Piha. She started to retreat, but it was too late.

"Jessalyn!" Danny jumped off his barstool.

"What are you doing here?" Wait! How had he found her?

"You're my girlfriend. It worried me when you disappeared. This woman said you'd gone overseas. I knew that couldn't be right."

Before she could blink, he grabbed her in an embrace and kissed her. The kiss was just as slobbery as the others, and she wrenched away to scrub her mouth with her fingers.

"Quit kissing me," she said, putting an extra foot between them in case he pounced again. He was fast. She'd give him that. "I'm not your girlfriend."

"Who have you been kissing?" The question emerged from him in a snarl.

"What?" How had he known? Oh! Of course. Taniwha senses. Could he tell she'd spent time with Manu? She gave a tentative sniff and discerned nothing but onions and Danny's aftershave. Too strong. After another sniff, she backed away in self-protection. If he had a taniwha within him, the strong odor hid his otherness, although maybe that was the point of the stinky aftershave.

Jessalyn needed to ask Manu for dragon-recognizing hints.

"You've got bruises on your neck."

Jessalyn adjusted her polo shirt. "None of your business."

"I'm your boyfriend!"

"I thought you were my friend," Jessalyn snapped back. "Obviously, I was mistaken." She whirled, intent on escape.

Danny grasped her forearm, preventing her escape. "Can we go somewhere to talk?"

"I have ten minutes before Chef is expecting me back at work."

Danny dragged her to a booth. He pushed her down on the seat and slid in, trapping her in place. She drew a sharp breath, ready to rain down home truths about his highhandedness.

"Why are you working here? Why did you leave without telling anyone?"

The bald questions pierced some of her indignation and raised her guilt. She should've told Danny she was leaving, yet the things she'd learned of the Waaka family and Karen stilled her apology.

"It was an impulse. I needed money to keep up with the mortgage payments. My job at the library was temporary. There was nothing to hold me in Piha. How did you find me, anyway?"

"I'm your boyfriend. You should have told me." His voice rose, attracting the attention of a group of businessmen sitting at a nearby table.

"You are not," Jessalyn snapped. "Let me out. My break is finished."

"No, we have to work this out. I want to marry you." Desperation coated his words.

"Let. Me. Out."

His eyes widened a fraction before implacability stamped into his features. "Not until you come to your senses. We're perfect together. You know it's true."

Jessalyn glanced at her phone and muttered a swear word. Her ten-minute break had flown. Danny's stubbornness was legendary in Piha and amongst his friends. Once he set his mind, he became intractable and infuriating.

"One last time. Let me out so I can go back to work."

"I want to announce our engagement. I've got the ring with me."

The second he took his gaze off her to fumble in his pocket, she leaped up and over the table, her agility taking Danny by surprise. Her too, but she didn't dwell on the how and made her escape. Danny moved with a preternatural hustle and grabbed her shoulder, his grip painful in its intensity.

She shook him off, her countermove also taking him unawares. With a burst of speed, she shoved through the door and into the kitchen. With her apron back in place, she turned to Chef.

"What would you like me to do next?"

"I'll show you how to pipe the filling into the pastry cases. I need one hundred for lunch in an hour." He demonstrated and watched her efforts, evidently satisfied when he moved to speak with the other two kitchenhands.

Jessalyn piped the savory filling on automatic, getting up a rhythm. Her mind went straight to Danny. How had he found her? His insistence they were engaged and getting married bothered her even more. Danny was laid back rather than intense. Someone else was behind his declaration, and it didn't bode well for her. It meant other Waaka taniwha were watching her, spying on her every move. She needed to contact Manu and ask his opinion.

After finishing her task, she moved on to making mini trifles in shot glasses.

A bartender—a male this time—ran into the kitchen. "Jessalyn, your boyfriend is making a scene in the bar."

"He's not my boyfriend. He's someone I know from Piha."

"I don't care. He's drunk and rude."

Jessalyn glanced at Chef. He gave a curt nod. "Get him to leave and come back to work."

She stomped after the bartender, temper simmering. She enjoyed this job and was learning new skills. If Danny wrecked this for her, she'd never forgive him.

Danny was sitting at the bar and had two shot glasses in front of him, one of which was still full of a golden liquid. Probably his preferred bourbon.

"You have to leave. You'll get me fired, and I like this job." She grasped his arm and tugged. He crashed off the barstool, knocking her off her feet. He picked himself up and staggered into a man carrying three draft beers. The glasses went flying, the beer splashing a group of women. Their screeches of protest hurt Jessalyn's ears.

A security man appeared, and Jessalyn cursed under her breath. This wasn't good. On a weekday, security never started until five, which meant the bar manager had called this man in specially.

Jessalyn sprang up and grabbed Danny's hand. "Come on, we need to leave."

"Are you coming with me?"

"Yes," Jessalyn lied and took him by the arm.

How much had he drunk while he'd been here? He didn't usually get this bad from alcohol. He and his cousins could drink anyone under the table and made a game of it with summer visitors to Piha. She attempted to haul him to the pub entrance, but Danny wasn't having any of the hustled exit.

"I'm not going anywhere until you promise to marry me."

"We're not that sort of friends," Jessalyn said, irritated by his insistence. "I know your bad habits. That's enough to put me off marriage. Besides, we'd drive each other crazy. You're bossy with your girlfriends. I wouldn't let you get away with that. Admit it. We'd be miserable."

"We're perfect together. We'll get married." Danny's face contorted with determination. He wrenched away, stumbled, and sent a table flying. With it, numerous drinks and three newly delivered meals smashed to the floor.

Shouts erupted. Insults. Tempers snapped, and fists flew. In the blink of an eye, Jessalyn found herself in the midst of a fight. A thin, tattooed man clipped her on the jaw and knocked her against the security man who'd waded in to stop the melee.

"Sorry," Jessalyn said. "He pushed me." She scuttled out of the way, appalled at the drama Danny had created.

"Jessalyn," a harsh voice drew her attention.

She turned to face Will, the bar manager, the man responsible for the smooth running of the entire pub. The early lunch crowd had thinned, and she quailed at the man's severe displeasure.

"Get your things. I'll send your final pay on to you," he bit out.

"B-but I haven't d-done anything," she stammered.

"This is the second disturbance your boyfriend has caused today. You're disrupting business and chasing away our customers." Will's implacable expression told Jessalyn this was his final decision.

"Jessalyn. Jessalyn!" Danny howled.

She glowered in his direction, gathered her fury around her, and stalked through the employee door.

"Jessalyn," Chef called. "What the devil are you doing? I need you in here."

"Will sacked me." She marched to the staff locker room to grab her daypack. When she exited, Chef and Will were screaming at each other.

The red-faced bar manager spotted her, and anger turned his features hard. "I thought I told you to leave."

"I'm going." Jessalyn stomped out the rear entrance and jogged to Britomart Train Station. Danny could be anywhere, and she had no interest in finding him. Much safer for him, too, because if she saw him anytime soon, she'd be tempted to pop him in the nose.

Her eyes stung, and she swallowed hard, determined not to cry. This was a setback, not the end of the world.

She'd find another job.

Her phone rang as she tagged her Hop card and walked onto the platform. The next train to Papakura left in ten minutes. She checked the number and didn't recognize it. At least it wasn't Danny intent on continuing his crazy demands of engagements and weddings.

"Hello, Jessalyn speaking."

"This is Amy from Waitakere Real Estate. I have a business couple who are interested in renting your house. They're willing to pay the asking price of nine-hundred-and-twenty-five dollars per week during the official summer period. They asked if you'd consider a reduced rental of four-hundred-and-twenty-five dollars during winter."

"So they require a long-term rental?"

"They do. She works from home. A writer, while he works remotely for part of the week. Your property is ideal for them. Close enough to the city but at the beach too."

"Done. Are they happy to keep the remaining furniture, or do you need me to clear that for them?"

"They're newly married and starting out. This situation works well for them," Amy said. "When can you sign the rental agreement?"

"Is it possible to email it to me? I can courier it back to you."

With the business details clarified, Jessalyn hung up, her bad mood lightening a fraction. She must've looked a little crazy because an elderly woman sitting nearby stood and shuffled farther down the platform, sneaking wary peeks to monitor Jessalyn's behavior.

"Have a little decorum."

"So now you make an appearance," Jessalyn said. Her taniwha's silence had worried her—not that she'd ever admit to relief at her presence.

"Shush! Don't talk aloud. The humans will think you're crazy."

"Point taken," Jessalyn murmured. "You've been quiet."

"Sexual hangover."

Jessalyn considered that for a second. "No comment."

The train arrived and the elderly woman paused for Jessalyn to enter a carriage before scuttling farther down the platform with a sharp *tap-tap-tap* of her walking stick.

"That lady didn't even want to share the carriage with us."

"Smart lady. She should try sharing a brain," Jessalyn retorted. "Quiet, I have to call Manu. No, maybe I'll send a text."

"Danny is trouble."

"He's also deluded."

Her taniwha sniffed. *"As if we'd consider him and his weakling of a taniwha when we can have Manu with his sexy black beast."*

Jessalyn snorted, although her taniwha made a good point. Unfortunately for Danny, there was no comparison between the two men. Manu had offered his help even though she'd been a stranger. Danny blew hot and cold, his behavior and attitude to her depending on his older and, as she'd recently learned, taniwha cousins. Now, because of Danny, she'd lost a job she enjoyed. She sighed and sent a text to Manu.

He called her as the train pulled into Newmarket Station. "Why are you coming home early?"

"Danny turned up at the pub and created a scene. He got kicked out, and I got the sack."

"How did he know where to find you?"

"I asked, but he didn't answer my questions."

"Too busy harping on about marriage," her taniwha commented with a sniff. *"It wasn't even a tempting proposal."*

"The only way he could've known was by tracking the registration of my vehicle or someone at the real estate agency told him," Manu said. "You're not wearing the relic?"

"No, it's in the box." Jessalyn focused and replayed his words. "The agency has my phone number, not my address."

"Crap. Your phone. I'll get Hone to check it. Danny might have added a tracker. Has he ever had your phone?"

"We spent a lot of time together, especially before Dad died. I suppose it's possible."

"Hone can tell us for sure," Manu said. "I'll pick you up at the train station in Papakura. Half an hour."

"The train has just left Newmarket."

"See you soon, sweetheart. I'm sorry about your job."

Manu rang Hone as soon as he'd finished speaking with Jessalyn. "How easy is it to put a tracking device on a phone?"

"Hello to you too, cuz," Hone said drily.

"Danny, our surprise visitor when we were at Piha, arrived at the pub where Jess works. He created a fuss and got her fired."

"Tracking software is easy to install. Jessalyn wouldn't even know it was there. But he could've followed us home or tracked your vehicle registration number."

"I thought of that, but I sensed no one following us. Are you at home?"

"No, I'm watching a wife in Botany. Her husband is convinced she's cheating on him."

"Could we meet you there and give you Jess's phone to check out?"

"Bring me something to eat."

Manu laughed. "You'll get fat."

"Not your problem," Hone said. "Crap, she's on the move. Call me."

Manu left his house, waving to his father and his father's cronies as he backed from the driveway. His father made a rude gesture but for once his parent's animosity failed to pierce his excellent mood.

It was Jess.

They'd made love. She might not be familiar with taniwha ways, but he and his taniwha were halfway in love with her. He admired her courage and her manner of straight speaking. Her struggle to find herself when others might have crumbled under the knowledge of their sudden otherness.

Her possession of the relic bothered him, though.

He hadn't asked to look at it after they'd left her mother's house, even though his taniwha had expressed curiosity. The reappearance of a long-lost relic spelled trouble. For Jess, and by extension, him since he wanted to keep her.

Manu stopped at the local bakery and purchased enough sandwiches to feed three, plus a selection of cakes. On the rare occasions he'd dated, his dates watched their diets and each would throw up their hands in horror on seeing the cream and fat in his box of cakes. Jessalyn wouldn't hesitate to gobble up two or three, and he admired her ease with her body.

A gorgeous curvy body he'd had the honor of loving the previous night. That it had happened before the full moon pleased him. While Jess's dragon had seemed dazzled by the moonglow, Jess had made the choice to share his bed. That pleased him most of all since he wanted her to have choices rather than regrets.

The last words he needed to hear were *my taniwha made me do it.*

Jess was waiting when he pulled up outside the Papakura Railway Station.

"I had to do a food stop for Hone," he said when she slid into the passenger seat. "Are you okay? I know you enjoyed that job."

"How did you know?" She sounded pissed, and he didn't blame her.

Manu pulled out into the traffic and turned onto the Great South Road. "Because even though you were struggling with your taniwha, you kept going to work. Never once did you skip your job."

"They won't give me a reference now. I'll have a blotch on my employee record."

"I have contacts if you want, or you can find another job on your own. You have a work ethic, and that will soon become obvious to any employer. Tell them the truth and say you'll work for a trial period. What type of job will you apply for?"

The piss-and-vinegar faded from her expression. "Honestly, my preference is to work with wood. I enjoyed making the wooden boxes and small pieces of furniture rather than the large pieces that were Dad's specialty. Toward the end, I made most of the ones he sold, and I finished the last large piece he'd started."

"Why didn't you do that? You have your father's tools."

"If I hadn't needed to sell Dad's vehicle to catch up on the mortgage, I might've taken that path." She shrugged, drawing his attention to her breasts. "Hey! Watch the road. Don't ogle my boobs."

"And very nice tits they are." He winked and did as she instructed. "You said instinct made you stay."

"Yeah. If I'd known spectacular sex lay in my future, I might have traveled south earlier."

"Spectacular, huh?"

"Perhaps that's overstating a little. It was hot sex." Her lips quirked as she tried not to escalate to a smile.

Manu hated to drive her focus back to taniwha stuff, but now that Danny had arrived on the scene, his gut shouted conflict ahead. "Jack sent me a list of storage places for us to check out once we hook up with Hone. If Danny is tracking your phone, he'll find Hone instead. Do you have the key to the storage unit?"

"I have it," Jess said. "Danny should keep his distance from me. I have a strong inclination to flatten him with my fist."

"That's my girl. Do you know the proper way to punch?"

"Huh! If we weren't driving, I'd show you my skills." She slid him a sideways look that held more than a hint of slyness. "Your nose is a little pretty for my taste. I prefer my guys on the rugged side."

Manu chortled and shot her an amused wink.

Jess's eyes sparkled, her mood considerably lighter. "Tomboy, remember. I tried several martial arts and did boxing for a while at school. I was the lone girl, and the school refused to let me box against the guys after I annihilated the younger boys."

"Annihilated, huh?"

His phone rang.

"Will you get that for me? It should be Hone."

Jess plucked his ringing cell from the console and pushed a button. "Manu Taniwha's phone. I am his secretary. How can I help you today?"

Jess gasped, and Manu signaled he was pulling over.

"Please hold while I transfer you," Jess said in a tight voice.

"Taniwha," Manu growled.

"This is Nelson Waaka. I believe you have something that belongs to us."

Well, he'd been expecting this since he'd glimpsed the relic. "Waaka," Manu said. "What are you hinting at?"

"Don't play dumb with me," Waaka barked.

"Explain," Manu demanded, channeling his mother at her most imperious.

"A member of my tribe is engaged to Jessalyn Brown. He says you are preventing him from returning to Piha with his fiancée."

"Who?" Manu asked.

"Don't play cute," Waaka snarled.

"Look, I don't appreciate you accusing me of what amounts to kidnapping. If your man can't keep hold of his fiancée, it's nothing to do with me."

"The woman is in Auckland."

"Auckland is a huge city with over a million residents. I have enough to do without keeping tabs on your people." Manu hung up.

"He won't like that," Jess said.

"Don't care." He tossed her his phone. "Block his number, will you?"

Before Jess could do that, his phone rang again. She glanced at the screen as if it were a poisonous katipo spider. As he watched her, she relaxed.

"It's Hone."

Manu pulled out into the traffic. "Can you answer for me? I'll be able to hear most of the call, anyway."

"Hey, Hone. It's Jessalyn. Manu is driving."

"You okay, sweetheart?" Hone asked. "Manu told me Danny caused problems at the pub."

"I'm still angry enough to punch someone."

"Not me, please. Cassie adores my gorgeous face."

Manu snorted, earning him a grin from Jess and a cackle from his cousin. "Remind me to tell you about Hone's courtship of Cassie." Some of his easy humor faded as he recalled the ending of that story. The truth—although it hurt, he doubted he could have done anything differently. His mother...

Manu pushed the ever-present guilt away and pulled up the

memory of the mother he'd loved—the parent of his childhood who'd been fair yet stern. She'd taught him leadership skills, given an example of how he should apply them. His current leadership style... Next to useless since he wasn't leading but hiding out.

Jess blowing into his life had changed his attitude and given him a reason to live instead of merely existing. Ironic, given he'd destroyed his father to get to this place in his life. For that, he'd always be sorry. Soon, he'd man up and talk with his father, but first, the Waaka family.

"Hello?" Jess leaned over to click her fingers at him. "Hone, he's zoned out on us. Hone said his lady has gone to Sylvia Park. He's in the mall but wants me to follow his target into the ladies' shops. Then you and he can sort out my phone."

Manu signaled a turn and drove onto the motorway. "We'll be there in ten minutes."

"You'll find me loitering near the Lush shop," Hone said. "Please hurry. I've had to start buying things so I don't look suspicious."

Jess ended the call and returned his phone to the console. "At this rate, we'll never find Dad's storage unit."

"We can always ask Karen again."

"No," Jess said, her face closing down.

Manu reached over and clasped her right hand in his left. "I'm sorry."

"I loved my father, but it's hard to justify his lies. Every time I think about it I get so angry. It's frustrating as hell he's not here to shout at."

"I hear you. My mother..." Manu broke off with a shrug. "We can't control our parents' actions. All we can do is influence our own. It's called adulting."

"Nelson Waaka is a scary dude."

Manu went with Jess's change of subject. "I can do scary."

"I only have your word for that."

His taniwha growled, and Manu grinned as he released the sound.

Jess blinked. "That wasn't you."

"No," her taniwha purred. *"That was the sexy black beast!"*

"Inside voice," Jess barked.

Manu cocked a brow at her as he took the Mt. Wellington exit from the motorway. "Sexy black beast?"

"Her words. Not mine," Jess said.

Manu didn't bother to hide his satisfaction. Things were looking up for him and his taniwha.

It was almost two hours later when he and Jess left Sylvia Park.

"You can't buy me a new phone," Jess protested.

"I just did. Hone's idea to leave the software on your phone intact will help us keep track of Danny or at least misdirect him if the need arises."

"I'll pay you back once I get a job, although why did we buy this one? It cost enough to fund the debt for a small country," she grumbled.

Despite her protests, Manu noticed the way she stroked the phone. "Here is the list of storage places. Work out which one to visit first."

Jess started their search with enthusiasm. The man in the office checked their key number against his records.

"No, this isn't one of ours," the burly Samoan man said. "The key is the same, but we don't have this number."

The story repeated with different variations until they reached the last one.

"If this isn't the right one, I guess I'll have to confront Karen again." Her moue of distaste told him of her opinion of that course of action.

Manu parked his truck. "Come on. Let's go."

They entered the office.

A scrawny, tattooed youth raised his hand in greeting. "Hey. What can I do for you?"

"My father has a storage locker. I found the key with his possessions after he died but not the address of the storage place," Jess said. "Is this one of your keys?"

"No," the guy said as soon as Jess handed it to him. "Have you tried the one on Jensen Street?"

"Yes, we've worked our way through the list."

"Can you show me your list?" the guy asked.

Jess handed it over.

"No, you've covered all the places in this area." He paused and tapped his finger on the page. "There is one place that closed two months ago. The owners intend to bulldoze the site and develop it for housing. From what Dad said, legally, they had to wait out those who have paid for long-term storage."

"Can we have the address?"

The guy rattled it off. "You can try their office, but I doubt if anyone is on site. They have a sign posted with a contact number. They should've sent you a notice about the closure."

"It might have gone to Karen's place," Jess said.

That made sense to Manu. "Thanks for your help."

"Remember us if you require ongoing storage," the guy said. "Here's my business card."

Jess thanked him and stashed the card in her pocket.

Toby's Storage was a five-minute drive away, and when they pulled into the parking lot, they found the place deserted. The owners had cleared half of the units, and a small block remained standing in the far corner.

"What do you want to do? Ring the owners or crawl through the hole in the fence and try our key."

Jess considered the hole before turning to him. "I'm owning adventurous today. That spying stuff has me jazzed."

"There is no reason you can't go into the spying business full-time. Hone or I could set you up for an interview with the boss."

"No thanks. Peeing in a bottle sounds disgusting. Let's go."

Manu held up the wire of the fence to make the gap bigger. He took a moment to admire her arse while she wriggled through the hole. A growl escaped him, attracting Jess's attention once she stood.

"Hey! Eyes on the prize, not my backside."

"She is the prize," his taniwha whispered through his mind.

No disagreement there. For the first time since his mother's death, he and his taniwha stood on the same page. Jessalyn Brown completed them.

"It's way more exciting than the rest of my surroundings. I'm imagining sinking my teeth into the fleshy spot where it meets your legs. That and more after last night."

"Manu!"

The flush in her cheeks delighted him.

Manu climbed the fence and tumbled over, landing beside Jess.

"Showoff," she muttered.

"Aw." He pouted, enjoying himself. "I was giving you a chance to eyeball my arms and chest. You should praise my easy strength and agility."

"Idiot," she said and stalked to the standing storage units.

Manu grinned like a fool while admiring the sway of feminine hips.

She scanned numbers and came to a stop. "I think this is it." Her fingers shook a fraction, and she took two tries to insert the key into the lock.

Manu held his breath, praying they weren't in for another disappointment.

The key turned smoothly, and Jess lifted the roller door. The scent of wood hit him first.

"Dad didn't sell the last lot of boxes," Jess said, surprise in her voice.

"Now we've found the locker, why don't we re-lock it and ring the owner?" Manu suggested. "We'll tell him we need to clear it, and if you work him right, he might offer a refund to get rid of you."

Jess brightened and straightened her shoulders. "I can do that. Then I'll repay you for the phone."

Manu wanted to argue. The cost of the phone was nothing to him since he'd sold his rights for his first invention when he was barely out of his teens. That one smart business move had netted him millions, ample funds to live out of the shadow of his parents and pursue his passion for inventing and tinkering to improve things.

Back at his vehicle, Jess made a phone call and told the man she spoke to that she wanted to get into her father's locker.

"Yes, I have the key," she said. "Empty it? Oh, no. I hadn't intended to do that. Didn't Dad pay for a year?" She paused to listen and frowned. "Really? I hadn't— Two thousand dollars?

Right now? A check for two thousand five hundred dollars? But... Oh, a bank transfer? Yes, I think I have a bank statement. All right. Let me think. Yes, that should work. Thank you. I'll see you in ten minutes."

Jess hung up, and Manu had seconds to brace himself before she threw herself at him. Her arms wrapped around his neck, and she kissed him with enthusiasm. Then, she released him and stepped back to beam at him, and every bit of blood drained to his cock. For an instant, he wavered, dizzy with the speed of his arousal.

"The owner will be here in five minutes. I'm sure I had my bank account details." She rummaged through a side pocket in her daypack. "Ah-ha! There it is."

"Well done with your negotiations. You handled him like a pro. Not only sexy but intelligent too."

A vehicle pulled up, and a man hustled over to them.

His bald head beamed in the afternoon sun, and he pulled out a hanky to mop his brow. "Ms. Brown?"

"Yes," she said. "I have my bank account number here."

"I'll unlock the gate for you so you can drive into the yard. While you're unloading your father's unit, I'll process the payment. I'll get you to confirm it before you leave, and you can sign this agreement and return the key."

"Thank you," Jess said.

She and Manu drove over to the locker and unlocked it.

"I guess it's better if we pack it in the truck and go through the boxes once we're in private," she said.

"You can store it at the warehouse. We don't have to worry about Danny now that Hone has confirmed he'd put tracking software on your phone. I have plenty of room, and the rest of your father's tools are there, anyway."

"Remind me to thank you later with a kiss."

Manu took a moment to grab her and plant a kiss on her rounded lips. "Call that interest," he suggested. "I'd prefer a naked kiss much later."

CHAPTER 13

Sexy Times And Fun

J essalyn prayed something in the storage shed provided answers. Expectation whizzed through her. On second thought, the exhilaration might be her taniwha and her hope of having the sexy black beast again. A blip surged through Jessalyn, frisking every nerve ending on the way to her pussy.

Holy fish and chips. With Danny's arrival, she hadn't had a chance to recall the events from the previous night. Manu Taniwha didn't require a map of a woman's body. He hadn't missed a single hot spot and had pointed out others during his tour.

She flapped her hand to disperse the heat blooming in her cheeks.

"There are so many boxes here. I assumed Dad had sold them all. And wood. This will keep me going while I search for another job."

"Or it could provide you with the opportunity to do what you love," Manu said. "I told you you're welcome to use a corner of my workshop."

"I'll consider it. So much has happened since I left Piha. Losing my job might be perfect timing so I can focus on the changes and adapting."

Manu stood and chucked her under the chin, his tender expression doing things to her insides. "Great attitude, sweetheart."

Her taniwha gave a little coo of contentment, thankfully quietly so Jessalyn's embarrassment never spiked, but she kind of echoed the sentiment. *Be still my heart.*

Ten minutes later, on their arrival at the warehouse, Jessalyn examined the boxes more carefully. Nothing stood out as unusual.

"Zilch in the clue department," she said once the boxes were stacked near her tools.

"All right. Let's head back to the house." He came to a sudden halt. "Had an idea. Wait there."

He returned and once he sat behind the driver's wheel, handed her a watch. No, not a watch. It had buttons of different colors.

"Hopefully, this won't be too big for you, and it will work with your European blood. This will be an excellent test. I made them for Hone and my brothers. Strap it on one wrist, and I'll explain the controls."

Interest and curiosity had her studying the gadget while she strapped it on her wrist. "Is this one of your stealth units?"

"It is."

She'd already observed how close-mouthed he was with her and others unrelated to him when it came to this invention. She felt... Honored. Excited, too.

"This blue button will make you invisible. The red button will turn you visible again, and the middle button is a boost button that aids camouflage in different circumstances."

"Got it," she said. "When will we use this?"

"I suspect Danny followed us last night. It's no secret where I live. He could've asked my father and his cronies or tracked your phone. I'll ask Dad if he saw Danny. It will give me a chance to check on him. Click the blue button now."

Jessalyn followed his instructions and didn't think the gadget had worked. She could see herself, and everything appeared normal. "It didn't work."

"Yes." His voice throbbed with satisfaction. "I can't see you, but I can sense your presence. Others won't see you."

"You truly can't see me?"

"No."

"How long have you been working on this?"

"Since I was eighteen. Being a taniwha in an increasingly busy world is difficult. Other shapeshifters face the same problems, and I wanted to make our lives easier." He sighed as he drove away from his warehouse. "The problem is my stealth gadget will tempt the criminal element. Humans and shapeshifters alike."

"Hmm," Jessalyn said, picturing the mayhem created by invisible thieves. "You could keep a tight control and rent units to vetted taniwha or other shapeshifters. Man, I can't believe there are other shifters."

"You believe me?" Manu's voice held humor.

"A month ago, I didn't believe in dragons. Other shifters aren't a far stretch. What do we have? Werewolves? Vampires?"

"There's a small vampire clique in Auckland. The South Island has more shifters because there are more open spaces. Mostly feline shapeshifters and a few wolves."

"Huh. Well, there you go. Back to your stealth units. Instead of selling them outright and losing control, rent them and make a kill switch. If you learn of any problems, you could render them useless. Maybe an anti-tamper switch too. You don't want anyone pulling them apart and stealing your secrets. If they start to pull them apart, you'd need to know."

"I'd considered the tampering angle already, but a control to disable the stealth unit remotely. That makes sense with a rental unit."

"Manu. Manu! You've missed the turn."

"What?"

This glimpse of his absent professor mode, another side of him, intrigued her. Mentally, he was in his warehouse, busy tinkering with his gadget. "You'd better let me drive."

"What?" He shook his head, alertness returning to his brown eyes.

"You zoned out and missed the turn."

"Crap. Sorry." He waited for the traffic to clear and did a U-turn.

"If you intend to do that again, I will get behind the wheel."

He took his gaze off the road for a sec, his eyes turning golden and giving her a peek of his dragon.

"Watch the road! You can't see me, so don't look."

"Bossy wee thing."

"Not so much of the little."

He laughed, a joyous sound that had her own lips curving. "A bet," he suggested. "If I drive to Papakura without mishap, I win oral sex from you."

"Interesting, but I'd like to point out you drive safely most days. What do I get if you lose?"

"Oral sex from me."

No way was that a losing bet. Both ways, she won. If she lost and drove him crazy enough, she'd get some for sure. "To clarify, if you drive home without going into your head, I get to touch dragon dick."

Manu's brows rose. "Put that way, it sounds kinky."

Jessalyn pondered the matter for a split second. "I'm fine with kinky."

"The full moon is closer. How are you feeling?"

"Actually, so much has happened today that my mind has kept busy. My stomach is fine. No burning sensation."

"You're eating more, and the sex probably helped."

"And we're back to sex," she teased.

"You're an attractive woman. I enjoy your company, even when we're not doing the sex thing."

She cackled, "I'm fluttering my eyelashes. You can't see, but I thought you should know. My taniwha is purring."

"So is mine," Manu said drily. "And my cock is hard."

They approached Manu's driveway, and several older men loitered near the mailbox. The instant they spotted Manu, they started yelling.

Manu slowed and lowered his window. The shouts rose a decibel. "Stand out of the way, and I'll come back to speak with you." Manu's powerful voice, backed by his taniwha, silenced the men.

Jessalyn caught the flickers of surprise.

Manu used the remote to open his garage and drove inside. He lowered the door and released a loud exhalation. "I should've done that earlier instead of avoiding them."

"I'll start dinner," Jessalyn said.

Manu strode to the side door before halting. He turned back. "I won the bet. Later," he said before he disappeared outside.

Manu strode toward his father, understanding his parent's frustrations and depression better now that Jess had entered his life. The problem of what to tell his father... How much detail did he give?

Bare basics, he decided.

He dipped his head in a show of deference since these elders were all experienced warriors.

"Will you do it?" his father asked with a trace of eagerness.

"No, I refuse to execute you," Manu said. "Wait!" He lifted his hand and pushed taniwha power to enforce the order. "I need to tell you something. Nelson Waaka called this morning. He insists I return one of his tribe to him."

He had their attention now since no one liked the Waaka tribe. Nelson's father had played a huge part in the fight for the relic during the last unrest. His behavior had caused resentment and outright anarchy amongst the taniwha tribes before Nelson took over.

"Who does he want? The girl who was staying here?" his father asked.

Manu ignored that. "Have you seen a young Māori guy in his twenties loitering around here?"

"I talked to a kid. Danny was his name," Frank Hohepa, one of his father's oldest friends, said. "He told me he was visiting a relation."

"Cousin to the Waakas," Manu said. "He's here to cause trouble, and I suspect it's related to the relic."

"But the relic went into the sea when the woman guardian drowned," his father said. "What was her name?"

"Humarie Brown," Manu said. "I'm not sure what's going on, but can you pass the word to your families and friends? I need everyone to watch and note anything unusual. We've always allowed taniwha from other tribes free access to the Auckland region, so pay attention to visitors, especially if they ask questions."

Auckland, as the biggest city in New Zealand, was important for trade. It wasn't unusual to sense other taniwha, but as long as they didn't create trouble, visitors traveled freely through their tribal boundaries.

"I intend to call a tribal meeting soon, and I should have more information by then." Manu paused, waiting for arguments, but not one elder offered one. "If you see Danny again, snap his photo and pass that around too. He's not to be trusted."

"What about this girl? What has she got to do with the relic?" his father asked.

"She is Humarie Brown's daughter," Manu said. "A half-caste."

One elder tut-tutted, the reaction much as Manu had expected. Given Jessalyn's European blood, they'd ignore the possibilities. They'd underestimate her, which was what the Waaka family had done. Their loss. His bloody huge gain.

His father leaned closer and sniffed him. "You're fucking her."

Manu bit back his instinctive protest. "It's almost the full moon," he countered. "I needed a woman." Crap, the wrong thing to say around his father.

"I don't have a woman," his father snarled. "Your fault."

"What would you have had me do? Could you have lived with yourself if Mum had murdered innocents? Jack and Emma. Hell, Emma has just had twins. Hone and Cassie. Ma intended to kill them all. If I hadn't stopped her, what might she have done next? She'd lost her mind, Dad. Admit the truth instead of giving me a hard time. It's difficult enough dealing with the situation and my guilt, but the truth is I had no other option. I'd do the same again. Tane and Kahurangi understand my actions. You were there and witnessed the same as us. Ma injured Emma, and she still bears the scars."

His father's face fell as if he was conceding the point. "I thought June was getting better."

"You knew she'd become dangerous?"

"I'd talked to her, told her I thought Hone and Cassie were mates. I thought she'd agreed."

"You *knew*," Manu repeated.

His father's shoulders slumped. "June's grandmother suffered from delusions. June seemed fine until we met Cassie. She became obsessed with growing our family. Grandchildren."

"You should have told us. The sword sensed her instability. That's why it deserted her and embraced me. Damn it, Dad. You should have shared this with us. Tane, Kahurangi, and I might have been able to help."

"I'm sorry, son." Chastised, his father seemed smaller, weaker.

"Dad, if there is a problem, you must tell me. That goes for all of you. If you have problems within your family, share them with me. As your leader, I'm here to help. We're stronger together. That's what makes us a tribe and enables us to survive in these modern times. That is the reason I'm telling you about the Waaka family. If trouble comes to town, we must work as a team. Speak to your families tonight. I'll post on our private bulletin board. Tell everyone to go online and check for details. Any questions?"

"No," Frank said. "We'll pass the word."

His father turned away with the others.

"Dad, wait. Can I have a private word before you leave?"

"Are you all right for the full moon?" Manu ignored the weirdness of discussing his father's sex life, but this was one area where he could help.

"I have a widow friend. We assist each other when necessary."

Manu forced himself to keep his gaze on his father instead of succumbing to embarrassment and a schoolboy foot shuffle. "If you don't choose to do that, I can lend you one of my stealth units. That way, you can fly in dragon form."

"Your invention really works?"

"It does, Dad."

"Thank you, son," Samuel said, his gaze flitting and

never settling. "Hinemoa and I are happy enough with our arrangement."

"Good. That's good," Manu said. "Call if you need anything. Tane or Kahurangi, if it's easier for you."

His father walked away without another word, and Manu watched him leave with his friends. After a quick scan of the street, he stilled and let his senses fly. Nothing.

Satisfied, Manu jogged up the path, eager to rejoin his mate.

"How did it go?" Jessalyn called. "I didn't hear yelling. Not after our arrival."

Manu grinned at the spoon that lifted in the air and stirred a pot. Jess had forgotten to make herself visible again. He'd done that a time or two when distracted by improvements or a brainwave for an invention. "No, he and his friends listened for once. I think..." He trailed off, wondering if he should share his inner thoughts. No! Jess was his mate. She mightn't realize it but he and his taniwha held not a shred of doubt. "Neither my father nor I dealt well with the aftermath of Mum's death. Me having to kill her, I mean. Now, after talking to Dad, I think he's struggling with the same guilt. We both wonder if we could've done things differently."

The spoon turned in his direction, and a meaty sauce dripped onto the counter.

"Oops." A dishcloth wiped away the spill. "Could you have gone down a different path?"

"No, not at the time."

"I don't pretend to understand taniwha ways, but from what you've told me, your mother wasn't in her right mind. You and your brothers tried to reason with her."

"We did."

"That's your answer. Remember her with respect for the good things she did for you, your family, and your tribe. If you and your father dwell on your guilt, you'll destroy any chance of a happy future. My father... That's what I'm trying to do."

"When did you get so smart?"

"I've always been intelligent. That's part of the reason Danny argued with me. He and his friends hated it when I did things better than them. Carving, for instance, and martial arts."

"I might've been cranky if a woman beat me at things in my masculine domain."

"*Pfft!*"

He hid his amusement. "What's for dinner?"

"Spaghetti bolognese. The sauce will improve if it sits for half an hour. Want to sit on the deck with a beer?"

"We could do that," he agreed. "Or you could pay me for losing your bet."

"Sex?"

"Yeah. I've been thinking about getting my hands on you again for most of the day."

"Really? You hid your desire well."

249

The spoon stirred the sauce, and the light showing the element in use flicked off. The spoon bashed against the inside of the pot and traveled to the sink.

"I'd hate to give you an opportunity to tell anyone I welshed on a crazy bet." Her voice held humor and perhaps a hint of lust.

"Uh, Jess?"

"Hmmm?"

He experienced a tug at the waistband of his jeans and his telltale groan almost escaped. "Please push the red button on the stealth unit. The visual is as much a turn on as the act."

"Oh! I forgot. Everything seems normal, and the unit flexes with my wrist. It's too big, though. You should design ladies' sizes."

"I'll start work on that soon. Red button, Jess."

She popped into view, and her mischievous expression drew his stare. Jess held out her hand, and dumbly, he entwined their fingers. She appeared happy, and the emotion simmered in him too. Sex—great sex was the perfect way to celebrate.

Hand-in-hand, they walked into his bedroom.

"I haven't done this much," Jess said.

"It would give me great pleasure to talk you through my preferences." Manu laughed, admitting the truth. "I enjoy acting bossy in bed."

"Do tell. What do I do first?"

Manu walked to the far side of the bed, where a thick mat covered the varnished floorboards. "We're gonna play a little game called using the five senses." He laughed when she wrinkled her nose. "A great time will be had by all."

"Promises. Promises." She fluttered her lashes, her brown eyes more golden than usual.

"Unzip my jeans and pull out my cock," he ordered.

Her eyes widened a fraction, and those lashes of hers lowered, screening her gaze. Manu waited, anticipation thrumming through his veins. Her gaze was on his groin now, and it burned like a physical touch. Her feminine hand intrigued him. The tremble. The scar on her thumb. Compared to most women, her hands were battered, yet he loved her calluses—the faint roughness—stroking his bare skin.

The button on his jeans popped open. His zipper rasped down, guided by her right hand. Mesmerized, he watched as she tugged his boxer-briefs and set the elastic band beneath his balls. She moved without haste, her leisurely speed ramping up—hell—everything. His expectation. His excitement. His erection.

Her gaze lifted and connected with his.

"Use your hands to explore my cock. My balls too. Keep your touches light but with enough pressure not to make me squirm."

Interest flared in her. "Are you ticklish?"

"Now is not the time to discover this," he stated, his tone final.

Her lips hitched up into a sexy curve, one that tempted him to greater mischief.

"No. You lost the bet. Pay up."

"Yes, master."

Every muscle in his body clenched at her sultry tone and tightened again when she yanked his clothing down his legs.

"Widen your stance," she murmured.

Before he could protest he was the one in charge, she kissed his inner thigh, her lips petal soft against his skin. She nuzzled his pubic hair, which was minimal due to his grooming routine. Her lips and tongue fired the tiny nerves in his other thigh, her sensual assault more arousing than any sexual act of the past.

"The male cock is ugly," she said.

Manu grinned. He couldn't help it since she kept surprising him. "Perhaps, but it gives great pleasure."

"Perhaps," she parroted.

Although most of her expression remained hidden, her gaze on his dick, he imagined her amusement.

With gentle fingers, she handled his balls, rolling them.

"Fascinating," she murmured and used her tongue to taste and stroke one. She trailed a finger from the base of his cock to the tip before measuring his girth with her hand.

Manu breathed carefully, every instinct screaming at him to pounce, but he refrained, the visual of her on her knees, one he'd pull out many times in the future.

Once she'd explored and observed his cock at close quarters, she glanced up at him. "Should I use my mouth next, oh master?"

"Not yet. We'll move this to the bed." He offered his hand to help her stand and drew her close to press a soft kiss on her parted lips. Before he gave in to the instinct roaring through him, he stripped off his black T-shirt and remaining clothes and, naked, planted himself on the mattress.

"Strip," he ordered. "We'll do the rest naked. Better visuals for me," he added.

Jess wasted no time in following his instructions. God, she did it for him. In the past, her peers might have teased her about her size, but she was in proportion. Sleek muscle and golden skin stretched over big bones. Perfect for him. Just perfect.

"What next? When do I get to taste?"

"Touching is important," he countered. "The tease arouses your partner."

"You sound like a talking sex manual," she grumbled.

Manu laughed. "I'm imparting wisdom. You asked for instruction. I'm merely giving you information to use in the future. If you learn one thing, it's this. A woman skilled at oral sex will have her man eating out of her hand."

"Okay. Okay. What's next?"

"After lots of touching with your hands and kissing plus, you can use your mouth to lick and tease. Touch the perineum. Give me your finger." He grasped her finger and guided it along the patch of flesh, barely holding back his groan. "This will get a man off faster. A few firm strokes together with your mouth."

"Ah, massaging the prostate," she said and suited action to words.

"Use your mouth now. Tease me with your tongue. Explore the head of my cock. Flick your tongue. Pay attention to the underside."

Jess was a quick student, and Manu ceased his avid watching, instead closing his eyes and letting himself settle into sensation.

She kissed. She stroked. She sucked.

"Perfect," Manu whispered. "Take me inside your mouth."

The wet heat of her hot mouth had him trembling like a virgin getting his first bout of oral. His pulse raced. His heart hammered. His taniwha's purrs of blissful enjoyment almost deafened him.

"Control the amount of cock in your mouth with your hands. Yes, that's it."

She did a sexy swirl of her tongue, catching the sensitive underside of his shaft, and his balls lifted.

"I'm close now, sweetheart. If you don't wish to swallow, finish me with your hands." Either way, he was fine. So thrilled with this half-dragon woman he'd discovered in his backyard.

Her mouth tightened around his shaft while her finger stroked. Helpless under her ministrations, his hips lifted, driving him deeper into her mouth. A tingle started in his balls and surged up his dick with a force that left him dizzy. His groan of pleasure echoed in his bedroom as Jess swallowed around his shaft.

Without being told, she gentled her touch, using her hands and mouth, her tongue to soothe him down from his climax. When she released his cock, his eyes popped open, and he met her gaze. A slow cat-got-the-cream smile curled his lips as he spotted a drop of his semen on the corner of her mouth.

His woman.

"Thank you," he said, his voice husky. "Let me kiss you. Please."

She entered his arms willingly, her breasts flattening against his chest. He cupped her face in his hands and kissed her eyelids, her nose. Tiny flutters of his lips against her cheek before he pressed his mouth against hers and sucked on her top lip. He repeated the action on her bottom lip, then used his tongue to widen her mouth. He tasted himself on her, a hint of wildness that was completely her. Content, he pressed against her and sipped deeply, intent on returning the pleasure she'd given him. He gloried in her sighs, her moans as he mapped her body.

And later, as he slid his cock deep, he reveled in the way she gripped him tight, the tiny strands of pleasure and enjoyment tying them together and strengthening the bonds of mating.

For him, she was the one. He'd have to tell her soon, sensed she would fight, and he understood. This world was new to her, and she was still finding her feet. Jess was learning of her abilities. Some in his tribe might disparage his mate. Her tainted blood. He cared little for their objections.

With Jess in his arms, he sampled the future, and it had never seemed sweeter.

CHAPTER 14

Time For Further Investigation

M anu settled his sweaty body on hers, and Jessalyn sighed, not with discomfort but with enjoyment. He stole a kiss before rolling out of bed.

"What should we do today?" he asked, his eyes bright with the same contentment that filled her.

She stretched, enjoying his gaze on her breasts, her power over him. "Are you going to the warehouse?"

"Yeah, I thought I'd work on adding some of your suggestions to my units and also make a smaller one for you."

"I get one?" Excitement and a warm sensation settled in the

region of her heart.

"I think it's best for you to keep a low profile when you're outdoors. We don't know if Nelson Waaka has other members of his tribe down here."

Some of her exhilaration faded. "Good point. I want to do a closer stocktake of the boxes and maybe work with the wood we found stored in the shed. I might research the different markets around as well since I never went with Dad. Now I understand why he never wanted me to come to Auckland with him." Huh! Not that she was bitter or anything.

"Plan. You take the first shower while I sort out breakfast," Manu said.

Danny was loitering around Manu's mailbox when they left his house.

Her friend's black hair lay flat against his head, long due for a wash. Which said something since Danny was vain with his hair. He wore the same clothes as the previous day.

On spotting them, he ran toward Manu's truck and thumped on the window.

Manu opened it. "Did you want something?"

Jessalyn had never heard that imperious tone before, and Danny's reaction to it surprised her. His shoulders straightened and his eyes grew more alert. It was practically an invisible salute—an acknowledgment of a leader.

"Where is my fiancée? Jessalyn has disappeared, and I'm concerned for her safety." His nostrils flared, and he leaned closer to Manu.

Jessalyn stared. Could he sense her? She'd showered and changed into clean clothes. A set of brand new clothes, in fact. Or was it the relic? As was her normal habit, she'd taken it out of its box and stroked the fishhook symbol on its face. This morning, she'd obeyed an instinct to wear the pendant, but she'd made certain she'd concealed it beneath her T-shirt.

"You bear the same citrus scent as Jessalyn did yesterday."

"Jess spent two days with me. She showered and used my soap. She might've used my laundry powder. No matter. She has gone now."

"She doesn't like people shortening her name."

True, but Manu's husky tones thrilled her, and the short form of her name coming from his lips pleased her. Of course, the man was skilled in satisfying her and made her entire body hum with pleasure. Heck, the sex last night had made her taniwha speechless, which was a skill in itself, and her taniwha still slumbered in post-coital bliss.

"Look, I have a meeting to attend. What do you want?"

"Where did Jessalyn go?"

"No idea. She mentioned signing papers. I understand a couple has rented her house."

Concern crept into Danny's expression. "She isn't coming back to Piha?"

Jessalyn frowned, not understanding his desperation or his assertions they were engaged. That was, of course, ludicrous. They'd never been more than friends. Never.

"Look, Danny. Jessalyn stayed two nights. That's all. It was a favor for someone who needed help. She thanked me and left. Stop loitering around my house or I'll call the cops the next time I see you."

Manu closed the window and drove off. Jessalyn stared back at Danny, who had pulled out his phone.

"He's reporting back to someone," she said. "I don't understand his persistence. Telling everyone we're engaged is ridiculous for a start."

"They suspect you have the relic. Once you took it out of the box, it released energy or a form of subtle power. They didn't find it in your house during their search and suspect you have it with you."

"I have it," Jessalyn said. "Will they try to steal it?"

"Yes."

"Why haven't you?"

"I believe the guardian should remain separate from the tribes. No one tribe should have more power or advantages than the others."

"But my mother left the relic behind. She wanted nothing to do with it."

Manu checked the rear-vision mirror before taking the back roads to Onehunga instead of the most direct route.

"Have you considered your mother was never meant to have the relic? That it was meant for you?"

"What?" Her voice emerged as a squawk. "Me? That's crazy."

"It calls to you. That's why you're wearing it around your neck right now."

Jessalyn's hand went to her chest. Manu wouldn't see the action because she wore his stealth unit, but he was right. An urge to protect the pendant drove her, and happiness—a bone-deep sense of confidence and well-being—filled her whenever she wore it next to her skin.

"How did you know?" she asked finally.

"It omits a..." He trailed off. "I guess I'd describe it as a power frequency, but that's not right. It's more a gut awareness."

"You said nothing."

"I hate the idea it makes you a target. That's my main concern. Nelson Waaka won't give up. He's single-minded, and he and his tribe believe they have a right to the relic. He won't change his mind nor give up in his efforts to claim it."

"What is the purpose of the relic? Why is it so important?"

"Our people believe the wise old taniwha guided us to Aotearoa. He kept us safe through storms, and the reward after the long journey was a land of plenty where we prospered. Some believe the taniwha held magical powers. Spiritual powers. He garnered people's respect. His mana was great."

"Mana?"

"His power. The respect others had for his authority. Some might say mana is almost a type of charisma. The holder of the relic gets all that by extension."

"I've met Nelson Waaka face-to-face. He rules by fear. I sensed that even though I was a kid."

"Which is the best argument for him not getting hold of the pendant," Manu said.

"Crap, what am I going to do?"

"You could give it to him. Things might settle down after that."

"No." The protest was instinctive. "Maybe I could donate it to the museum. Offer it to Te Papa, the national museum so every taniwha could see it."

"What if it was stolen?" Manu pointed out.

"Double crap."

"I'm sorry, sweetheart. Your decision. There is nothing stopping you from putting it back in its box and locking it in a bank safe."

"Perhaps." That solution didn't sound any more ideal than the others when every part of her ached to have the relic next to her skin. The dilemma—by keeping the relic she put herself, Manu, and everyone else of her acquaintance in danger from the Waaka family.

Manu halted in front of his warehouse and opened the security gate to enter. Once it closed behind them, Jessalyn made herself visible again. She unstrapped the unit and handed it to Manu.

"I'll make the strap for you today. How would you feel about going flying with me tonight?"

"Yes! I'd love that."

"Then that's what we'll do. I'll be busy working. Call if you need anything, and make sure you eat plenty of snacks."

"I didn't breathe any fire last night."

"I noticed," he said, his approval clear in the quick squeeze of her shoulder.

Manu unlocked the warehouse, and they walked inside before he closed the door and switched on the lights. He turned to her and drew her closer, wrapping his arms around her. He cupped her face and kissed her—a slow and thorough exploration of her mouth that soon had her pulse racing. Gradually, he backed away, his eyes glowing as he caressed her cheek.

"Later," he said and nonplussed with the emotions and reactions coursing through her, she stared after him. He fascinated her, infuriated her at times, and intrigued her. And he was so easy on the eyes.

He might carry baggage and lingering guilt at what happened to his mother, but he was a decent man and an able leader. This man drew her like no other. Unfortunately, the relic would attract problems for both of them unless she placated Nelson Waaka and his tribe.

She drew out the pendant and clasped it with her hand. Warmth emanated from the old bone while the greenstone inlay soothed her. The Māori fishbone signified a safe journey. She'd require every bit of the power behind the relic to navigate the future that lay ahead.

Jessalyn pushed her worries aside and strode over to the corner of the warehouse that now housed her father's woodworking tools and the boxes of things they'd removed from the storage unit. Hers now.

Working with wood had always calmed her and, in a weird way, connected her with her emotions. So that's what she'd do now. Work to make special boxes to store jewelry and other precious knickknacks, and she'd mull over her possible courses of action.

Happier now, she sorted through her pieces of wood. All offcuts of native timber were too small to make the larger items of furniture her father had favored. Rimu, totara, kauri, and rewarewa. Her hand settled on a piece of rimu, and she separated it from the pile, her eye drawn to the grain of the reddish wood.

The process was instinctive, her mind's eye clear on what she wished to achieve. She found protective eyewear, connected the saw to the power and made her first cut. With the wood cut into four equal pieces, she commenced the next step, her mind full of the relic.

Karen Baker.

Jessalyn pulled a face. Her mother was the obvious source of information. If she could speak to her and get answers to a few questions, it might set her on the right path to make decisions.

That was one idea.

Another—she could research the myths and legends of the Maori people and try to find information within them. Possibly helpful.

Jessalyn worked and sanded the wood until the sides and the lid of her emerging box was smooth to the touch and pleasing to her eye. Once she finished the first, she moved on to the next and continued with her sanding until her belly gave a protesting rumble. A glance at her watch surprised her. Four hours had passed.

Jessalyn set down the fourth box and went to investigate the fridge. She ended up making two plates of sandwiches and a pot of tea.

At Manu's lab, she knocked on the door before entering. "I've made a snack and tea if you're interested. I didn't think I should bring them in here in case something spilled."

"Perfect timing." Manu plucked something off his workbench and stood. "I've finished a unit for you." He fastened it on her left wrist. "Perfect fit." He unfastened the unit and set it on his workbench. "Now lead me to that food."

While they ate, Jessalyn told Manu she needed to go to the library to research the taniwha species and associated myths and legends.

"I might make one last effort to talk to Karen Baker."

"I'll take you," Manu said.

"No, I'd prefer to go on my own this time. I'm hoping she might speak more frankly if I'm alone."

"All right. When do you want to go?"

"This afternoon," Jessalyn said. "I'll visit the library after I go to see her."

"You can use a stealth unit."

Jessalyn froze, her breath catching in her throat. She coughed. "You'd trust me with one of your units? You haven't known me for long. What if I do a runner?"

Manu winked at her. "You like my sexy black beast. You won't flee."

Five minutes later, Jessalyn was on her way to the railway station, invisible to everyone. Luckily, it wasn't rush hour, but even so, an elderly lady almost sat on her lap during the train journey to Manukau. The bus to Botany Town Center challenged her even more, and she ended up standing near the door midway in the bus to avoid someone sitting on her.

She walked the final bit to Karen's house and came to an abrupt halt. A for-sale sign sat on the grass verge. A car was parked in the driveway. Someone was home.

Jessalyn ran up the front path and knocked on the door. Footsteps heralded an arrival, and the door opened. It wasn't Karen.

Jessalyn slid inside before the woman—a real estate agent,

judging by her badge—closed the door again. The house was empty, with no sign of the previous occupants. Karen Baker truly had uprooted her family and disappeared, as she'd threatened.

The real estate agent's phone rang. "Bettina Whiting," she said.

Jessalyn overheard the woman phoning inquire about the house.

"I'm here at the moment if you'd like to do a walk-through," the real estate agent said. "The owner has moved to Australia."

Jessalyn didn't wait to hear more. Karen had left, taking Jessalyn's siblings with her. That she'd never get a chance to know her family hurt as much as the rejection. She didn't understand her birth mother. If she ever had children, she'd never treat them as disposable commodities.

"Sexy black beast," her taniwha piped up.

"Hello to you too," Jessalyn muttered.

"I had a sterling sleep. Where are we?"

"Good for you. We're going to the library to do research."

"Road trip!"

"Shush," Jessalyn said, seconds before the real estate agent poked her head out of a bedroom door, a tape measure in hand.

Jessalyn let herself out of the house.

"Where is the sexy black beast?"

"In his den," Jessalyn said.

"Oh. What did I miss?"

"Nothing. I've been making wooden boxes this morning."

During the bus ride to the Panmure Railway Station, Jessalyn stewed. Karen could have helped her or offered advice at least. Instead, she'd acted belligerent. Terrified enough to pack up her household and flee to Australia. She was learning that Karen never made threats. Instead, the woman took action.

Jessalyn tapped her chin. *Hmm*, she was running out of options.

Let's hope she found something to help her at the library because Nelson Waaka loomed like a volcano ready to blow.

CHAPTER 15

A Flying Date

M anu waited at the warehouse until six-thirty. He sat at his workbench, pretending to concentrate when his mind danced from gloom to excitement. What if Jess didn't return? A snarl echoed through his mind, his beast bearing the same concerns. Had he trusted too easily? What if she was in league with the Waaka family?

"Good grief, man. Get a grip."

Just as he lectured himself about jumping to outrageous conclusions, the alarm bell rang on the gate. Long strides took him to the security screens, and he spotted Jess waiting for entrance. Once he opened the gate, she jogged through, and relief at her appearance left him dizzy. Man, he had it bad.

"I'm so sorry I'm late," Jess said, her tone breathless and her cheeks flushed from her haste. "The stupid train was late, and I missed the connecting one to Onehunga. I didn't want you to think I'd taken off with your stealth unit, and I left my phone here."

"You're here now," Manu said, not wanting to admit his mind *had* gone there. "Did you speak to your mother?"

"No. She made good on her threat, packed up her belongings, and skedaddled for Australia. The house is for sale."

"Crap, I'm sorry. That must hurt."

"I checked books out of the library. Maybe I'll find a nugget to help."

But her demeanor told him she didn't truly believe that.

"What will Nelson Waaka do if he finds me?"

"My gut instinct says he'll force you to marry into his tribe, and you'll be kept a virtual prisoner."

"And if he discovers you're hiding me?"

"He might issue a challenge, depending on how pissed or determined he is to possess the relic."

"That's disturbing."

"Yes, but instead of letting Nelson Waaka worry us, let's go flying."

"Now? It's still light."

"Stealth units, remember? I've packed a picnic dinner. I thought we'd fly to Great Barrier Island, have our dinner, and make love on a secluded beach under the stars."

"*He-haw!*"

Manu chuckled at Jess's embarrassment.

"Inside voice," she chided her taniwha. "You're lucky your taniwha is well-behaved."

"Remember, we've been together longer," he said. "We've come to terms."

"*My sexy, black beast!*"

Jess groaned and hid her face while Manu grinned so wide the muscles around his mouth protested. Jess's taniwha wanted them. That was half the battle won.

"How is this going to work?" Jess asked. "Is it cool to admit I'm incredibly excited? You won't drop me, will you?"

"I'm beginning to see where your taniwha gets her chattiness."

Jess pressed her lips together.

"Not going to comment?"

"Shut up," she said, lifting her nose into the air.

"You'll need to carry the backpack. That will leave my claws free if I drop you." He kept a straight face at her flash of concern. "Come on. We'll go out the back, so I can shift with no one seeing me."

Jess preceded him, and he took delight in the sway of her hips and her rounded buttocks. Touching her, loving her hadn't been enough. His taniwha was pushing him to claim her. It was becoming harder and harder not to stake his rights. Jess's possession of the relic stood in his way.

How the hell could he inform her about mates and what they were to each other when her life was in upheaval?

He couldn't. So he remained silent, trying to show her with actions how much he cared for her. She was his other half, and while their taniwha accepted this, the human part of Jess required wooing rather than decisive action.

While her clambering onto Manu's back wasn't graceful, she perched securely enough as they arrowed through the air.

"Keep an eye out for planes."

The words, uttered in Manu's voice, echoed through her mind.

"Manu?" Planes? She glanced over her shoulder toward Mangere International Airport.

"Excellent. You can hear me."

"Wow!" She thought the word instead of speaking aloud.

"Flying is incredible. It's the coolest thing about being a dragon."

Manu flew toward central Auckland, the evening lights spread out before them. From his back, Jessalyn spotted the green hills—all dormant volcanoes. The wind tangled her hair and stifled her hearing but neither dimmed her enjoyment. The salty tang of the harbor grew stronger as they approached Rangitoto, the youngest of the dormant volcanoes in Auckland at around six-hundred-years. From above, it was easy to see the crater, now full of plants and small trees.

"Have you been to any of the islands?"

"No. I hadn't visited Auckland much before this trip. I'd done a school jaunt to the zoo and one to the museum. That's it." And now she understood why. Her father hadn't wanted her to learn about her mother, her brother, and sister.

"That's Waiheke Island there. I'll take you to visit soon. We'll go wine tasting and have lunch at a vineyard."

"I'd enjoy that." Normal date things. Come to think of it—that was also a rarity in her life. Since the incident with the rugby captain, her relationships had been short-term summer flings with no wasted emotion.

They flew onward until, through the dimming light, she spotted land again.

"That's Little Barrier Island. It's a closed island and requires a permit to visit."

"Have you landed there?"

"I have. I've stayed overnight and listened to the kiwi call and watched the morepork as they hunted for prey."

"You rebel, you."

Manu's amusement came through loud and clear. *"This is Great Barrier Island. We're traveling to the far end. They've just had the island declared a night sanctuary. Wait until you see the stars. It's magical. Hold tight. We're landing, and the wind has come up."*

Jessalyn tightened her grip on the knobby scales that ran down

Manu's spine when he was in his taniwha form.

Despite his warning, the landing was smooth and without a hitch. Jessalyn clambered down to study the private bay. Two gnarled pohutukawa trees clung to the nearby bank, their roots a tangled mass, while one tree bore the strange spiky beards typical of the older trees. Along with the stretch of sandy beach, this bay had a flat grassy area. Beyond that, patches of native bush crammed the spaces, and ferns grew in a green mass of ordered chaos. Jessalyn turned to the sea. Jagged rocks edged the shore, and the waves tumbled over them, creating white froth.

"You can become visible now," Manu said from behind her.

"Oh!" Jessalyn pushed the red button and glanced at Manu. "It's beautiful."

"His human half is sexy too!" her taniwha squealed.

Jessalyn winced. "Shush. Inside voice." Parents must experience this same exasperation when they repeated instructions to their children. "Are you hungry? I forgot to take snacks with me."

"We'll eat straight away," Manu said, drawing the backpack off her. He unpacked a rug and spread it on the grass. "A glass of white wine?"

"Yes, please. Can I do anything?"

"You could strip off your clothes so I don't feel weird in my nudity."

"Will there be a reward for compliance?"

"Count on it," he said as he pulled containers and plates out of the backpack.

The area was private, and the moon provided illumination. Almost full, she noted. A tingle swept her torso and landed in an ache between her thighs. Yes, removing her clothing sounded perfect. She'd bathe in the moon's light while she waited for her dinner.

She stripped off her clothing and footwear and stacked them in a tidy pile. If anyone came, she'd hit the stealth unit button, and the interloper would see nothing but a discarded picnic.

"You're gorgeous, Jess," Manu said as he handed her a glass of wine. "I enjoy watching you."

She wrinkled her nose at him and fluffed up her hair. "Well, my hair is behaving for once."

"*Pffff!*"

"Did you snort at me?"

"Your beauty is more than your hair. It's your gorgeous brown eyes and full lips, the glow of your brown skin, but most of all, it's your courage and determination, the way you've accepted the things life has chucked at you. Instead of whining, you're trying to discover a solution. Your work ethic is impressive as is your independence." He smiled and the sincerity in him stole her breath. "And then there is your curvy body that fits mine perfectly, your sassy comebacks, and the way you tease me. You've given me a reason to get out of bed each morning."

"Oh." Mostly, when people commented, they insulted her size

or her build. She was too Māori or not enough Māori. Like a square peg, she'd never fit properly with her peers in Piha. Heat gathered in her cheeks. "Thank you."

Manu's smile was wide and happy and contagious as he dug in the backpack for food. "I visited the bakery before you arrived back at the warehouse. There's a bacon and egg pie, beef and horseradish sandwiches, and an apple pie for dessert."

"Great, what are you having?"

"You," he replied without missing a beat. "A toast. To the future."

"The future," Jessalyn said, lifting her glass. Her mind traveled to the Waaka family, their persistence and tactics. A ticking time bomb, with the countdown underway. She forced away the thought, determined to enjoy this unexpected picnic treat. "How often do you fly?"

"Several times a week, but I'm lucky because I have a stealth unit. Most taniwha of the flying variety are limited to a few flights a year at best. How did the unit go today? Did anyone sense your presence?"

"No, the worst part was when an elderly lady tried to sit on me on the bus. After that, I picked seats at the rear. Rush hour would've been impossible, but the train is workable if you keep your wits about you. Danny seemed to sense something this morning."

"Yes." Manu frowned. "Some more tweaks required to disguise

the scent."

"Why? If a taniwha is trying to commit a crime using your stealth unit, it's best other taniwha can sense them. You, as the inventor, might require the special capability, but for the normal person, the news that it doesn't mask scent might be a deterrent against bad behavior."

"Good point." Manu handed her a slice of pie. "I'll pay George Taniwha and Sons to do a background check on each dragon who wishes to rent a unit. That will give notice of gambling problems, financial issues, or anything else that might make the rental a risk."

"You wouldn't want an abusive husband or stalker to get their hands on a unit."

"Exactly. The units are tamper-proof. I've installed emergency kill switches to use as a last resort, and rather than purchasing the units outright as I originally intended, I'm sticking to rental. I thought weekly at first and longer after each taniwha proves his or her trustworthiness."

"Have you worked out your costings?"

"Yes, I'll recoup the cost of making the unit in the first two weeks and make a small profit for each week after that."

"What about your time? You must've spent years working on this."

"I have, but I've invented other things for the engineering industry that bring in consistent royalties. I'm not hurting for money. My reasons for starting were selfish. I wanted the freedom to fly whenever I wished instead of being compelled to find a sexual partner every full moon."

"I haven't breathed fire for the last two nights. It's so relaxing—this perception of control. It has only been two days, but that's promising. Right?"

"My theory is you've accepted you have a taniwha, and you're taking better care of yourself. Also, sex has helped your influence over your dragon."

"That's not the reason I agreed to share your bed," she blurted.

"Pleased to hear it," he said. "It's not my main aim either. I have my unit and can fly at any time."

"So we're having sex because…"

"We're attracted to each other and want to express our mutual lust and liking." His voice was firm, his gaze direct. "I enjoy spending time with you."

"Where is my sexy, black beast?"

A growl burst from Manu, and he and Jessalyn stared at each other in mutual consternation.

"Also, our taniwha appear to favor each other," he said, his tone dry.

They ate most of the food and drank another glass of wine each. When she should've blushed and fidgeted with self-consciousness in her unclothed state, Manu's presence both relaxed and stimulated her mind.

"Your description of the stars didn't do them justice." Jessalyn set aside her empty glass and lay back on the rug. Without the interference of man-made illumination, the vast number of stars and the beauty of the night sky stole her breath. "This is stunning. Magical."

Manu settled beside her, their bodies touching, and they watched in silence until Manu turned on his side.

"What?"

"I'm going to kiss you."

"Have at it." She licked her lips, her gaze going to his mouth as he rolled slightly to cover her. His solid weight against her torso electrified her, and she wound her arms around his neck, holding him close.

Their lips touched, and the kiss was slow and dreamy. Full of pleasure and promises and shared intimacy. His confident skill and easy strength fired her body and left her hungry for more. An outing to remember. Then, Jessalyn stopped thinking and surrendered to Manu's experience and magic.

Best first date ever.

CHAPTER 16

The Cops Visit

The week unfolded for Jessalyn, full of research in which she discovered absolutely nothing. She worked on her wooden boxes, using delicate tools to carve the lids. Instinctively, she etched in Māori symbols: the koru and the fishhook. One box she left natural while she painted the lids of the others in black, white, and red.

Manu strode from his office. His demeanor told her something was wrong, and alarm surfaced. Her instincts suggested their days full of easy camaraderie and nights of passion were at an end.

A piercing whistle shrieked inside her head, and she clapped her hands to her ears. "Stop!"

A brief grin flickered across Manu's mouth. "Your taniwha."

"Yup. Showing her appreciation of a mighty fine man. What's up?"

"Nelson Waaka has requested a face-to-face meeting."

"Can you refuse to meet him?"

"He has adhered to our protocol, and to rebuff him will be an insult. He is bringing a group of six with him."

"I'm sorry. This is my fault. I'll leave. You can tell him you have no idea of my whereabouts."

"No!" Manu seized her hands, forcing her to look at him. "I don't want you to leave. Besides, if you go, you'll always be looking over your shoulder and wondering if you can trust the people you encounter."

The truth.

"You're right." She eased out a shaky breath. "This needs to stop. What do you think his visit means?"

"My best guess is he wants to push your marriage to that Danny bloke. A marriage to a Waaka will cement his hold over the relic."

"He'd try to take it from me," Jessalyn said.

"Yes."

She pulled the pendant from under her shirt, her thumb tracing the familiar curves of the fishhook. "I can't give it up. It's a part of me."

Manu's focus was on the pendant, yet his interest didn't alarm her because he'd shown no sign of wanting it. He didn't covet the pendant like Nelson Waaka, but she sensed his respect for the relic's history and magic.

"There must be something I can do or find to help or at least guide me in the right direction. The librarian I spoke to in Auckland said they hold the older, original texts at the National Library in Wellington. Although she did say, some of the papers and books were old and valuable and are restricted to those doing special research projects."

"Nelson wants to come next week. Wednesday."

"Could I borrow money from you? I can fly to and from Wellington in a day."

"What if we both went? Tomorrow. I should be able to purchase two seats on a plane. I mean, we could fly the taniwha way, but holding on for that length of a flight might be taxing and cold. Safer to fly on a plane."

"Can I borrow a stealth unit in case the library staff refuses to allow me access?"

"Definitely. We should use the units, anyway. Can you research the layout of the library and the places where the books you require are stored?"

"Internet," she said.

"Do as much research as you can beforehand, and I'll help you once we arrive at the library."

Jessalyn set aside the third box she'd intended to varnish. "I'll start now."

Manu's phone buzzed. He picked it up and frowned at the number of the incoming call. "Richard, this is an unexpected pleasure."

Jessalyn left him to his call and entered the kitchen. She'd make tea before she started her research. Her belly rumbled. Something to eat as well. She opened the fridge to survey the contents. It was full since Manu had ordered groceries and supplies online. The delivery had arrived the previous day.

She pulled out a loaf of bread, cheese, ham, and mayo.

"The word is out," Manu said from the kitchen doorway. "I've had phone calls from both leaders of the South Island tribes. They'll be in Auckland on Wednesday too."

His phone rang again, and after a glance at the screen, he pulled a face. "Wellington. I need to ask permission to enter their territory, anyway."

"Go to your office. Talk taniwha politics. I'll bring you a sandwich."

Manu was still speaking on the phone when she entered his office with tea and a plate of sandwiches.

"See you on Wednesday." He ended the call, rubbed his hands across his face and groaned. "God, I loathe taniwha politics."

"How did the tribes discover the relic has returned?"

"I'm uncertain," Manu said. "Every leader I've spoken to has acted cagey. Also, the leader of the Lower North Island tribe refuses to let me enter their territory."

Jessalyn frowned. "Is that normal?"

"No, and he declined to give me a reason why he is denying me access."

"Can we get on a flight this afternoon or tonight? The afternoon is better since breaking into the library doesn't feel right."

"Excellent idea." Manu dragged his laptop closer and pulled up the Air New Zealand site.

Jessalyn wandered back to the kitchen to eat her sandwiches and finish her tea. She tapped into her phone and started researching the library's layout and available resources.

"Done," Manu said five minutes later. "We leave in two hours. Let me call Dad, and I'll ask him to arrange a meeting for tomorrow night for our tribe."

"Will the Wellington tribe be watching the airport?"

"Possibly. We'll hire a car, and you can drive. Each of the leaders asked me what you look like," Manu said with a trace of disgust.

"Why? What have my looks got to do with anything?"

"My best guess is they're hoping to arrange a marriage with you. An arranged marriage will be more acceptable to the single men if you're not a dog—to put it bluntly."

"Don't I get a choice in the matter? I don't want to marry anyone. This isn't the eighteenth century. I'm a responsible legal adult, and no one can force me to do anything." Jessalyn half-expected Manu to laugh and tell her he was joking. That didn't happen.

"Unfortunately, marriage might be your best bet if you want to stop the tribes hounding you." Regret shone in Manu's direct gaze.

Jessalyn stared at him, waiting for a better punch-line. "You're kidding."

"I'm sorry."

Jessalyn could see he was genuinely apologetic at the situation, but it was one neither of them could change.

"Not one of them will have my well-being at heart," she snapped. "They'll marry me because matrimony gives them control of the relic and, therefore, power and bragging rights over the other tribes. *Because of the supposed magical powers embedded in the relic.*" She used her hands to do air quotes, disgust filling her. These men intended to move her around like a chessboard piece while they beat their chests and decided her future.

"Over our dead body," her taniwha snapped.

For once, her taniwha didn't project and confined her pithy observation to Jessalyn.

I agree, Jessalyn thought. *Let them think they've won. They can't force us to do anything.*

"You will find a way to best them," her taniwha said with confidence.

Jessalyn wasn't so certain, but she'd exert her brain and outmaneuver these men who sought to control her, starting with this research trip.

"I've called a cab," Manu said. "Here's money to pay for the fare."

I will stay invisible from now until we get inside the library. Wear your unit in case someone in Wellington decides you're a person of interest. They don't know what you look like at present, but you can bet they'll be working to correct that."

"Good point. I'll wear a hat and pull back my hair instead of leaving it loose."

The journey to Wellington proved fruitless, and the promising books held nothing to help Jessalyn. She'd even strolled into the staff areas. While she'd discovered source material, not one book mentioned the first taniwha or the relic. This was one legend that had remained in oral history rather than passing into the written language.

Disheartened, she and Manu returned to his house and crawled into bed. They'd fallen asleep, curled together.

A loud noise woke Jessalyn. Confusion filled her until her senses completed the gaps.

"It's the door." Manu rolled out of bed and rubbed his hands over his face.

His black hair stuck up in all directions, and the instinct to run her fingers through the dark locks had her sliding from bed too.

Manu pulled on a pair of jeans. "Stay here. I'll get rid of whoever it is."

"It's time to get up anyway," Jessalyn said and headed for the shower.

Ten minutes later, dressed and marginally more alert, she went in search of a cup of tea.

"Jessalyn," Manu said, his face expressionless. "These two policemen want to speak to you."

"Me?" She entered the lounge, and the two cops straightened, their gazes watchful. One policeman was older with a stomach paunch straining his light blue shirt and leather belt. He reeked of tomato sauce. The other cop was younger and of Asian descent, and surprisingly his scent was spicy and green. Fresh. She also identified Manu—a musky, manly aroma along with a hint of citrus from the body wash in the shower. Delicious.

"Jessalyn Brown," the older cop asked.

"Yes." Something about the vibe in the room put her on guard.

"You are acquainted with Danny Ngataki?"

"Yes, he was my best friend when I lived in Piha."

"Was?" the Asian cop asked, his brown eyes narrowing in suspicion.

"He turned up at the pub I worked at two days ago and made such a scene the manager fired me. I haven't seen him since." She decided seeing him while she was invisible didn't count.

"So that was the last time you saw him?"

"Well, Manu told me he was hanging around outside here the next day, but I never saw him. Manu said he left."

"Danny Ngataki was found dead this morning," the elderly cop said.

"Dead?" Jessalyn didn't have to pretend shock. "But how? Why?" She swallowed hard, then she got it—their meaning. "I didn't do it! Yes, I might have been furious at Danny for getting me sacked, but he was my friend. I'd never kill him." Her legs didn't seem to want to hold her up, so she tottered to the nearest chair and fell onto it. "Are you sure it's Danny?"

"His cousin Karl Waaka made an identification," the older policeman said. "Can you tell us your whereabouts from yesterday afternoon until this morning?"

Jessalyn glanced at Manu and caught his faint nod. "I flew to Wellington and spent a few hours there and arrived back on the ten o'clock plane. Then, I came home and went to sleep."

She couldn't tell them Manu had been with her the entire time because he'd been invisible.

"Why did you go to Wellington?" the younger cop asked, piercing her with his brown gaze.

She glanced at Manu, her mind working busily. She couldn't exactly mention anything taniwha either. No matter what she told them, her visit would raise flags. She clasped her hands in her lap. "I'm researching Māori mythology. I needed to check the records at the National Library." Too late, she recalled no one in the library would've seen her because she'd used the stealth unit.

"All right," the older cop said. "We might have further questions for you."

Manu showed them out, and Jessalyn stood and followed. Manu

partially closed the door. "Wait here until I come back or call you. Close the door after me."

He turned invisible. The door opened wider and Jessalyn waited a few seconds before she closed it.

Now, she truly needed that cup of tea.

CHAPTER 17

Accusations

It was almost three hours later when Manu returned. Jessalyn had spent the time cooking and brooding. A sense of doom had settled in the pit of her stomach as she worried about what had happened to Danny and why.

A quick series of taps sounded on Manu's front door.

"Yes," she called.

"It's me," Manu said.

She opened the door.

"Let me inside," Manu said. "No, stay out of sight. There's a cop car parked opposite the house, and I'm certain the guy loitering at the end of the street is a Waaka."

Jessalyn pressed against the wall and let Manu close the door. As soon as it shut, he materialized before her.

"Are you okay?"

She rubbed the back of her neck, tears pressing behind her eyes. "Is Danny really dead?"

"Yeah." He sniffed. "Have you cooked? I missed a meal."

Jessalyn followed Manu to the kitchen and served him a huge piece of Quiche Lorraine. She refreshed her cup of tea. "What happened?"

Manu hesitated.

"Tell me," she said.

"The cops think you murdered Danny. The problem is they checked the flights and discovered you were on the plane to and from Wellington, and this doesn't fit with the window they have for the time of death."

Jessalyn swallowed hard. "What happened to him?"

"They found his body near here. Someone thumped him over the head and fractured his skull."

"How did they know about me?"

"He had a picture of you in his wallet, and his cousin told the cops you'd had a fight."

"When?" Jessalyn demanded. "We had words after we got kicked out of the pub, but that's the last time I saw him."

"Karl told the cops you have a nasty temper and often hit Danny."

Jessalyn's mouth opened and closed, and her indignation climbed to mountainous levels. "Karl Waaka has never liked me ever since I showed him up during our kickboxing class. The other boys teased him about getting beaten by a girl. I'm not violent. My temper is no worse than anyone else's."

"There is another guy with Karl. Martin Tamaki. He backed up everything Karl said."

Jessalyn spluttered, gripping her cup so hard it was a wonder the china didn't give with the force. "Martin Tamaki is a worm."

"No one saw anything. They have no witnesses, but both Karl and Martin told the cops you rang Danny and arranged a meeting."

"But that's a lie."

"The cops are confused because you were in Wellington, and the time of the alleged meeting was before our plane landed back in Auckland. I told them I was with Jack and Hone."

"That's something at least."

"The cops think you paid someone else to kill Danny."

"What? I don't have any money."

"They're wondering if I'm involved," Manu said. "Although Jack and Hone confirmed my story to the cops."

"What are we going to do?"

"Well, first, I need to lock up the stealth units."

"I'm so sorry," Jessalyn said, immediately understanding the wider repercussions. The police presence would put a dampener on anything taniwha related.

"It's not your fault." Manu stood and walked around the table to hug her. "I think this is Nelson Waaka flexing his muscles and attempting to get you out of the way."

"You think he's responsible for Danny? He wants the relic that badly?"

"He craves the prestige and the mana," Manu corrected. "Those connected with the relic via marriage have prospered. The Waaka tribe prospered in the short time they held it. Nelson will seize the relic and throw away the guardian."

"I'm the guardian."

"Yes."

Jessalyn pulled from Manu's comfort. "I'm winging it with no idea if I'm doing the right thing. What sort of guardian does that make me?"

"You're doing the best you can. Jess, there is something else. With the senior members of all the tribes coming to town next week, you can't stay with me any longer."

"What? Why?"

"The other tribes will accuse me of using you for my own ends. I can't have that."

"You're kicking me out?"

"No! I enjoy spending time with you. Cassie and Hone suggested you stay with them to avoid talk of conflicts of interest. If anyone asks, we'll say you're Cassie's friend."

His face had turned expressionless, and Jessalyn wasn't sure what to think. She craved his touch, his comfort, yet despite their body contact, a palpable distance stretched between them.

Jessalyn stepped out of his embrace. "What will happen after this meeting?"

"One tribe will win over the others," Manu said.

"Win how?" Her voice grew sharp, her mind jumping to nasty conclusions.

"If talking doesn't reach a result, each tribe will pick a champion, and there will be a fight until one dragon remains."

"In other words, you're going to fight over me like a bone."

A knock on the door halted Manu's reply. Jessalyn froze before instinct had her using her senses. Not the cops. A more gamey scent with a similar freshness to that of the Asian cop.

"It's Hone," Manu said. "He's here to pick you up."

Taniwha. She listened carefully to the murmur of voices. Hone wasn't alone. She followed Manu but kept a healthy distance, hurt he was sending her away. If the other tribes wanted her, then why had Manu turned remote? She'd thought he liked her. Obviously, she'd misread the situation.

Manu opened the door to Hone and Cassie.

"Are you ready to go?" Hone asked.

"Manu just informed me I was leaving. I'll pack my bag." With stiff shoulders and her nose in the air, she retreated before she blubbered. And she never cried, so that pissed her off further.

"Nice going, numbskull," Hone said once Jess had disappeared from sight. He lowered his voice. "Why the hell didn't you tell her she is your mate—a true mate—and you want to marry her? Why not admit you'll be miserable without her?"

Manu sighed and didn't dodge the truth. Jessalyn was it for him, and he'd never stood a chance with her because she was the guardian of the relic. If he claimed her, the other tribes would cry foul, and the last thing he wanted was to drag his people into a war. The rumors swirled now because of his mother's abrupt death. He was loath to add to the dung pile.

"Manu!"

Manu winced at the demand in Hone's voice, but his cousin was the one man who understood the challenges he faced, both before and after taking up the leadership role. He trusted Hone with his secrets.

He centered his mind and inhaled before replying. "Jess is under enough pressure. I didn't want to add to it, not with the tribes meeting next week. She'll have enough to deal with then. Besides, her taniwha is a mere babe. Jess doesn't experience the same pull as me."

Hone released a derisive snort. "So you intend to step away and suffer in silence. Have you realized the full moon is on the day of the meeting?"

"Emotions will be high. I'm certain the date was chosen to cause trouble," Manu said.

"But what about Jessalyn? How is she going to cope with the

added pressure of the moon? Everyone will watch her closely as it is. Have you thought of that?"

"Hone, stop picking on Manu," Cassie said. "You need to prepare her as much as possible for what she can expect during the meeting. Give her every advantage so she can acquit herself well. Jessalyn is young. My guess—the tribal leaders will attempt to bulldoze her and order her to take specific actions. Help her prepare."

"Cassie is right," Hone said. "With your permission, I'll describe the meeting and give her an idea of what she might face."

"I'm ready," Jess said.

Manu had the absurd impulse to grab Jess and fly her to Great Barrier Island, where they could be alone. A normal courtship. If he had time, he could take her to a movie. They could act like a regular couple before he asked her to marry him. Unfortunately, her importance meant the other tribes would fire accusations of him using his inside position for gain.

He and Jess could never have an ordinary relationship now, even though he'd liked her and known she was his mate before he'd learned of the relic.

A healthy knock on the door had him turning. He cast out his senses and frowned. Now what? He opened the door to glare at the two cops standing there—the same cops who'd visited earlier.

"We'd like to speak to Jessalyn Brown," the older cop said.

Jess stepped forward, her pack on her back. "Yes?"

"Are you going somewhere?" the Asian cop asked.

"She is coming to stay with me and my husband," Cassie said. "We're going shopping."

"Let Jessalyn answer," the older cop demanded.

"I'm staying with Hone and Cassie for a few days," Jessalyn said.

The older cop eyed her with skepticism. "We'd like you to come down to the station to answer a few questions."

Jess scowled. "What sort of questions? I've told you everything I know."

"Go with the police," Hone said to Jess. "Cassie and I will wait until you're finished."

"Does Jess need a lawyer?" Manu asked.

"What? I can't afford a lawyer," Jess squawked.

"Jess will be out in a few minutes," Manu said to the cops.

They shared a quick glance before the Asian cop answered. "Two minutes."

"Jess," Manu said. "They think they have something on you if they want to question you formally. It's fine not to use a lawyer but use your judgment. If things get sticky, tell them you want to stop until you have a lawyer present. Don't worry about the cost. I'll cover it for you. Okay?"

"Yeah, thanks."

"One more thing. I'm not sending you away. I want you with me, want to be with you, but the shenanigans of the other tribes make our relationship difficult. They'll accuse me of trying to possess the relic." He sighed and squeezed her shoulder. "You'd better go. Call if you need that lawyer, or tell Hone."

She stared at him for a long time, then dipped her head in acknowledgment. The next minute, she was gone.

Jessalyn sat in the rear of the police car, reeling from the discussion she'd overheard between Hone and Manu. Of course! If she'd used her brain, this obstacle would've been obvious. It was something else to consider before this tribal meeting that was becoming bigger and scarier as the days passed.

Mates. That hadn't cropped up in her research either. She required more information.

The police car parked outside the Papakura Police Station. The two policemen escorted her inside and directed her to an interview room.

"Wait here," the Asian cop said.

Jessalyn claimed a seat while she mulled over what she'd learned. Yes, she was young in years. She'd turn twenty-two in two months. Her mind did a dash to Manu, and she wondered how old he was. It hadn't occurred to her to ask since he never treated her like a kid. During her research, she'd discovered taniwha generally lived a long life—over one hundred years—if they weren't killed for eating people.

The door to the interview room opened. A plain-clothes female detective, dressed in a smart navy trouser suit, entered along with the Asian cop. They took the other side of the table to Jessalyn, making her feel as if she sat in the principal's office. The detective read Jessalyn her rights and told her they intended to record the interview.

"Do you understand these rights?" the sharp-eyed detective asked.

"Yes," Jessalyn said.

The detective stated aloud her name and Jessalyn's. The Asian cop added his name, and the session began.

"Tell me how you know Danny Ngataki," the detective started.

"I met him when I was six. We went to school together and became friends because we enjoyed doing the same things. We've been friends ever since."

"Yet you had a disagreement at the pub. He made you lose your job. Didn't that make you angry?"

"Of course it made me angry. I liked working in the kitchen and the chef was teaching me stuff. I enjoy cooking, and because of Danny, the manager sacked me." Jessalyn kept her voice even and answered the question truthfully.

"So when you met later, you lost your temper and struck him on the head with a hunk of wood. You killed him."

"No, I didn't. I haven't—didn't see Danny again after I shouted at him at The Viaduct and stormed away. I didn't kill him."

"Who did you pay to kill him for you?"

Jessalyn gaped at the detective and the silent cop. She snorted. "Don't be silly. First, I don't have the money to pay for that. I didn't pay anyone to kill Danny. He was my friend, even if he had started acting weird."

"Weird, how?"

"He insisted I was his fiancée, and he kissed me." She shuddered. "It was slobbery and horrible."

"Witnesses at the pub say he told them you were engaged."

"They are wrong. I don't—didn't think of Danny in that way. We were friends. Nothing more."

"You withdrew ten thousand dollars in cash from your bank account. What did you do with it?" the detective asked.

"What?"

"Who did you pay the money to? Who did you pay to kill Danny? Tell us, Jessalyn. We can help you."

Jessalyn bit back a second snort with difficulty and focused on her clasped hands. These idiots truly believed she'd killed Danny. Heck, she'd been tempted to punch him, but she'd never kill him. Even if his companionship had been erratic, they'd been friends. She glanced up, her gaze connecting with that of the detective's. The woman's determination glinted in her eyes, but she didn't have the right person.

"I didn't kill Danny or pay anyone to do it. My father died

recently, and I received ten thousand dollars when I sold his vehicle. Since the bank check was made out to me, I paid the money into my bank account. I withdrew it the next day in cash because the fee for a bank check is outrageous. I walked out of the ANZ bank with the cash and into Westpac next door to deposit the money in my father's business account. Along with my father's house and vehicle, I inherited a mortgage, which was in arrears. The ten thousand cleared the amount owing and left extra to cover payments for a few months until I could get a job. I never saw Danny after I left him at The Viaduct. I neither killed him nor arranged anyone else to do the deed for me. Honestly, I wanted to flatten his nose for his rotten behavior, but I didn't even do that. I ignored his shouts and walked away, leaving him standing outside the pub."

"Interview suspended at 11:03," the detective said.

The detective and the Asian cop rose and left the room.

Ten minutes later, the detective returned. "You may go, Ms. Brown."

"Thank you," Jessalyn said, her voice stiff. She followed the detective out to the visitor room and spied Hone and Cassie waiting for her.

"Everything okay?" Hone asked.

"I'm allowed to leave," Jessalyn said.

She didn't speak until they left the police station and sat in Hone's SUV.

"They're idiots. They accused me of putting a hit on Danny. I was more likely to punch his nose than waste what money I had to pay someone to kill him."

Cassie laughed. "I am woman. Hear me roar."

"*Pffft!*" Jessalyn said. "Hone, explain what a mate means in the taniwha world."

"Damn. Heard that, did you?"

"My senses have improved," Jessalyn said.

"What about your taniwha? Can you shift?" Hone asked.

"I don't think so."

"Has anyone ever told you how to shift?" Cassie asked, her curiosity obvious.

"No."

"Do you have a kick-arse outfit to wear to the meeting?" Cassie asked, redirecting the conversation.

"I own jeans, T-shirts plus a denim jacket. I donated my one dress to Hospice."

Cassie glanced at her husband and swiveled in her seat to wriggle her eyebrows at Jessalyn. "You've come to the right people. This is gonna be fun."

Preparing For The Worst

J essalyn sat outside with Hone and Cassie, replete after a huge
    steak dinner and a dessert of apple-and-plum crumble with
thick cream. Her mind drifted to the upcoming meeting, which
would take place the following evening.

She hadn't seen or spoken to Manu since she'd left his house.
Now she understood the mate concept, had Manu been playing
her? Doubts had crept to the surface and had her second-guessing
everything. Her taniwha offered no advice and remained silent
as if she'd slipped into the same coma she'd slept in for most of
Jessalyn's life.

Hone and Cassie had been great, even though Hone hadn't

answered her questions about Manu's meeting. Cassie had helped her choose an outfit for the leaders' meeting and decide on a hairstyle and makeup. The latter items weren't something Jessalyn ever considered, but Cassie—who had confessed her secret identity as a popular country singer—informed her appearances were everything. Jessalyn must walk into the meeting projecting confidence and cool class if she had any hope of defeating these bossy and demanding taniwha.

If only she could decide what else she should do.

Her gaze lifted, drawn by the massive orb of the moon. Pale and lustrous. Beautiful. Watching it soothed the angst residing inside her, the uncertainties the following day would bring. But also, a faint edge of sensual awareness sizzled through her limbs, and that worried her.

The truth—she didn't want any man except Manu.

Which was strange, considering the wretched man had separated them. Setting her free, according to Hone.

"Is that the relic?" Cassie asked.

"What? Oh, yes." Jessalyn hadn't been aware she'd pulled it from beneath her shirt. Her fingers glided along the raised greenstone emblem. She froze and removed the pendant from around her neck for a better look.

The symbol on the face had transformed into a manaia—a monstrous mythical creature. The bird head represented the sky, the fishtail indicated the sea and the body between depicted the land. Combined, they gave the wearer a guardian status and protected against evil.

"That's strange," she said, studying the new design with awe. The relic *was* magical.

"What?" Hone sat alert, but Jessalyn didn't fear he'd seize the relic.

"The greenstone design has changed. When I found the pendant, the greenstone was a koru. After a while, it changed to a fishhook, and now it is a manaia."

Hone cocked his head. "Interesting."

"Explain it," Cassie ordered.

"From my research, the koru represents new life and growth. It can also mean peace. The fishhook is the symbol for safe travels—usually over water—and prosperity, while the manaia is a guardian," Jessalyn said.

Hone tapped his chin, his gaze distant as he pondered. "It's almost as if the relic has transformed with you, Jessalyn. Your life was changing when you found it. You were growing and learning skills. Safe travels might indicate your journey of discovery to Auckland. The arrival of the manaia indicates you've matured into your powers."

"I don't feel different."

"But you've grown in confidence," Cassie said. "What would've happened if this meeting was forced on you say, two months ago?"

"I'd have run," Jessalyn said. "Or burned the meeting place

down with my fire."

"This week, you've done everything you can to prepare," Cassie said. "You're ready, and I think you're going to kick their shapely Māori backsides."

Hone's brows rose. "Whose backside are you checking out, sweetheart?"

Cassie giggled. "Just yours. Jessalyn, could I look at the relic? Hold it for a few seconds?"

Jessalyn hesitated.

"Do it," her taniwha whispered.

Surprised by the sudden appearance of her dragon, Jessalyn obeyed the quiet *inside* order. "It gives off an energy that makes me happy when I wear it. It will be interesting to hear what you experience."

A pulsing silence had fallen with even the persistent click of the cicadas diminishing. She placed the pendant in Cassie's outstretched hand, and her new friend started.

"It sort of buzzes, and it's warm to the touch. Oh, it's beautiful. You can tell it's old." Cassie used her forefinger to trace the manaia motif. The pendant darted off Cassie's fingers and floated back to Jessalyn. The relic hovered until she held out her hand, and the pendant settled against her palm. Strangely, the spurt of anxiety she'd experienced on handing over the pendant faded, and a sense of wellbeing flooded her.

"Well, that's interesting," Hone said. "Did you know that would happen?"

"No." Jessalyn stared at the relic, surprised by the faint purring that echoed through her mind. A quick glance at Hone and Cassie suggested they hadn't heard the satisfied sound. "I'm learning as I go along."

Hone frowned. "I hope it's enough."

"Hone!" Cassie chided.

"It's all right," Jessalyn said. "This meeting will challenge me. For a start, the attendees hold enough male testosterone to ignite the city. If anything, Hone is understating the difficulties I'll face. All I have is my research, the relic, and my determination not to bow to tribal pressure. I understand the elders will force me to choose a mate."

"Oh, Jessalyn." Cassie reached for her hand and gave it a commiserating squeeze. "What will you do?"

Jessalyn sighed. "Play it by ear. My one option." A thought occurred. "Each tribe is bringing an entourage of their most important people. Can I bring a support team?"

Hone frowned. "Who did you have in mind?"

Jessalyn turned to Cassie. "I'd like to take Cassie. She has already helped me with my appearance. Feminine advice will help me balance out the testosterone."

"No," Hone said.

"I accept!" Cassie said at the same time.

"No, it's too dangerous. She's pregnant."

"Oh! Congratulations." Jessalyn's shoulders slumped.

"What if I asked Manu if I could use one of his stealth units? Jessalyn needs someone on her team," Cassie said.

"No, absolutely not. Tempers will be high. Lots of male posturing."

"Look at it this way." Cassie's chin lifted in determination. "Our son or daughter should grow up in a world where women are respected. If these tribal leaders get their way, Jessalyn will find a marriage forced on her. This would end her freedom. She'd be little more than a prisoner. If I can help her prove she is the guardian for a reason and deserves her freedom, then I can lift my head in pride."

"Do you think I can beat them?" Jessalyn asked in a faint voice.

Cassie's eyes flashed with yet more determination. "You will kick dragon butt."

Hone groaned. "I'll call Manu, but if he vetoes this plan, you're staying at home."

"Yes, Hone." Cassie's smartarse tone hovered near sweet as she turned to Jessalyn. "We'll work on tactics in the morning."

"Cassie, thanks. I appreciate the support." Jessalyn hoped it was enough and concentrated on standing her ground and embracing positivity. It was difficult when the urge to follow her mother and flee to Australia gnawed at her gut.

CHAPTER 19

Male Testosterone

U nexpectedly, the meeting was scheduled during the early afternoon, and it took place at a marae—the sacred meeting grounds—on the banks of the Waikato River.

"This marae is designated as neutral ground," Hone explained as the limousine they'd sent to collect Jessalyn pulled up outside. "Are you clear on the protocol?"

"Yes, I've got this." While her life had been outside the marae and the local community, she'd seen a pōwhiri—the Māori welcome—several times.

"All right. I'll let them know you've arrived. Cassie, sweetheart. If everything turns to shit, you get out of the marae. I'll come for you."

"Jessalyn will protect me," Cassie said.

The utter conviction in Cassie's voice had Jessalyn's stomach twisting. She inhaled and eased the breath out in slow increments.

"Jessalyn can't shift," Hone said.

"Go," Cassie ordered. "I promise to keep our baby and myself safe. I will not be that girl who acts with reckless abandon."

Jessalyn waited for Hone to leave before she exited the limousine. "Will this plan work?"

Cassie's invisible fingers squeezed Jessalyn's arm. "At the very least, it will keep them off balance."

"True that," Jessalyn murmured. "If this turns to shit, please follow Hone's orders. I'll do my best to protect you. I've been practicing my fire-breathing."

"Yep, I've watched. Most impressive. How come you don't burn your throat and face?"

A nervous giggle burst from Jessalyn. "A mystery. I wish my taniwha was awake. She's been silent."

"I am here!"

A gasp came from Cassie.

"Inside voice." Jessalyn straightened her shoulders. "Let's do this."

With her pulse racing, Jessalyn stalked to the carved gateway at the marae's entrance and waited for the men to notice her.

Manu and the myriad strangers no longer wore the garbs of

civilization. Each man was bare-chested and barefooted. They wore the traditional piupiu—a skirt made of dried flax—and the strands swished and parted, giving peek-a-boo sightings of hard male thighs. Dragon tattoos covered chests and backs, and tribal bands curled around biceps. Some of the men had moko or facial tattoos. Others wore cloaks to display their mana or carried a taiaha, which Jessalyn knew had been used as a weapon in the past. These days, the long wooden spears were for ceremonial purposes.

"Oh, my," Cassie whispered at her side. "What a pretty sight. Be still my heart."

"Beauty is skin deep," Jessalyn murmured, taking in the different faces amongst the crowd of taniwha warriors. She spotted Nelson Waaka, and anger expanded, writhing through her body like a fast-growing vine. Although she didn't have proof, Danny had died because of this man. Nelson's greed had led to this meeting. Her gaze crawled over the other men. They were equally to blame for this situation.

Manu.

Her heartbeat blipped when she sighted his bare chest. She continued her scan of faces, committing them to memory. Some men, she recognized from the pictures she and Cassie had discovered online.

"The sexy black beast," her taniwha whispered.

"He is not our friend today," Jessalyn murmured.

Manu parted from the mass of men, starting with the traditional pōwhiri or greeting issued when visitors came to the marae. Hone had told her to expect this, although this would be a male-only greeting. Manu pranced toward her, twirling his taiaha.

He stole her breath with his strong voice, his melodic words in the Māori language, and his traditional facial expressions of wide eyes and poking tongue. He approached and dropped a piece of greenery at her feet.

This was Jessalyn's signal to accept the token to show she came in peace. She gritted her teeth, knowing as all of them did, this situation held the potential to explode. Peace, indeed!

When Jessalyn stepped forward to scoop up the greenery as protocol demanded, an invisible Cassie began to sing a song in the Māori language. Jessalyn waited until Manu gestured her to advance, and he retreated deeper into the marae as she followed.

Jessalyn remained impassive, although she took pleasure from the uneasy looks exchanged amongst the men. *What kind of trickery is this?* She could practically hear their thoughts as she strode onto the marae. As she entered the large meeting house, Cassie's waiata, or song, trailed off.

"That is our seat over there," her taniwha said in disdain.

Jessalyn didn't reply but strode to the lone seat facing the crowd. She sat, and the men scrambled to take their own seats. Ah! Now that she studied the arrangement, she could see the five separate areas—one for each tribe.

In a traditional pōwhiri, there would be speeches and songs, and she—the visitor—would offer a koha or gift. They would greet each other with a hongi by pressing their noses together.

Not this time.

"They do not respect us," her taniwha stated.

Silence fell, and the slow-burning anger in the pit of Jessalyn's stomach flared higher.

"Calm," her taniwha whispered.

"Don't let them get to you," Cassie whispered. "Imagine them naked."

They were already half-naked. Imagining them nude pushed her mind to sex.

Her taniwha hissed, and Jessalyn forced herself to relax and wait.

Let the games begin.

Anxiety filled Manu as he studied Jessalyn. He couldn't read her mood, but he imagined she might feel overwhelmed at appearing amongst the people who'd rejected her half-blood pedigree. Perhaps smugness or a *take-that* thought or two. Definitely stress. Yet she broadcast none of her emotions to the crowd of judgy taniwha. Pride had settled on him as she'd walked onto the marae, her dignity and calm settling his taniwha's unease.

From the moment she'd left his place, he'd missed her presence, and his taniwha had moped. Stupid beast. Both of them needed their A-game today. And now, Hone had threatened him with dire consequences if Cassie got hurt in the crossfire. His two favorite ladies stood in danger today, and somehow, he had to trounce the leaders of the other tribes in such a way that the peace deals brokered half a century ago remained intact.

Yeah, he could do that without breaking a sweat.

"She is impressive," his brother Kahurangi said at his side. "She looks like a queen."

Nothing less than the truth. She wore a matching bronze jacket and trousers with a blouse that reminded him of the color of the full moon. The bronze of her suit made her eyes glow amber, and his tongue had tangled briefly while offering the welcome. Her black hair was long and loose but the front was braided, giving her a more feminine look. She wore the relic in the open, the bone-and-jade pendant attracting attention.

Nelson Waaka stood, cockiness in his expression and body language as he strutted his way to the front. He approached Jessalyn, and every muscle in Manu's body tensed.

"Stop there. No closer to the guardian."

Nelson halted at the barked order from Cassie. Manu restrained a laugh at the burst of astonished whispers.

"Her mouth didn't move," a man from his tribe whispered. The man's awe resounded through the tribes.

Manu had hesitated on hearing Cassie's suggestion via Hone, but now he was fiercely glad. If his invention gave Jessalyn an edge, all the better.

He leaned closer to Hone. "What other *magic* do they have in store?"

"They refused to tell me, but they have a strategy."

"You mock us with stunts and trickery," Nelson Waaka spat.

"You will respect the guardian," Cassie stated, her voice lower than normal. "Please begin. Others have the right to speak, and I do not wish to be here all night."

"Fuck." Hone tensed at his side, only relaxing when the audience of taniwha murmured their agreement.

"This woman comes from my tribe, and I demand you return her to us. She was engaged to one of my tribesmen, but someone murdered him during his visit to his fiancée. I believe a member of the Auckland tribe committed the murder, and I fear for her safety in this territory."

A wave of objections came from the audience, but Manu remained stone-faced, not rising to the bait.

"Quiet," Cassie ordered.

The men fell silent, most uneasy with this ghostly voice issuing orders. Jessalyn stared over the audience, her expression impassive, her carriage proud.

"Have you finished?" Cassie prompted.

"N-not yet." Nelson Waaka gathered himself. "The guardian was promised to my ancestor, and I believe that now the relic has reappeared, the holder..." He raked his gaze over Jessalyn, his distaste clear. "The holder of the relic should make good on her mother's promise." With his piece said Nelson returned to his seat.

Jason Hohepa, who led the southernmost tribe, rose and walked to the spot Nelson had recently vacated. "My name is Jason Hohepa, and I lead the Southern Otago tribe. I believe each tribe should choose a candidate as a prospective mate for the guardian."

He retreated, his position claimed by another leader.

"My name is Hemi Hoete. I'm the leader of the Southern Canterbury tribe. I agree with Jason Hohepa's suggestion.

The North Wairarapa leader repeated Jason's suggestion. Helpless to do anything else, Manu stood.

"My name is Manu Taniwha, and I'm responsible for the Auckland tribe. I have had the honor of meeting the guardian, and I believe her fair and able to make her own decision as to a mate." God, this politics crap was so hard. His taniwha growled softly, the sound ringing through Manu's head. They were of one accord. Each wanted to snatch Jess and take her to a place of safety where they could make love to her until she fell with child.

"Caveman, much," he muttered as he returned to his seat.

Shouts rang out, the various entourages shouting their opinions. Manu didn't take his gaze off Jess, worry for her curdling his gut. This situation would not end well. That, he knew with certainty.

Jessalyn rose, her contempt for them showing in the curl of her lips. She held up her right hand in a stop motion and waited for the shouting men to notice her demand for silence.

Finally, she rolled her eyes. "Enough!" she roared, her voice deeper than normal and holding a magnetic power that drew him.

Every other taniwha too. Several men gaped. Most regarded her with more respect, and they fell silent.

"I have listened to your posturing. I'm aware some of you wish to hold the relic and nothing will stop you in your quest. Lying. Stealing. Cheating. *Murder.*"

Jess's voice rang out, mesmerizing him and every man in the meeting house. He wanted this woman at his side but had no idea how to achieve his desire without causing a war. His shoulders drooped momentarily. Snatching her and fleeing to Australia looked good right now.

"You believe I should give up the relic because I bear mixed blood but understand this. The relic called me. The relic claimed me." She thumped her chest with her fist. "*Me.* A half-caste."

"Your mother cheated our tribe of the relic," Nelson shouted.

"Quiet!"

When the hubbub didn't die, Jess threw back her head and blew a stream of fire toward the ceiling of the meeting house. The flames danced along the carved ceiling before flickering out, and the scent of smoke filled the air. Shocked whispers, uneasy whispers, urgent whispers spread among the delegates.

Manu's admiration surged. While he'd seen her fire before, he'd never seen her control it in that manner.

"It is my preference not to ally myself with any tribe. The guardian should remain an impartial outsider, his or her presence for the benefit of every tribe. While this is my preference, I understand the Waaka tribe feels hard done by because of my mother's decision to marry another instead of going ahead with the arranged marriage. I understand they and others will not rest until I have a mate and the relic comes under *male* protection."

Her tone stressed the word *male* with disgust. She'd lost respect for the taniwha males present, and it showed in her demeanor.

"Each tribe will select two men—two candidates to put forward as my mate. I will let the relic choose from amongst those selected."

Shouts and protests filled the room.

Jess shot another stream of fire above their heads, and the flames arranged themselves in the shape of a fiery dragon. The meeting house grew quiet—the silence absolute.

"That is my final decision. Choose your candidates. I will wait outside in the sun. You and you." Jess pointed at Hone and a man from the Southern Otago tribe. "Bring ten chairs and arrange them outside in a line. When my alarm sounds in half an hour, your candidates will have their backsides on those chairs. After I switch off my alarm, any empty seats will remain that way."

With that announcement, Jess strode from the meeting house and disappeared outside.

Hone scooped up five chairs and followed in her wake, no doubt to check on Cassie.

"Who will you choose?" his father asked.

Manu stood and gestured his tribesman closer. "Volunteers?" he murmured.

"You, as the leader, must be a candidate," his father stated.

To Manu's relief, the others all radiated approval of the suggestion. "All right. One more from among the unmated males."

At least half of the men stepped back.

"I'm not sure I want this drama," one man said and joined the ranks of the mated.

The remaining ten men, including his two brothers Kahurangi and Tane, weren't exactly leaping to volunteer. Time was ticking, and Manu needed someone from his tribe at his side.

"Right." Manu came to a decision. "I'm giving you all a number. One. Two. Three." He continued around the group. "Change positions and mingle so you're out of order." He strode over to his father and his father's offsiders.

"Joseph," he said to the nearest man. "Pick a number between one and ten."

"Three," Joseph said.

Manu returned to the group. "Who was number three?"

Each of the men stepped back, leaving Kahurangi in the line of one.

"Crap," Kahurangi said. "My bad juju senses are spiking."

"Mine too," Manu muttered. "Let's go."

Manu exited the meeting house to find all but two chairs taken. Kahurangi took one, leaving the final on the end for him. Behind Manu, the other tribesmen flowed outside. Nelson Waaka and his oldest son sat near him and Kahurangi. Now a widower, the man was determined to seize the relic by honest competition or far worse. Fear took hold of Manu. He had no idea what Jess had planned. Whatever it was, he prayed it was enough to beat Nelson.

"You will remain behind this line," Cassie stated in a firm voice.

A stick floated from Jessalyn's side, and every taniwha watched as a line formed on the gravel between the row of chairs and the meeting house. Uneasy murmurs filled the air, and Manu ignored Kahurangi's elbow to his ribs. Surreptitiously, he dragged in a lungful of air and tested it for scent. There was nothing to suggest Cassie was behind the voice, even though he knew she was.

"Are you ready?" Jessalyn rose and removed the relic from around her neck.

Once again, the group of taniwha males fell silent, and Manu, along with the others, held his breath.

Jessalyn scanned the row of taniwha males. Each appeared interested. Eager. Curious. She met the gaze of Nelson Waaka who sneered at her, confidence oozing off the man who always snatched any prize he desired. Others backed down and made way for him because of his status.

His oldest son, Hika, sat at his side, and it was clear he held little respect for her either. Hika was several years older than her and had always treated her like something nasty on the sole of his boots.

Her stomach did a rollercoaster swoop, and she swallowed hard.

If her idea didn't work, she refused to mate with either male. Somehow, she'd escape their clutches. Her gaze darted back to Nelson, and she met his stony expression with a respectful nod. Never let it be said she didn't possess manners.

Nelson's scorn blazed in her direction, highlighted by his hands across his broad chest and his wide stance even when seated. Jessalyn fantasized about stalking over to him and slapping that derogatory attitude of his right off his ugly mug.

"He's wearing underwear," her taniwha whispered. *"Thank goodness. Bet his dick is as old and shriveled as his face. We're not letting it near us."*

She choked back a nervous laugh. *Pfft!* She needed to scrub her mind free of that thought.

"Focus," her taniwha chided. *"Let us begin."*

"You. Number One. Stand and state your name and tribe," Jessalyn said. Somehow, she kept her voice steady while inside, she was a whirling mass of anxiety and trepidation. What if her idea failed? What if she ended up trapped with a man she loathed, nothing more than a broodmare?

A tremor spread through her. What if a Waaka won her?

"John Ake. Southern Otago tribe."

Like all the ten chosen taniwha, he was a big, strong man in his prime.

"Unlike some of you," Jessalyn said. "I believe the relic chooses me to be its guardian. I also believe the relic will guide me to choose a worthy taniwha to stand at my side." At least, that was what she hoped. This idea of hers might go spectacularly wrong. "To that end, I will send the pendant to each of you. If the relic rejects you, please leave your position in the row and return to your tribesmen."

Jessalyn forced herself to meet the gaze of each of the ten chosen men. Last was Manu, and she couldn't read him. Her skin prickled, and she wrenched her gaze free, strangely breathless. She gave herself a mental shake.

"Let us begin." Jessalyn held the pendant until she bumped Cassie's invisible outstretched hand. "John Ake, hold out your right hand. Once the pendant settles on your palm, you may close your hand."

If Jessalyn hadn't known of Cassie's presence, she would've crossed herself against magic and evil spirits. Instead, she watched her pendant float through the air and drop onto John Ake's hand.

He closed his hand over the ancient bone and greenstone pendant, then let out a strangled yelp. The relic floated back to her and settled on her hand, and some of her tension drained away. She straightened further as confidence flowed through her.

This might just work.

"Number two," Jessalyn prompted as the first man rejoined the large group of taniwha. "Name and tribe."

"Arepeta Davis, Southern Otago."

"I'm standing right in front of you," Cassie whispered.

They made the transfer, and once again, the relic allowed Cassie to transport it to Arepeta Davis. He held the relic for longer, but then, he, too, released a shout of pain.

She and Cassie continued the process until there were four taniwha left: Hika and Nelson Waaka and Kahurangi and Manu.

Hika stood without Jessalyn's prompting. "Hika Waaka, Northland tribe."

The man held out his right hand with an arrogance that echoed his father's.

Cassie carried the pendant to Hika. Every taniwha focused on the unfolding scene, the pregnant silence sending ripples of unease skittering across Jessalyn's skin. Cassie dropped the relic on Hika's palm, and his strong fingers enclosed the bone. When nothing happened, a smug expression filled him, and he lifted his triumphant gaze.

His initial celebration left, and strain etched onto his handsome features. Smoke poured from the fist that clenched the relic. Hika fought. A growl burst from his straining throat, and he fell to his knees.

Whispers flooded the marae as the pendant slipped from Hika's grasp and darted back to Jessalyn. Hika slinked over to join his tribe.

Jessalyn swallowed and turned to Nelson Waaka.

The man showed not a shred of concern for his son. "Girl, you know who I am. Send the relic."

Nelson was fit, and she supposed handsome for his age. He had myriad tattoos etched into his skin. Still confident. Overconfident, actually, after his son's failure. Avarice hardened his features along with impatience.

"Please don't let the relic choose him. *Please,*" she muttered under her breath. Reaching up to seek the calming touch of her pendant, her hand froze halfway to her neck when she remembered she wasn't wearing the relic. Instead, she rolled her shoulders in a quick release of tension.

Cassie walked toward Nelson. Halfway to the man, the relic lifted off her hand and floated back to Jessalyn.

Someone from amongst the group of taniwha laughed, and Nelson snarled his displeasure.

"Give me a proper opportunity," he snapped.

Jessalyn handed the relic to Cassie. She walked two steps this time before the pendant sailed to Jessalyn.

"Stop fooling around," Nelson snarled at her. His beast glittered in his eyes as enraged as his human side.

"I'll take it myself," Jessalyn murmured.

She ambled toward the man, each step slow and steady. His top lip curled, indicating his lack of respect for her, which was on par with his treatment of other women. In his imperious way, he stuck out his left hand and waited for her to give him the relic.

Tension filled her limbs, an unwillingness to hand over the pendant. She wet her lips, knowing she had to continue despite every part of her screaming this was wrong.

"Go on, girl."

His words, his expression taunted her and goaded her to rudeness.

Jessalyn inhaled and let the pendant settle on his palm, managing not to touch him during the transfer. She turned and strode away from the man, her skin writhing in aversion at his proximity.

Behind her, a man laughed. A second man laughed. An infuriated roar had her whirling. Oh! The relic had followed her back.

Her taniwha sniffed. *The relic refused that taniwha outright.*

Nelson's face flushed and Jessalyn saw the whites of his eyes. His chest swelled, his nostrils flared, and his lip curled upward to display his sharp teeth. "I will have the relic!" Nelson thundered.

Uh-oh. Jessalyn backed up as Nelson's taniwha exploded from his body—an olive-green beast with malicious intent.

"Kahurangi!" Manu shouted.

Manu sprinted toward her, flinging his body to cover hers as Nelson spat fire.

A red dragon attacked from the side, shoving Nelson before he could gather breath for more fire.

Manu had fallen, burned by Nelson's flames. Jessalyn rushed to him, anger filling her on seeing the blisters already forming on his bare chest. His piupiu bore scorch marks, and several flax strands had dropped free of the waistband to reveal his black undershorts.

Her right hand fluttered as she hesitated. Jessalyn was unsure of what to do to help him. Cold water. They needed to get cold water on the burns. The relic floated before her, nudging her hand, and the sudden coolness coming from the pendant gave her an idea. Obeying her instinct, she pressed the relic to his burned skin. Manu moaned, and she feared the worst, but when she lifted the pendant, the blisters had vanished. Quickly, she repeated the move, doctoring Manu's burns, even as she marveled at this miracle. With the process completed and reassured by the lack of pain on his face, she hung the relic around her neck and rose slowly to face Nelson.

An edgy, twitchy sensation crawled through her mind, her vision narrowing in on the green dragon until it was as if she stared through a tunnel. Confidence and strength had her standing tall. If Nelson wanted a fight, she'd play dirty too. Her pulse raced, and heat roared through her. She flung off her jacket and stomped over to the green dragon.

Following instinct, she summoned her fire and let rip.

Her flames shot into the green dragon's face. Everyone froze. A glance at the main group of taniwha showed their clear astonishment at her abilities. Shock, intrigue, and curiosity collectively etched into their features.

From the corner of her eye, she spotted another dragon. A green one. *Hika Waaka.*

Jessalyn backed up a wary step. Her party trick might work

once, but her ability to spit fire weakened the more she did it. She required rest between her fire-breathing sessions. And for her next trick...

Heat crawled across her skin, burning her from the inside.

"Let's do this!" her taniwha shouted.

Before Jessalyn could scold her dragon, the pressure on her skin increased. Her body seemed to swell, and panic flooded her mind when her clothes ripped at the seams.

Her taniwha whooped. *"Never fear, taniwha is here!"*

Before Jessalyn could ask, her bones cracked. The sounds had a croak of disbelief escaping while panic had her squeezing her eyes shut and hoping for the best. Her rapid breaths came close to hyperventilation as her garments tore under the stress, falling to the ground and leaving her naked.

Unexpectedly, the pressure gave. The murmur of voices, the amazement, and the shock had her eyes opening. She glanced down from a greater height than normal and spied pale limbs and lustrous scales the color of the moon.

"OMG!" a voice blasted through her mind. *"We're gorgeous!"*

Jessalyn turned her body, all sleek elegance despite her larger size. She stretched out her arms—wings. She had wings!

What the heck did she do now?

"We fly. We attack. We punish," her taniwha stated.

"For Danny," Jessalyn thought.

The two green dragons flew at her, their talons outstretched. She dodged one, but the other gouged her shoulder. Temper rushed through her ears, and she let instinct and her taniwha take over.

Jessalyn flapped her wings and lifted off. She did a slow circle to maneuver and started when she discovered five other dragons flying at her back. A red dragon. Two blacks. A gray and a royal-blue.

"Friend," her taniwha stated. *"Attack!"*

Despite the fear stalking her mind, she darted at the two green dragons, trumpeting her fury at their audacity in trying to claim her and the relic. Determination had her holding her course. She inhaled and released the breath in a roar of fire. Instead of pulling back, she flew through the flames and smoke, attacking with her claws. She collided, the body contact rattling her teeth.

One of the green dragons toppled, and the other issued a keening cry. It flew after the falling dragon.

Jessalyn hovered, waiting for the smoke to clear and for any other dragons to decide to attack. Not a single strike came. She continued to hang in the air, the tiring exertion making her muscles shudder with fatigue.

A black dragon glided from the group of taniwha who had joined the battle. Jessalyn tensed, but the taniwha didn't attack. He approached with caution.

Jessalyn felt her eyes blink. Her eyelashes flutter.

"There's my sexy black beast!"

Jessalyn cringed, but the black dragon opened its maw and

trumpeted out a roar. He flew to her and gently nudged her with his head, silently directing her back to the land. *"Time to rest now, sweetheart."*

Instinct had her flapping her tired wings and gliding after him. Her landing was more of a stumble than anything, but at least she managed not to face-plant. Reaction set in, and a tremor slid through her massive body.

"We're so pretty," her taniwha crowed. *"In both forms."*

"I'm glad you're pleased with us, but we have no clothes. You ruined our new outfit."

Manu shifted back to human form, apparently unconcerned with his naked state. The other dragons who had flown with her settled on the open space near them. They also shifted while she hesitated.

"You don't expect her to shift with all these men gawking at her," Cassie's voice said from her right. "Find her some clothes and go and have a cup of tea or something to calm your nerves."

Kahurangi chuckled, unfazed by the invisible voice ordering them around. "A beer might hit the spot."

"I could do with something stronger than tea," Jason Hohepa said. "If I hadn't seen that with my own eyes, I wouldn't have believed it. Wait until I tell my tribe."

He and Kahurangi drifted toward the building to the right of the meeting house and most of the other men followed.

"Move along," Cassie snapped. "Nothing to see here."

The rest of the men peered around uneasily, and when Cassie growled, they moved with alacrity until Hone and Manu remained.

"Why didn't you tell me you could shift?" Manu asked. He sounded hurt she'd keep this from him.

Jessalyn rubbed his shoulder with her head. *I had no idea.*

Manu's hand smoothed over her shoulder. Her scales tingled beneath his touch. "Jess, you'll set tongues wagging amongst the taniwha tribes. Not only are you a rare white and the same color as the original taniwha, but you have skills and powers no one has ever witnessed."

"Get the girl some clothes," Cassie ordered. "And the pair of you should cover up. All this male goodness is too much for a pregnant woman."

"Cassie!" Hone said, but there was laughter in his tone.

"You're pregnant?" Manu asked. At Hone's broad grin, Manu drew him in for a man-hug. "Congratulations to both of you. Emma must be excited she'll have playmates for her kids."

"You're the first ones to know after Hone," Cassie said. "We'll tell Emma and Jack tomorrow."

"I have gym gear in my vehicle," Hone said. "It will be big on you, but it is clean."

"I can guarantee that," Cassie said. "I cured him of stinky gym clothes."

Um. Okay. She had clothes, but how the devil did she get back to her normal size so she could wear them? *"How do I get back to a human form?"*

Manu laughed, the joyous chortle of a happy man, and her taniwha purred in reply. Jessalyn smooched his shoulder, and his hand caressed her scales. Her taniwha purred even louder.

"When the pair of you have finished." Cassie cleared her throat. "Jessalyn, you still have work to do."

A reminder that her problem remained—the tribes fighting over her like a group of determined women during a sale at a designer store.

Jessalyn backed away from Manu. *"Tell me how to shift! I require a nap. I am tired!"*

She cringed. *"Inside voice,"* she reminded her taniwha. Maybe soon, they'd become comfortable in their working relationship, but some days Jessalyn struggled to deal with her toddler of a dragon.

Cassie giggled while Manu and Hone shared a grin.

"The shifting process is easy. Think of seeing yourself in a mirror," Manu said. "Imagine your reflection and what you look like and keep focusing on it. We'd better step back. Cassie, stay next to Hone so we know where you are. Jess, are you imagining that? You'll find once you fix the image in your mind, your taniwha will pay attention and help you focus on your task."

A pain streaked along her spine, and the image in her mind fractured.

"Keep concentrating. Push away the discomfort," Manu ordered.

Discomfort? Had a kiwi pecked his brain? It was bloody agony. Jessalyn nodded her taniwha head and got sidetracked when she and her taniwha studied her moonglow-white scales. They were so pretty.

"Jess! Focus. As Cassie pointed out, you have things to do."

Hearing the urgency in him, Jessalyn pulled up a vision of herself again and attempted to breathe through the beginning twinges and the fiery aches that soon followed. Then—to her great relief—the cracks and reshaping started. Her transformation was much slower than Manu's and Hone's, the aches and throbbing soreness lingering.

Finally, she stood in front of Manu, naked and trembling from the shift.

"Please tell me that gets easier," she said.

Manu folded his arms around her trembling body. "It gets easier."

She frowned at him. "I'm unsure if I should believe you or not."

"Here are the clothes," Hone said.

Jessalyn gratefully pulled a green T-shirt over her head and stepped into a gray pair of sweatpants.

Cassie started laughing.

"What?"

"Hone, you couldn't have picked a better T-shirt for Jessalyn."

Jessalyn pulled the shirt away from her chest and read, *I'm not in a bad mood. Everyone is just annoying.* "Works for me," she said. "Let's do this."

The chatter coming from the smaller building next to the biggest meeting house was louder and more natural. Men shooting the breeze.

"Hold the door for me," Cassie whispered at her side. "I've got to witness whatever happens next so I can report back to Emma."

"Stand against the wall so no one tries to walk through you," Jessalyn murmured back.

Most men sat with members of their own tribes, but a few mingled, taking seats at several of the long tables with the bench seats. Huge platters held sandwiches and most taniwha had a beer bottle clasped in their hands. Conversation ceased when she entered after Manu and Hone.

A loud groan—the sound of a man in pain had Jessalyn turning in that direction. Hika Waaka lay on the ground, one of his legs bent in an unnatural position. His chest bore scrapes and cuts, one on his right shoulder deep and oozing blood. She strode over to the groaning man.

"This is your fault, woman." Nelson Waaka fired the words at her like Māori spears intended to wound the enemy. He flung out his hand as if he intended to stop her from coming closer to him and his son.

The relic cooled against her skin, and she lifted the cord over her head. She walked around Nelson and crouched by his son. "Let me try to heal some of your wounds."

"Why would you help me?" Hika asked, his words strained. "I've always treated you with disdain because of your mixed blood."

"I am the guardian. I care for all my people," Jessalyn said. "Let me help."

Hika's head jerked in assent, but every muscle in his body tensed as if he feared she'd injure him further. She laid the relic over the worst of his wounds—the one on his shoulder—and held it there. To her awe and amazement, the flesh knitted together. Healing Manu hadn't been a fluke. Once the injury transformed from an angry red to a healthier pink, she moved on to the next wound. Finally, she tackled his damaged leg.

"My taniwha is healing us, but his exhaustion means it's a slow process," Hika explained, less confrontational now.

"You'll need someone to hold the limb in the correct position," Manu said from behind her. "Will you let me help?"

"Here's what I want to do," she said to Manu and Wiremu, one of Hika's friends. "I'll use the relic to numb the pain a fraction. You must pull his leg into the correct position, and I'll attempt to heal it."

Jessalyn made no mention of the extreme lethargy that had crept into her, sinking to her bones. The healing sapped her strength. Still, Hika was in pain. She could rest and hopefully recover soon.

The relic settled on the site of the break and cooled beneath her fingers. Hika let out a sigh that turned into a groan when Manu and Wiremu carefully repositioned the bone. It took long minutes before the tension left Hika, and his muscles relaxed.

Jessalyn nodded at Manu and Wiremu and concentrated on holding herself upright. It was obvious the healing weakened her body. A problem. If the taniwha leaders learned of this limitation, it gave them a weapon.

"Sugar," her taniwha whispered.

Excellent idea. "Could I have a pot of tea, please? I'd like tea with milk and plenty of sugar."

"I'll make you tea," Wiremu said and hurried to the kitchen area at the end of the long room.

Jessalyn walked around the scowling Nelson and sank onto the nearest empty seat, unsure if her knees would continue to hold her upright.

"Thank you," Hika said, sounding genuine and grateful. "The discomfort is minimal now."

Jessalyn slipped the cord of the pendant back over her head. Wiremu returned in an impossibly quick time with a tray. He'd made a pot of tea and added a milk jug and a rose-patterned cup and saucer—the type grandmas produced from their china cabinets. He'd also included a matching plate of chocolate biscuits.

"The tea won't be ready yet," he said. "I can get you a can of L & P meantime."

The citrus-flavored soda made in the New Zealand town of

Paeroa appealed to Jessalyn. The lemon tang, along with the sugar content, might help to cure this pervading weakness. "That sounds perfect."

As soon as Wiremu produced the glass of soda, she swallowed the contents, the tart sweetness soothing and just the thing. It didn't take her long to finish the entire can.

"Are you intending to heal my hands?" Nelson Waaka shouted into the low murmur of male voices.

"Dad!" Hika protested.

"Can't you see she's exhausted?" another of the nearby men said.

"She injured me. She should fix it," Nelson countered, his jaw sticking out in a pugnacious manner.

Jessalyn glowered at the man with dislike. If he'd ever seen her and her father in Piha, he'd crossed the street to avoid them. Unplanned meetings between her and Nelson had always ended with rudeness on his side. She'd done her best to avoid the man and the other family members. In a small community, that hadn't always been possible.

"More sugar," her taniwha said.

Jessalyn picked up one of the chocolate biscuits and popped it into her mouth. She swallowed, almost moaning at the energy hit. "Is my tea ready?"

Wiremu added a dash of milk to the cup and topped it up with strong tea. He added three spoons of sugar and stirred the liquid before handing it over. Jessalyn took a sip and then another.

"Thank you." She finished the cup and smiled her thanks when Wiremu produced the teapot. Praying her legs would hold her upright, she rose and walked over to Nelson, where he stood by himself near a smaller table for four. Her right leg ached, and she focused on even strides and concealing her limp.

"Show me your wounds," she said.

The sneer on Nelson's face never shifted as he held out his hand for her to observe. Unease slid through her seconds before Nelson grabbed her and produced a knife. He held it to her neck, hauling her toward the door with easy strength.

"Dad!" Hika shouted. "Don't be stupid."

Several of the other men shot to their feet while Hone and Manu advanced on her and Nelson.

"Stay where you are," he warned, and thankfully, his knife hand lowered a fraction. "If you come any closer, I'll slit her neck."

Jessalyn froze, fear pumping through her muscles. A warm breath near her ear had her twitching.

"He's flipped. I'll jab his hand and hope he drops it," Cassie whispered. "Best I can do. Be ready."

Jessalyn agreed with Cassie's assessment. The man's eyes bore a crazed glint. Either he hadn't considered the consequences, or he didn't care. She let him tug her toward the door because, with his concentration split, he'd shifted the knife downward.

An unearthly howl rippled from him. Blood spurted from his right arm, and the knife clattered to the ground. Jessalyn stomped on his bare foot, pleased to propel another pained shout from the man. Manu, Hone, and Wiremu rushed to restrain Nelson while Jessalyn beat a quick retreat.

"Sugar," her taniwha whined.

"More tea," she announced and hustled back to her tray. She shoved a chocolate biscuit into her mouth and washed it down with hot tea. She glanced up on hearing a *whoosh*. A glowing sword floated past her and toward the chair where Hika now sat. To her right, Nelson threw back his head, and an anguished howl emerged. Manu and Hone had released him and now Hika's friends kept him prisoner. Nelson fought the three taniwha restraining him, struggling to follow the weapon.

"No. No!" Nelson screeched.

She and the other taniwha watched the sword press against Hika's chest and melt into his flesh.

A sob burst from Nelson, and the fight seeped from him.

"Heal his hand," her taniwha ordered. *"Show him mercy."*

The second cup of sweet tea and a biscuit had helped. Jessalyn's energy levels were stronger and her strides measured as she wove in and out of the tables to reach him.

"Let me see your hand," she ordered.

When he stared at her, one of the taniwha holding him forced him to extend his hand. His flesh on the back looked as if someone had pounded it full of nails and then removed the iron spikes. Jessalyn hurriedly laid the relic on it, and coolness spread up her arm. When she lifted the relic, his hand was no longer a bloody mess, but the newly healed skin bore the same manaia as her pendant.

Nelson never spoke, but she glimpsed the respect in the eyes of the two taniwha who held him prisoner.

Jessalyn returned to her tea and drank another cup.

"It is time," her taniwha said. *"I need sleep."*

"All right." Jessalyn set her cup down with a clink. She stood. "I am going home now, but before I leave, I have something to say." She waited until she was the center of attention. "I am the guardian of the relic. Although I come from the area of the Northern tribe, I claim allegiance to no tribe, and no one tribe may rule over me. Instead, I belong to all five tribes in New Zealand. Even if I marry—whether I marry a human or a taniwha—I will remain neutral. You cannot use me as a bargaining chip.

"The original taniwha guided the first canoe to New Zealand, hoping to find a new and better world. We have prospered here in the land of the long white cloud. All of us. We have adapted to new ways and must continue to change to fit in this modern world. We must follow the taniwha's legacy of peace and unity and not let greed blind us to the right path.

"I will visit all and offer service, but I bow to no man or woman. I am my own taniwha and will remain outside the tribal system. That will make the powers of the relic available to all, should they have a need.

"If you have any questions or concerns, please nominate one spokesman per tribe. I will see these spokesmen at two o'clock tomorrow afternoon. That is all."

Jessalyn strode from the building with her shoulders back, and her head held high. Despite her casual attire, she aimed for dignity and prayed she wouldn't fall flat on her face.

CHAPTER 20

Jessalyn Lays Down The Law

Manu rushed after Jess with Kahurangi and Hone on his heels. He found Jessalyn staggering toward the parking lot and obviously leaning on someone.

"Stand back, Cassie. I've got her."

Manu scooped her off her feet and strode toward his truck. Kahurangi jogged ahead and opened the doors.

"Sweetheart, you should've admitted your fatigue."

"Couldn't let them see me weak. Pride."

"You were incredible," Kahurangi said.

"Jessalyn," Cassie said, still invisible. I'll visit you tomorrow. Will you be at Manu's house?"

"Hopefully, I'll be working on my carving, so you should find me at Manu's warehouse," Jess said.

"You should rest," Manu said. His mate looked exhausted, and no wonder, given she'd stopped a war between the tribes and garnered respect in the process.

"Carving wood is restful for me," Jess said. "I'm terrible at sitting around and doing nothing. I like to keep busy."

"Oh!" Cassie sounded excited, a little breathless. "Manu, can I visit Jessalyn at your warehouse? I'd like to write a song to commemorate today. The ballad of Jessalyn. Can I do that? Can I?"

Manu grinned at her enthusiasm. Jess exchanged a glance with him and checked Kahurangi's and Hone's reactions.

"Even if a human listened to the song, they'd think it was fiction. I was there and participated, yet it doesn't feel real," Jess pointed out.

"Write your song," Manu said. "But I and the other taniwha leaders will want to hear your completed version before you go public with it."

"Deal," Cassie said with enthusiasm. "Hone, we should go home."

"Cassie, don't forget to add in your part in the battle," Jess said.

Cassie's laughter drifted on the air as Hone headed for his SUV. Kahurangi climbed in the rear seat while Manu settled Jess in the front. He clicked the seatbelt for her and closed the door. By the time he rounded the hood and settled in the driver's seat, her eyes were closed, and it sounded as if she was asleep.

"She's amazing," Kahurangi murmured.

"Yes, she is," Manu agreed. "She stopped a bloody war today."

"And garnered the respect of the tribal leaders with her healing powers."

Manu nodded, a bit shaky, as he considered everything that could've gone wrong. He sucked in a breath and started his vehicle.

"She's your mate," Kahurangi said.

"Yes, but I don't think she feels the same way."

"Bull crap," his younger brother said. "She likes and trusts you. You sexy, black beast, you."

Manu glanced at Jess and laughed. "Heard that, did you?"

"It was hard not to hear. I think most of those present got an earful of her taniwha. Her taniwha accepts your beast and flutters her eyelashes at you. She understands the mate concept, but don't you see? Jess's half-European blood combined with her Māori half is what makes her special. She laid down the law before she left and earned their respect because now they understand she won't stand for their posturing. Court her. Take her on dates like a regular human male instead of dragging her to bed and huffing and puffing like a typical taniwha."

Humor shaded Kahurangi's advice, and Manu snorted. "If you're huffing and puffing, it's no wonder you're still single."

"So what have you done so far, smartarse?"

"I took Jess on a flight to Great Barrier Island. We had a picnic on a private beach and watched the stars." Manu tried not to sound smug but suspected he'd failed.

"Damn!" Kahurangi sounded impressed. "I need to up my game."

"Are you still job-hunting?"

"Yeah. The garage owner refuses to give me a reference."

"You shouldn't have fucked with his wife."

"I didn't know she was his wife, and I didn't fuck her. Her scent repelled me."

Honesty rang in his brother, and Manu believed him. "I'm ready to go to market with my stealth unit. None of the taniwha suspected Cassie's presence, or that she was the invisible voice, so I've got the right balance for masking scent. It's not the mechanic work you prefer, but would you like to help me with sales?"

"What about Tane? He hates his job," Kahurangi said.

"I intend to ask him too. I've decided to rent the units and have fitted kill switches to use if a taniwha uses them unlawfully. Taniwha must apply to rent a unit, and the rental period will be weekly at first because I suspect the demand will be high."

"You've considered this carefully," Kahurangi said. "How much will you charge?"

"I want every taniwha to fly unhindered, not just the rich, so I thought I'd offer a discount on one unit each week. I'll keep the other units at one thousand dollars per week."

"Considering the years you've spent designing your units, that is peanuts. Are you sure that is enough?"

"I don't need the money. I have plenty."

Kahurangi laughed. "Sucks to be you."

Manu sobered. "It does. I had to execute our mother."

"Manu! We've discussed this. She gave you no choice. Even Dad, deep down, understands. She placed you in an intolerable situation. We loved her. All of us, despite her faults but look at it this way. If she had worn your shoes, she wouldn't have hesitated to kill you. She wouldn't have given it a second thought and would've strutted around afterward, trumpeting her tough stance and the greater good. You know this, Manu. She would've killed you—her son—without a blink. Hell, she tried to kill me and Tane when we attempted to stop her from flying to Cassie's place in Clevedon. Forgive yourself and move on. The tribal sword passed to you before this happened, just as Nelson's passed to Hika today. The sword of leadership never stays with an unworthy leader."

Manu indicated agreement because his mind understood the logic, but his heart... His heart mourned the mother he'd lost who'd taught him and his brothers right from wrong and turned them into half-decent men.

"Mum was old-fashioned in her ways. Already, the tribe is prospering from some of your changes. The young kids have a purpose. Once the tribes learn of your stealth units, they'll be beside themselves." Kahurangi's tone turned sly. "And your mana will grow when they see you've wooed and won the guardian."

Manu dropped Kahurangi off at the family home before turning his vehicle toward his house. Jess slept still and didn't wake until he pulled into his garage and used the remote to close the door.

She stretched and blinked at him like a sleepy ruru.

"We're home," he said. "Come on. Let's get you fed and into bed. Shifting exhausted me at first."

"I feel as if a truck flattened me. Every muscle in my body hurts."

Manu wrapped his arm around her waist, and when she staggered, he scooped her off her feet and carried her inside. He set her down in the kitchen. "I'd suggest you have a bath, but I don't want you to fall asleep and drown."

She frowned. "I guess I can find my own place now that Nelson Waaka is no longer in charge."

"I enjoy having you here," Manu said, his heart racing at her declaration. She couldn't leave him. "Jess." He waited until her eyes focused on his face. "I care for you. I want you in my life and, if you agree, my bed. You've gained my respect, and I like you. A lot." There. He couldn't speak any plainer.

The truth—in this short space of time, he'd fallen for her. He loved Jess although she wasn't ready to hear his declaration. He watched her, eager for her reply and working hard not to fidget.

"*Woohoo!*" her taniwha shrieked.

A tremulous smile formed on Jess's sexy lips. "I like you too."

"Excellent. We've settled that then. Can you manage a shower on your own while I cook dinner?"

"The wall will prop me up," she said with a yawn. "I'm starving."

Manu watched her stumble away and waited until the shower started running. He bustled around the kitchen and popped a cottage pie in the oven. He pulled a packet of snap-frozen vegetables from the freezer and got them ready to microwave. For dessert, he had a red velvet cake, and he was glad he'd thought to stock up the fridge before he'd left for today's meeting.

The shower switched off before he checked on her, and he figured her hunger kept her upright. She burst into the kitchen, a towel wrapped around her dripping body.

"Manu," she said, her expression determined.

His stomach swooped in sudden fear, and he swallowed. He had to clear his throat before he could speak. "Yes?"

"I've been thinking about what you said. I don't like you."

His stomach dropped, and his shoulders slumped. His taniwha's growl of displeasure broke free and echoed in the kitchen.

"I love you," she continued. "We haven't known each other long, but you're the first person I think of when I wake in the morning. Nelson shifting to his dragon horrified me, but my terror magnified when he spat his fire. His hurting you made me furious, and that is when my taniwha exploded from me. I care for you too, but it is with love and friendship. If you don't feel the same way, I understand, but I had to be honest and tell you."

Manu stared at the fierce woman standing before him in a towel. His warrior woman. "Jess," he finally said with reverence. "I love you so hard. *So much*. My taniwha claimed you as his mate when we first met, and my human side toppled into love with you not long after."

"Why didn't you say something?"

"I wanted to give you time to get used to me. And then the guardian stuff got in the way. It wasn't right to tell you my taniwha had claimed you when you were already under so much pressure."

"Were you going to tell me?" she demanded.

"I'd decided to ask you out on dates and give you more time. The last thing I wanted was for you to suspect your guardian powers were the attraction. I wanted *you* before I learned any of this. You're pretty and determined. You have courage, and the more I learned, the more I liked and admired you."

"I'd enjoy dating," she said. "I've never had that."

"Another reason to romance you," he said.

"Feeding me would be an excellent start. I'll dress."

She returned shortly after, and Manu closed the distance between them and hugged her.

Jess held him as tightly. "Mine," she said with a sigh of contentment.

"Yours," he agreed, laughter filling him.

The taniwha women often grumbled because of the he-man

mentality and the bossiness of the males of their species. His Jess moved a step ahead of his less agile he-man thoughts.

He pulled away a fraction. "Just so you know, I want to marry you. Not straightaway because you need the freedom to find your feet."

"Yes," she said. "Excellent plan. What have you cooked me for dinner? Lots of delicious meat?"

"No kiss?" Manu held back his laughter with difficulty. "To seal our promises of a future together."

Her belly gave a thunderous rumble. "My legs feel like cooked noodles, and only your grasp on my shoulders and feminine determination is keeping me upright. I'm desperate for food."

Manu guided her to the breakfast counter where he'd set two places. He grabbed a can of soft drink from the fridge for her and studied the contents since the cottage pie required another ten minutes to cook. Ah!

He gathered a pot of hummus and a packet of crackers. In seconds, he had several on a plate for her, along with some cheese.

"Thanks!" She fluttered her eyelashes at him and beamed before falling on the food. A sense of contentment filled Manu while he put the vegetables in the microwave. Looking after Jess made him happy. Making love with her was better, but there was a soul-deep satisfaction in making certain she ate and rested.

The oven timer dinged, and Manu removed the pie. He served a portion with the vegetables and handed it to Jess before getting his own. He sat beside her.

"This is delicious."

"I can't take the credit. One of the ladies in the tribe makes them."

"You should hire her as our housekeeper. Does she cook cakes and biscuits?"

"She made our dessert. Red velvet cake."

"Can you afford a housekeeper? I can help once I get a job, but Cassie said I can't go around in jeans and a T-shirt all the time. I have to buy clothes. She said people judge, and first appearances are everything. That and confidence."

"We should be able to swing enough money for a housekeeper," he said, holding back a laugh. That was one problem he didn't have. "I could give you money for clothes."

"No. I prefer to buy my own things. Something Dad taught me." She forked up a mouthful of pie. "I think I've finished being angry at him for not telling me about my... About Karen. The mortgage." She sighed. "My biggest regret is not being able to get to know my brother and sister. Maybe one day."

"They'll want to meet you," Manu said. "If it were me, the abrupt move to Australia and leaving friends would've made me stubborn and curious. I bet they're asking questions. You and your siblings looked alike."

Jess shrugged. "Perhaps."

"Are you certain I can't lend you money for new clothes?"

"No," Jess said. "I'll pay for them myself. I know! If you want to pay for something, you can foot the bill for the food."

Manu chuckled. "Smartarse."

Jess went to bed straight after dinner, and by the time Manu cleared the kitchen and joined her, she was sound asleep. He stripped, slipped between the sheets, and embraced her. Jess never stirred, but Manu smiled, that contentment and satisfaction blooming in his heart again.

His mate.

Her role as the guardian would bring challenges for both of them, but if they could have private dinners and quiet moments together, he'd be more than pleased with his lot.

A kiss on her shoulder brought Jessalyn awake. "What time is it?"

"Eight-thirty."

"I guess it's time to get up."

"Not yet," Manu said. "How are you?"

"Much better, although I could eat."

"Newsflash," Manu said. "Did you realize a tattoo has formed on your back?"

"What? Really? Let me see." Jessalyn hurried for the en suite and the big mirror. "There really is a tattoo on my back. *Ooh!* When can I practice flying?"

Manu laughed.

"What's wrong?"

"I've said it before. I know where your taniwha's inspiration for her chattiness comes from," he said. "Turn around. Let me get a good look at your tattoo."

Jessalyn obediently turned. The delicate caress of his finger over her back made her shiver with delight.

He laughed again.

"What now?"

"Your taniwha winked and blew me a kiss."

"She can move in her tattoo form too?"

"If she wants to reposition. Mostly they sleep. Come back to bed."

His heavy-lidded gaze hinted at what he had in mind. A tingle sprang to life between her thighs as she crawled back into bed. An instant later, his lips claimed hers.

Jessalyn sighed against his mouth, thrilled with the force of hard muscles and the press of his cock. A thought occurred, and she pulled back to frown at him. "Did the guardian guide me to you? I mean, you were the perfect person to help me through my confusion. Even though you acted grumpily, you never turned your back. The fire-breathing scared me half to death, and your directions calmed me."

"I was terrified, too," Manu said drily. "My taniwha decided he wanted you—an out-of-control dragon who didn't recognize her species. Not your fault, I know, but still confusing for both of us and our taniwha."

Jessalyn kissed the tip of his nose. "Luckily for you, I'm a quick learner."

"I'm proud of you. Most people would've buckled under the pressure. You're strong, and I have every confidence you'll make this guardian position your own."

Exhilaration sped through her at his praise, his belief in her. If she hadn't sold her father's vehicle and had stayed in Piha, things might have gone differently. She wriggled against him, drawing a husky groan from her lover.

She sought his mouth and tried to show him the depths of her emotions. They ran deep—she admitted that—but selfishly, she wanted dates and to learn the small, intimate things about him.

"Mine. Mine. Mine!" her taniwha cried, thankfully in an inside voice.

A groan escaped when Manu lifted and repositioned her body. Now, she gazed up at his sparkling eyes. One of his hands caressed her breast, and she moaned at the hint of pain that reverberated through her when he pinched her nipple. She kissed his neck, his shoulder and dug her fingernails into his back, urging him to hurry.

"Now," she urged.

"Not yet," he countered and moved down her torso.

He nibbled on her hipbone and rimmed her belly button with his tongue. His eyes gleamed as he glanced up at her, his mouth wreathed in happiness. Her heart turned over at the sincerity, the openness in him, and love. The emotion blazed from him as he maintained their visual connection and lowered his mouth with intent.

Her eyes fluttered shut, and seconds later, the warmth of his mouth teased at her slit. He used firm pressure on her nub before backing off. Instead, he pushed a finger inside her and stroked her. He hit the perfect spot, and pleasure roared through her—not the main event but a precursor of what would come.

"Manu," she whispered, a pleading in his name.

Manu gave her clit another slow lick before he rose up her body and kissed her. Their lips clung, and she gripped his broad shoulders, holding him to her.

"Happy. So happy," her taniwha whispered.

Jessalyn smiled against his lips, and he parted their mouths to regard her quizzically.

"Inside joke," she said.

Manu grinned. "My taniwha is communicating happiness too."

"Did you hear?"

"I guessed." Manu reached over and plucked a strip of condoms from the bedside drawer. He discarded all but one. An instant later, he rolled onto his back and lifted her over him.

She stared at him, startled for an instant.

"I want to see your expression when you come." His grin was decidedly naughty. "And I'd love to watch your tits bounce."

A laugh burst from Jessalyn. She guided his cock to her and slid down, impaling herself with a sensual twist of her hips. Setting the pace exhilarated her, and she experimented with slow and fast, all the time under his appreciative gaze.

Manu lifted her off him, and she groaned, empty and unfulfilled. He rearranged her on her hands and knees.

"You'll get an excellent view of my backside from that angle."

"Yes," he said, unrepentant. "In this position, I get to tease you, and I can watch the antics of your sexy taniwha."

She glanced over her shoulder, and his gaze was more golden than usual and full of heat. He notched his cock to her entrance and pushed inside her. One of his hands cupped a breast while the other traced a pattern on her back.

A purr burst from her when he began purposeful strokes. Instinct had her reaching to massage her clit.

"That's it," he said. "Jess, you feel so good squeezing my cock."

She tightened her internal muscles and laughed at his groan. One sweep later over her clit and she was coming. Manu quickened his thrusts before he, too, shuddered with his orgasm.

Long moments later, Manu separated their bodies. He removed the condom and drew her into his arms. A safe harbor.

The two o'clock meeting arrived before Jessalyn was fully ready. Deciding a neutral place for a meeting would work in her favor, she booked the private meeting room of the local McDonald's fast-food restaurant. While Hone had cackled like a hyena when she'd asked for his help, he'd agreed to her logic once she'd explained her choice.

Food to keep the taniwha happy and a public place amongst humans to ensure everyone behaved with decorum.

This time, dressed in a pale blue sundress that reminded her of something out of a fifties movie, she sat awaiting the five tribal representatives.

Hika arrived first. "Interesting meeting place," he said, and he actually smiled at her.

"Strategic," she replied. "How is your father?"

Hika dropped onto the seat next to her, his expression troubled. "You haven't heard. He admitted to killing Danny. A witness turned up, and the police arrested Dad a few hours ago."

"I'm sorry," Jessalyn said.

"You have nothing to apologize for," Hika said. "Danny didn't deserve the punishment Dad meted out. While we're alone, I want to apologize for my behavior toward you and that of my tribe." His mouth twisted. "There was much handwringing when the elders realized the guardian had been living amongst us for years, and we'd treated her with ridicule and disdain."

"I didn't know either," Jessalyn said.

"It doesn't matter. We will not forget your selfless act in healing us when we gave you cause for mistrust. I promise you this."

The other three leaders and Manu entered the meeting room. Hone and Cassie arrived bearing trays of food.

"Cassie will stay to take notes of this meeting," Jessalyn said. "I wished an impartial representative to aid me."

Jessalyn hadn't mentioned this to Manu, but he never blinked. The other four leaders remained silent, so she assumed they had no objections.

"The first order of business," Jessalyn said. "My taniwha has chosen Manu. While this means I will have a closer relationship with the Auckland tribe, I promise I will not ignore the needs of your tribes." She made eye contact with each of the leaders, a small part of her amazed at her impudence in laying down the law to these older and more knowledgeable men. "While I don't have experience, I will learn and serve where you need me. First, I will spend one week with each of your tribes."

Manu frowned at this, but she continued.

"I will make this a regular visit—at least twice a year—to ensure the guardian meets the needs of your tribe. It will be up to you to decide how you wish to use my time. I can heal or perhaps make judgments to settle disputes. I can teach woodcarving or spend time with your younger tribal members and share with them my research on the original dragon. Is this acceptable to you all?" While she waited for a reply, she grabbed a burger and bit into the juicy meat patty.

"Yum!"

"Inside voice," Jessalyn said once she'd swallowed her mouthful. "We're in public."

Her taniwha's enthusiasm broke the ice and the grinning men reached for burgers and fries while Cassie took a drink order and rose to give it to Hone, who had remained outside the meeting room.

"This is more than I expected," Hika said. "I appreciate your offer and accept."

"All I require is a willingness to keep the peace and accommodation when I visit your tribe. I expect that Manu will come with me sometimes," she said. "I understand you're protective of your boundaries. Will this be a problem? I promise that if Manu is with me, he will not interfere in your tribe, nor will he be part of any private meetings we might have. I will not share confidential business with him. While I am in your region, I'll become part of your tribe, and as such, your secrets will remain with you and your people."

"May I make a suggestion?" Cassie asked.

"Sure," Jessalyn said.

"Perhaps each tribe could make you a special shirt to wear while you spend time with them. Um, like a rugby jersey with the local tribal design."

"I like it," Hika said. "That is a practical and inexpensive way to show solidarity."

"And the final thing before I turn this meeting over to Manu who has something important to tell you all—I don't expect you to provide me with an expensive hotel when I visit. Nor do I wish to create a financial burden for anyone. I expect a comfortable bed and a room where I can have privacy when I am not with the tribe. That is all for now unless you have questions."

The Southern Otago leader spoke. "No, I think you have made your position clear. I suspect questions might arise later during your visits. You can deal with them then."

"Could you set up an email address for us to contact you?" The Wellington leader asked.

"I'll do that for you," Cassie said. "Does Manu have your contact details?"

"Yes," Manu said.

"I will enjoy this next bit," Jessalyn said as she reached for another burger. "Prepare to have your minds blown."

She finished her second burger and nibbled on fries. Hone knocked on the door and walked in carrying a tray of drinks.

"Hone, you can stay now," she murmured while Manu described his invention.

"Invisible!" Hika blurted.

"You're kidding us," the Wellington leader said.

"No, I will hold a demonstration at my marae this evening," Manu said.

The Southern Otago leader narrowed his eyes. "I knew your voice was familiar," he said to Cassie. "You were at the marae yesterday."

Cassie winked. "You guys were all ganging up on Jessalyn. I was her secret weapon."

"You're willing to rent these units to other tribes?" the Southern Canterbury leader asked.

"After the applicants pass a security test. If these get into the hands of the criminal element, it will be a huge problem," Hone said.

Manu sipped his drink. "Each unit has a kill switch. If the renter misuses them, they will cease to work."

The questions flew quick and fast, and Jessalyn sat back, watching Manu.

Cassie tapped her on the shoulder. "You're proud of him."

"I am."

"You love him."

Jessalyn tested the emotion, even though she knew it to be true.

"Yes. Yes. Yes! Sexy black beast!" her taniwha crowed.

The leaders fell silent and turned to Jessalyn. Heat surged into her cheeks as she met their gazes one by one.

"You have got to stop doing that," Jessalyn muttered.

Manu wove their fingers together. He lifted her hand and kissed the back, his eyes golden and twinkling and his taniwha peeking through. "Nine o'clock tonight at the marae in Papakura. We will demonstrate the stealth unit."

Jessalyn had expected Manu would drive to the warehouse in

Onehunga, but he didn't. Manu drove them toward the inner city.

"Where are we going?" she asked.

"A surprise." He winked at her. "I thought I'd get started on this dating business."

Manu pulled into the foyer of an exclusive hotel on the Auckland waterfront. Jessalyn's eyes widened, and she was glad she'd listened to Cassie and worn the sundress and sandals. "Are we having lunch?"

Manu laughed as he handed the keys over to the valet. "Are you hungry again already?"

"I could eat," Jessalyn said, her tone rueful.

"Then it's lucky for me I've organized a private meal up in our suite."

"A suite? Wow!"

"You're worth everything," Manu said and, taking her hand, led her into the foyer.

The check-in took mere minutes and soon an elevator whisked them up to the top floor, a keycard letting them into the suite.

Jessalyn followed Manu inside, their hands still clasped. Her shoes sank into the thick carpet as she took in the cream furnishings with punches of ruby and forest-green accessories. And the view—the harbor, blue and sparkling, spread out before them. Half a dozen yachts sped across the water, their sails full of wind. In the distance, the familiar volcanic cone of Rangitoto pushed from the sea. Although dormant, it was still imposing.

"This is beautiful," Jessalyn said. "I can't believe you did this for me."

"We're staying here tonight, and even better, there is a deck where we can take off and land with no one any the wiser."

"We're flying to the meeting," Jessalyn squeaked.

"I thought we'd make an entrance. You did say you wanted to practice flying, and it's a short flight from here to Papakura. Are you still sore? A soak in the hot tub might fix that. We have our own private one."

"Let's do it!" her taniwha shrieked.

Manu chortled as Jessalyn rubbed her ears. "I'll take that as approval."

A knock sounded on the door.

"Ah, perfect timing," Manu said. "That will be our afternoon tea." He opened the door to let in the room attendant.

Sausage rolls. She caught a whiff of meat and pastry and chocolate. Definitely chocolate.

Once the door closed behind the room attendant, Manu went to her.

"There is one more thing," he said. "Before we eat." He produced a small navy blue box from his pocket. "I promised I'd give you time before I pushed our relationship, and I mean to take things slowly." He kneeled and opened the box to display a ring with golden diamonds. "But my taniwha is just as pushy as yours. You don't hear him because he's well-mannered," Manu added.

"Please, Jessalyn Brown, guardian of the taniwha, will you marry me?"

"Yes! Yes! Yes!" her taniwha shrieked.

Jessalyn rolled her eyes. "You're a good man, Manu Taniwha, and even though we haven't known each other for long, I love you. My answer is yes."

He closed his eyes for a moment, but not before she glimpsed the gold of his taniwha. "She said yes." He pushed the band onto her ring finger and stood to pull her into an embrace.

"I loved you from the moment we met," he said. "I can't wait to make you my wife."

Jessalyn's stomach rumbled, and she groaned. "I guess we'll be eating first instead of celebrating our engagement in that big bed over there."

Manu drew her over to the table where their afternoon tea awaited. He poured two flutes of champagne and offered her one. "Let's do both," he said.

So they did.

The Wedding

Six months later

J essalyn stood on the banks of the Waikato River, dressed in a cream and gold wedding gown. Manu stood beside her, resplendent in his charcoal-gray suit.

"I now pronounce you man and wife. You may kiss your bride," the wedding celebrant said.

"Jess," Manu whispered. "I love you."

Then his lips were on hers, and she clung, overwhelmed by the depth of her feelings for this man who accepted her for what she was—the taniwha guardian and an ordinary woman.

The crowd cheered behind them as their lips parted, and they turned to face family, friends, and taniwha.

The leaders of various tribes approached and each of them pressed their noses to hers in a hongi. A formal welcome and acceptance.

Pleasure rushed through her at the open approval and recognition of the work she'd done for the tribes during the last months. Manu, sensing her emotion, squeezed her hand.

"I love you too. So much," Jessalyn whispered.

Since she'd burst onto the scene in her taniwha form, life had become very different. Of course, her engagement to Manu had been part of it, but learning more about her people and helping them to have better lives brought fulfillment and confidence she'd never possessed.

"Congratulations!" Cassie waddled toward them in an advanced stage of pregnancy. Hone hovered at her side, tall and protective.

Emma and Jack joined them, carrying a baby each.

There were hugs all around and hearty congratulations from the guests. Jessalyn smiled often. She also surreptitiously pinched her inner wrist to ensure this wasn't a wondrous dream.

Manu and Jessalyn led the joyous group into the dining room because, of course, everyone was hungry. The strident chant of a haka echoed with appropriate ferocity, and tears of happiness blurred Jessalyn's vision, gratitude that she'd found her place and truly belonged.

Cassie thrilled them with two songs before the band took over, and they danced and partied.

It was almost midnight when she and Manu left.

"Our destination?" she asked.

"I booked the suite at the waterfront hotel again. I thought we'd hole up there for a few days and enjoy our new roles as husband and wife."

She reached over to pat his hand. "Sounds like a plan, husband."

"Mrs. Taniwha has a nice ring," Manu said.

As happened last time, checking in was fast and efficient, and they were soon alone in their suite.

Jessalyn sashayed toward Manu, putting an extra sway in her hips. She turned to present her back to him. "Will you unzip my gown?"

"In a minute, sweetheart. There's something we need to discuss first."

Jessalyn turned back to face Manu, her happy contentment slipping from her lips and settling in her gut when she noticed his serious expression. "What is it?"

"A letter arrived for you from Australia last week, but selfishly, I refused to let anything impede our wedding. I wanted to marry you in the worst way, and I hope you'll forgive me for holding back the letter."

"From Australia?" Jessalyn eyed the envelope he pulled from his inside jacket pocket with disfavor. "Is it from Karen?"

"Yes, she sent it with a note that asked me to forward it to you. She sensed we were mates."

"I'm not sure if I want to open it."

"You're angry at her. I get that, but she might answer some of your remaining questions."

"True." Jessalyn pushed out a hard sigh. "Let's have a celebratory drink, and we can read it together."

"Plan," Manu said and stalked over to a champagne bottle that nestled in an ice bucket.

While she waited, Jessalyn studied the room and let a host of wonderful memories of their last visit bloom. A large vase of roses, the petals the color of her taniwha, released a delicate perfume. A basket of snacks sat near the tea-making station, along with a caddy of her favorite Russian Caravan tea. Manu had planned everything, and he made her life easier with his care and advice. His love. She'd enjoyed her engagement and eagerly awaited their life as a married couple.

Manu handed her a glass and lifted his in a toast. "To my beautiful wife."

"My sexy black beast," her taniwha shouted, her tone gleeful.

Jessalyn groaned before she lifted her glass. "To my handsome husband and his sexy black beast."

They sat together on a cream two-seater. Manu kicked off his shoes and Jessalyn followed suit, delighting in wriggling her toes in the thick, luxurious cream carpet.

"Open the letter and read it aloud," she suggested.

"All right." Manu made quick work of the envelope. "'Dear Jessalyn,'" he started. "'This is a hard letter for me to write since it brings back the past and every one of my insecurities. Best to start at the beginning, I think.

"'I inherited the relic from my cousin who had married into the Waaka family. This caused an outrage, and the ripples reverberated within the tribe for years since I was ten when the relic chose me as the guardian. As I grew toward a marriageable age, my father signed an alliance with the Waaka family and betrothed me to the tribal heir. His name was Ngahoe, Nelson's brother, and I loathed him on sight.

"'My favorite thing to do was to go fishing or swimming. I loved the water and swam or fished at every opportunity. That's how I met your father, and my taniwha wanted him. Later, I learned it was love at first sight for him too. I went to my father, but he refused to entertain my marriage with a pakeha. Your father and I didn't care. We spent every moment together, and one weekend, we went to Auckland, obtained the correct license, and married since by that time I was of age. I fell pregnant with you almost straight away, much to my father's shame. Ngahoe, Nelson, and their family were furious, but there was little they could do.

"'We were outcasts, but we lived happily enough until the relic showed favoritism toward you. You were scarcely six months old, and I feared the Waaka family would learn of this and kidnap you, gaining control of the relic. Your father and I talked and planned. James made a special box that made the relic invisible. He disposed of the pendant, the location secret from me.

"'Between us, we staged my death, and everyone believed the relic had disappeared into the sea. But James and I were mates, and my taniwha was inconsolable without my husband. Each full moon was hell, so we met every few weeks. We were both happier and rejoiced in our togetherness. Eventually, we had two more children.

"'The one bump in our marriage was the huge secret we kept from you. James said it would come back and bite us on the bum. He was right, and I'm sorry for the way I handled our meeting. I panicked because, selfishly, I didn't want your brother and sister pulled into taniwha politics.

"'I doubt we'll ever return to New Zealand. The children love the lifestyle over here, and I'll admit, I enjoy the warmer weather of Queensland. Of course, I miss your father dreadfully as I am sure you do too.

"'Judging by the gossip on the taniwha dark web, you have pulled the tribes together and you're doing a stellar job. I'm proud of you and know your father always saw these leadership qualities in you.

"'Congratulations on your upcoming marriage. Manu Taniwha is a strong and worthy partner for you.

"'Karen Baker.'"

There was a moment of silence while Jessalyn considered the contents of the letter. She sipped her champagne and frowned. "So she and Dad staged her death because the relic favored me."

"They saw trouble," Manu said. "Think of Nelson Waaka. He wanted the relic. Hell, he probably watched you during your younger years, waiting to learn if you could shift. He would've grabbed you if the chance presented itself and forced you to follow his orders. A child is malleable."

"We're never having children," Jessalyn blurted.

"I hope you'll change your mind. You'd make a perfect mother. Besides, events might not necessarily repeat. You're an able and fair guardian. The leaders respect you." Manu took her empty glass and set it aside. "We can talk later. It's time to celebrate our marriage."

Jessalyn shifted until she sat on his lap. She released a surprised *eep* when he stood. She clutched his neck and laughed as he carried her to the bedroom.

"I'm ready for the honeymoon stage," he whispered. He made quick work of her zipper and helped her remove her dress. Soon they were naked and lying on the bed. Their mouths met in a powerful kiss, and passion claimed them. They shuddered in each other's arms, declaring their love and commitment in a bodily way.

"I love you, Manu." She kissed his jaw and aimed a second one at his mouth.

"Sweetheart," Manu murmured, his kiss indicating another round lay in their near future

"He-haw!" her taniwha shouted. *"Again, my sexy black beast. Do it again!"*

Manu's big body shook as he contained his laughter while Jessalyn grinned. She couldn't have expressed it better herself. She gave a happy sigh as Manu pleasured her, and they both embraced their newly married state.

Thank you for reading **Black Moon Dragon**. I hope you enjoyed Jessalyn and the sexy black beast! **Snow Moon Dragon** (https://shelleymunro.com/books/snow-moon-dragon/) is the next book in the Dragon Investigators series, written after I was

lucky enough to visit the island of South Georgia and Antarctica. I fell in love with both places and had to use the setting in a book. Snow Moon Dragon is the result.

Shelley xx

Glossary

Taniwha – a dragon from Maori mythology. Some—water dragons—live in lakes, rivers or the sea. Legend says a taniwha lives at every bend of a river. Other taniwha are cave dwellers and have the ability to fly. Some are benevolent while others are mischievous tricksters or true villains.

Hone – Maori for John, and a very common Christian name.

Manu – Maori, meaning man of the birds or a person held in high esteem.

Kahurangi – Maori, meaning sky blue or precious.

Koru – A spiral pattern inspired by native ferns. Denotes new beginnings.

Manaia – Another pattern used in carving. Denotes guardian.

Pakeha – A New Zealander of European descent.

Lake Taupo – A large lake in the middle of the North Island of New Zealand.

Ruru – a native owl, often called a morepork after the sound it makes.

Haka – a ceremonial dance. Often associated with war to stir passion for the coming battle. If you're a rugby fan, you'll see the haka performed by the All Blacks before each international game. Facial features can be contorted and tongue poked out as part of the rhythmic performance.

Tohunga – an expert in their chosen field.

Mana – a person's prestige or influence. Their status.

Aotearoa – Maori name for New Zealand (Land of the Long White Cloud)

Te Papa – The museum of New Zealand, which is in Wellington.

Marae – an open courtyard where meetings take place. It can also mean a collection of buildings.

Powhiri – a traditional greeting to visitors entering a marae.

Piupiu – a garment made of flax. It also means to move, swing or sway, which is what the dried flax does when a piupiu is worn.

Taiaha – a long, spear-like weapon made of wood. These days used in ceremonial greetings.

Waiata – a song.

Koha – a gift.

Hongi – a traditional greeting where noses are pressed together.

L & P – Short for lemon and Paeroa. A New Zealand soda made in the town of Paeroa. It has a citrus taste.

Moko – traditional tattoos on the face.

Kauri – a native tree that was prized for building.

Totara – a native tree, which is popular for carving.

Rimu – a native tree with distinct red wood. Red pine.

About Shelley

USA Today bestselling author Shelley Munro lives in Auckland, the City of Sails, with her husband and a cheeky Jack Russell/mystery breed dog.

Typical New Zealanders, Shelley and her husband left home for their big OE soon after they married (translation of New Zealand speak - big overseas experience). A twelve-month-long adventure lengthened to six years of roaming the world. Enduring memories include being almost sat on by a mountain gorilla in Rwanda, lazing on white sandy beaches in India, whale watching in Alaska, searching for leprechauns in Ireland, and dealing with ghosts in an English pub.

While travel is still a big attraction, these days Shelley is most likely found in front of her computer following another love - that of writing stories of contemporary and paranormal romance and adventure. Other interests include watching rugby (strictly for research purposes), cycling, playing croquet and the ukelele, and curling up with an enjoyable book.

Visit Shelley at her Website

https://shelleymunro.com

Join Shelley's Newsletter

https://shelleymunro.com/newsletter

Also By Shelley

Paranormal

Dragon Investigators

Blue Moon Dragon

Blood Moon Dragon

Black Moon Dragon

Snow Moon Dragon

Middlemarch Shifters

My Scarlet Woman

My Younger Lover

My Peeping Tom

My Assassin

My Estranged Lover

My Feline Protector

My Determined Suitor

My Cat Burglar

My Stray Cat

My Second Chance

My Plan B
My Cat Nap
My Romantic Tangle
My Blue Lady
My Twin Trouble
My Precious Gift

Middlemarch Gathering
My Highland Mate
My Highland Fling
My Elusive Mate
My Valiant Princess
My Highland Wedding
My Highland Billionaire

www.ingramcontent.com/pod-product-compliance
Lightning Source LLC
Chambersburg PA
CBHW032142010726
47494CB00002B/319